Elders of Eventyr

Book Two

by Ellias Quinn

ISBN 978-1-944755-04-1

Published by Second March, LLC | THE WOODLANDS
www.elliasquinn.com

For those ever young.

Table of Contents

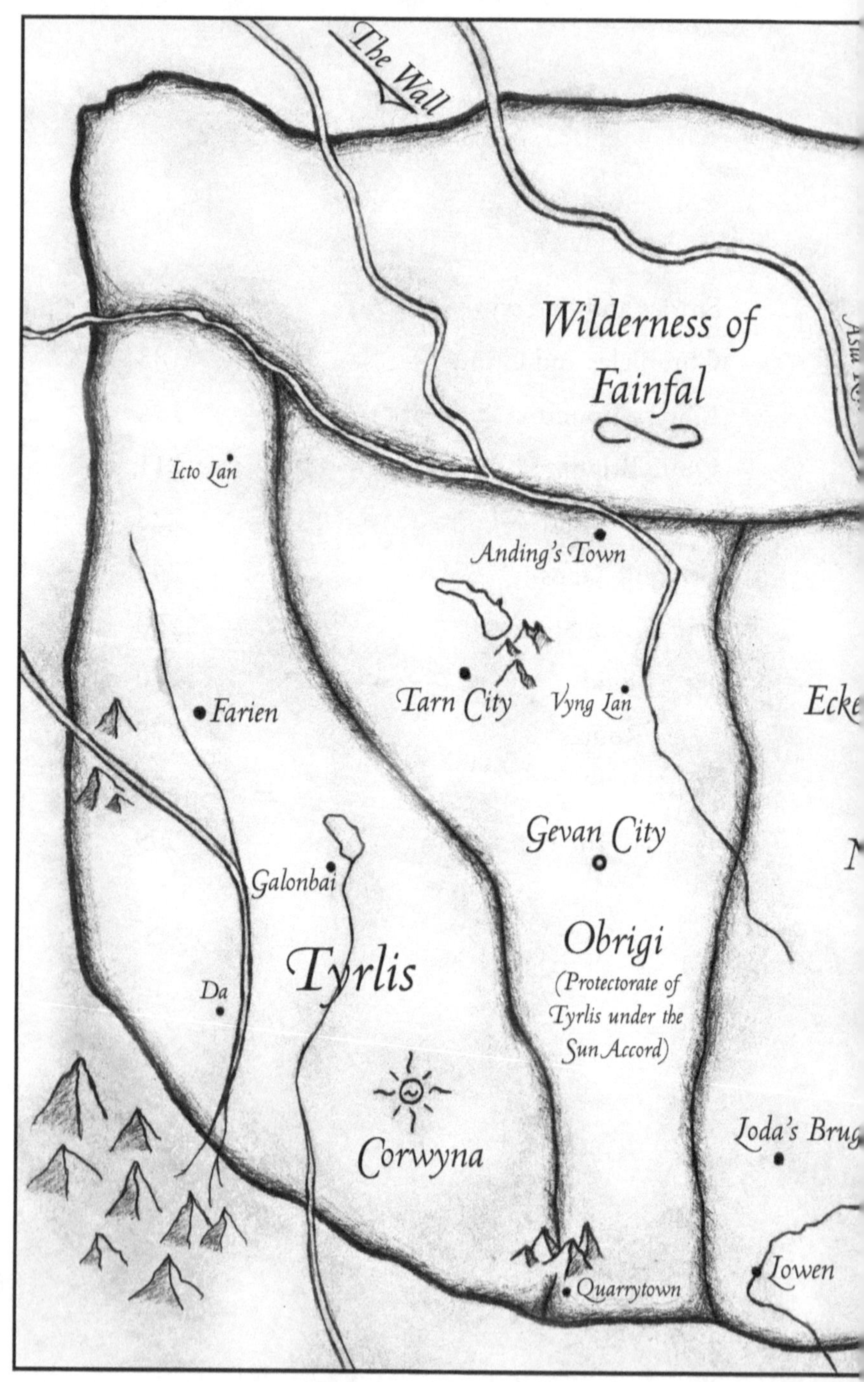

The Wall
Wilderness of Fainfal
Asta Re
Icto Lan
Anding's Town
Tarn City
Vyng Lan
Ecke
Farien
Gevan City
Galonbai
Obrigi
(Protectorate of
Tyrlis under the
Sun Accord)
Tyrlis
Da
Loda's Brug
Corwyna
Quarrytown
Lowen

Eventyr and its nations
Depiction by Viscount Jonyn Sang
Corwyna Councilman, Senior
rders Unknown
Vangara
Wilderness of Deepest Valdingfal
well
fal Region
Brotinnfjol
Goska
Asta River

Velana dri alva,
drimesk ermoli.
Dri dyri ajarten,
driskur erusi.

Velana dri alva,
kothym ervanoss.
Den hjardan erglir,
den valdri erveross.

Velana dri alva,
olakot, kodu.
Eletsol
Ranycht
Nervoda
Brandur
Sangriga
Obrigi
Kyndelin
Skorgon

Velana.

Awaken the fairies,
the forest is young.
The animals await,
the sun is new.

Awaken the fairies,
their home is alive.
Its heart is clear,
its guardians are true.

Awaken the fairies,
all of them, rise.
Life
Night
Water
Fire
Light
Earth
Animal
Crawler

Awaken.

Prologue

She had erased her fear. After that frantic night, testing all of her skill and finally gaining the Book of Myrkhar's power, she had been certain the fear was gone. The Book told her as much, and it even granted the ability to wield her fear against her enemies. Maybe she *hadn't* cast the spell perfectly, but what did it matter that some magic escaped? She had been strong.

She had been free. But that wretched thing – her other self – turned up and brought back her fear. Nychta remembered how close the knife had come to succeeding. How the fire then stole away her thoughts. She pulled the down-filled blanket tightly around herself and opened the curtains covering a window over her bed. It was dark out, past sunset. The Ranycht village below would have awakened to begin their night already. She knew she should leave.

The Book's voice, deep as the night sky, crept into her mind. *Get up. Prepare yourself for important work.*

The slimy black cover of the Book of Myrkhar stood out in an otherwise soft, dry bedroom. It lay on the bedside table and seemed to stare at her through the darkness with its circular metal symbol. Feeling a twinge of annoyance, Nychta pushed the blanket away and let her feet touch the floor.

"You aren't angry anymore?" she asked in a low voice.

Oh, child. When one has lived long enough, one constantly

feels anger. I am giving you a final opportunity to prove your-self. If you serve well, punishment may turn into reward.

"I'm not your servant. I'm your partner. You know I only care about one thing, and it isn't reward." She did enjoy the benefits of power, though. Her hand stroked the warm blanket.

I understand. Allow me to rephrase: Everything I ask of you will greatly help your cause. However, if you find yourself unwilling or unable to fulfill my requests, I will…withdraw my sponsorship.

"Fine," she said, scratching the edge of her large, pointed ear. "I'll do it."

I would not mourn your death, but it would put off your own plans considerably. You are keeping that fact in mind, yes?

She stirred uncomfortably. "Yes."

How clever of you. Now get up. Tonight we begin the hunt for our long-banished allies.

Nychta stood and stretched out her brown feathery wings as the Book began explaining its plan to her. After dressing for the night, she bound her dark brown hair in a braid. She had almost finished when she heard a knock.

"Lady Nychta," hissed a Skorgon soldier through the door. "Your meal is prepared downstairs. The general and the high priest await command."

"Good." As usual, hearing the formal title in front of her name prompted her to use a brisk, authoritative tone. "I'll be down soon with new orders." She caught herself almost thanking the Skorgon. Some undesirable habits had also been brought back by her lesser self.

Looking around the richly-appointed room, occupied by this town's mayor until recently, a large mirror drew her attention. She walked over and appraised her dim reflection, slightly warped by the cheapness of the looking glass. She didn't need lamps or moonlight to see herself in the dark – no Ranycht had to rely on them, something that made their kind strong where others were weak. Her eyes, once entirely purple but now cooled by a white tint, flashed against her brown skin in a commanding way. Alva throughout Nychtfal knew her by those eyes. A wary hunch to her shoulders was promptly straightened, and she turned to see her face in profile. That pointy little nose made her look like a girl. She wondered if the Book held any magic that could change her appearance. She needed to look strong, like a leader. Like a lady.

Like a queen.

Nychta smoothed down her green-and-brown tunic. She should get something in red. She donned the Book's satchel and opened the door. The Skorgon guards outside bowed at the waist, each one stretching its four arms behind itself in a gesture of subservience. These alva had insect-like features: most with hard plates over their skin and mandibles instead of jaws, some with spines and antennae at various places on their bodies. Their papery skin was usually brown or gray. Two of the Skorgon guards had protruding black eyes while the others had irises and pupils like other alva. Their appearance alone often terrified other kinds of alva. She smiled with satisfaction. A growing army of Skorgon was at her disposal. Father and Mother would have their justice soon.

After breakfast, Nychta stepped out onto a great balcony that presided over the moonlit town. Rustic buildings made of twigs lined the tree branches above and cozied up to each other on the ground below. This town was like so many others. It reminded her of…home.

A crowd of Ranycht with avian wings and brown skin, like Nychta's, had congregated on the ground to view their new ruler. They looked up at her curiously, whispering to each other. Beyond them, she could see cookfires and tents that merchants had set up in order to capitalize on the gathering.

Fires. Too many. She tried to move on, but the pinpricks of radiant flame wouldn't leave her sight. Her skin turned cold. Crush the fires, smother them, anything, anything, she just wanted them to stop *burning*. Air was suddenly precious as she struggled to get enough.

The Book pulsed. There was a tense moment, and then cool calm spread through Nychta. Her fear floated away.

I have always relished the challenge of playing with pieces I cannot control.

She chose to ignore its chuckling voice. How could a book be so arrogant?

1

Forest of Petals and Leaves

The wild plants of Fainfal coiled and tangled around each other and snagged on Matil, Khelya, and Dask as the alva and their two riding beetles moved through the undergrowth. Colors were more vivid in this part of Eventyr, and there certainly were a lot of them. Blossoms in purple, white, red, yellow, and blue peppered dense green bushes that rose high all around, and other flowers grew in clumps along the travelers' way, some at head height and some casting shadows over them. Off to the right, glistening ants marched parallel with the alva and, overhead, fat bees lit from flower to flower. Tree branches high above shuffled and bent with the weight of birds and other critters. The trees themselves were monstrosities mantled in ivy. They blocked much of the sunlight, but it wasn't as dark as Valdingfal, something that Khelya had praised.

Matil didn't care for the sunlight. Shade suited her just fine, but that was natural for a Ranycht: bat-eared and brown-skinned, with bright, sensitive eyes much larger and rounder than other kinds of alva. She would have kept nocturnal hours in their homeland of Nychtfal, but the group had to stay away from other Ranycht as much as possible. The three of them woke with the sun and traveled when most Ranycht would be asleep. The group had left Nychtfal a few days ago, but they continued to travel during the day.

Matil blinked as she passed through a ray of leaf-filtered light. Her eyes were rich purple, her hair long and dark brown. She was an oddity, because all Ranycht except her had bird-like wings. The wing holes in the back of her blue tunic showed skin – no feathers, scars, or any other sign that wings had ever grown there. Her lack of wings was the outward counterpart to her bare mind on the inside. Until recently, Matil hadn't known who or what she was. Even after uncovering the truth, the only things she remembered from her past life came back to her piece by piece in dreams.

Her ears drooped at that thought and she pressed her eyes shut to clear it away. When she opened them again, she saw that while she'd been thinking, Khelya and Dask had gone farther ahead, lost in a conversation about food. Dask and his beetle passed under a fern, and he absentmindedly stood in the stirrups to whack a frond. He was also a Ranycht, with green eyes and glossy, feathered wings the same color black as his shaggy hair.

Khelya was quite different from both of them. She stood much taller, twice the size of her friends, and her dark eyes could look toward bright light without making her wince.

Her skin was tanned and freckled, used to sunnier lands. She was wingless like other Obrigi Matil had seen, but there was one thing very strange about her. Khelya's entire body was half-invisible, as translucent as glass. She hadn't always been that way.

Obrigi had no magic of their own. The stories said that a thousand years ago, they had lost the blessing of Falgar the Elder which had given them their incredible creativity. Besides the Obrigi, most other alva could fly in some way and use magic, each kind with their own element. Matil and Dask's Ranycht magic allowed them and those with them to fade into the shadows, disappearing from sight. And after they had used too much magic on Khelya, the Obrigi had gotten stuck halfway. She was like a ghost – see-through and moaning about it. Over the past few weeks she'd regained *some* solidity, but it wasn't even close to normal.

Before the group had left Nychtfal, Dask bought two large ground beetles with shiny green shells and some supplies on one of his trips into town. Khelya walked while her friends rode atop the beetles. Endowed with Obrigi endurance, she wouldn't get tired until the end of the day.

So far the beetles had been a great convenience, and they saved Matil's feet from getting sore and tired. Their splayed legs could tramp over rocky ravines or fields of moss, terrain that she couldn't easily cross without wings. Dask said the beetles were known as caterpillar hunters, and Matil had seen the truth in the name – up close. She grimaced at the memory.

Matil rode Dewdrop, named for a dent in the strikingly blue shell plate behind the female beetle's head. She stroked Dewdrop's shell and wondered if the insect could feel her touch. Dask's beetle was a male named Olnar. The beetles currently tromped northwest through Fainfal, swaying their riders gently from side to side. The group had entered this wilderness three days ago on their way to Eventyr's impassable border to look for the human, Mr. Korsen. They weren't sure whether he actually existed, but they hoped to ask him for help.

Supposedly, the alva in these parts were more dangerous the farther one traveled into Fainfal. Matil had a hard time imagining it. Nothing at all had happened to them since they arrived. There was no sign of other alva except for some border-dwelling Ranycht. Dask had told Matil and Khelya that the alva of Fainfal, the Eletsol, went about during the day unlike their southern neighbors in Nychtfal, but maybe he was wrong.

The conversation just ahead was carrying back to Matil.

"Why don't you actually *try* fried mushrooms before saying they're disgusting?" Dask said.

Khelya hunched over to look at Dask. It was difficult to read her transparent face, but she seemed to be giving him a hard glare. "Because I hate mushrooms! The only food worse than mushrooms are worms, and it's hard to tell the difference sometimes. They're the exact same texture!" If she'd had large Ranycht ears instead of those short ones that came to the barest points, she would have flattened them back with the intensity of her opinions.

Slumping forward and resting her chin on the beetle's shell, Matil began talking in a low voice. "I promise they're not always like this, Dewdrop."

The beetle's antennae twitched skeptically as if in response.

Dask clambered to his feet on the saddle, bringing him up to a head shorter than Khelya. Olnar kept moving. To the big beetle, the alva with flapping wings was just another supply pack piled on his back.

"Okay, well, you know what?" Dask said. "If you're going to insult a traditional Ranycht dish – *the* traditional Ranycht dish – I have something to say to you and every Obrigi. Barley porridge tastes like snail slime, but even blander. And Obrigi ale," he paused to smirk up at Khelya, "is nothing but water!"

Khelya straightened her back calmly. "Water?"

"*Pond* water."

And then Khelya had something loud to say about Ranycht mental health, based on their cuisine.

Matil sighed. The reins lay coiled on Dewdrop's back and she reached for them, but a faint whisper made her raise her head. She listened for a moment, moving her ears around and hearing nothing but the forest's – and her friends' – cacophony.

"Arrow. Face." Khelya pointed from her new bow to Dask. "That's what'll happen if you don't take everything back." Because the bow was only Ranycht-sized, she had tied it to her belt with a blade of grass.

"Ha! Funniest joke I've heard all week," Dask said. "You couldn't even hit me at *this* range."

She held up the bow and twanged its string. "Yeah? I've been practicing. A lot."

He poked her bow-holding arm. "Hey, who was it that risked his wings sending a letter to your family?"

"I already thanked you! This is a whole other matter!"

The whisper Matil heard might not have been danger, but she supposed it didn't hurt to be cautious. She shook the reins tied around the bases of Dewdrop's antennae, urging the beetle to go faster until they rode between Khelya tugging at her brown headband on the left, and Dask about to give the whole forest an earful on the right.

"We should be quiet," Matil said. "What if she finds us?"

Dask and Khelya immediately knew whom Matil meant by "she". They quieted down, mumbling agreement. Dask climbed back into his saddle.

Matil glanced at both of them with a small smile. "I think someday I'll try fried mushroom *and* barley porridge."

"Both?" Khelya sounded revolted.

She nodded. "It's going to be delicious."

Dask wrinkled up one side of his nose. "What, are you gonna plop the mushroom bits into the porridge and eat it that way?"

"No, I didn't mean that," Matil said. "Although mushroom porridge might actually taste good."

"Hm." He clapped. "I applaud your adventurous spirit and can only hope that it won't kill you."

"You're so kind." She checked to see if there was any difference in Khelya's appearance today. The group had moved carefully through Nychtfal, trying to avoid the use of fading for the Obrigi's sake. However useful Khelya's transparency happened to be, she elaborated at length on its downsides. Among them were bad coordination, tingly hands and feet, and the feeling that she wasn't herself.

"But doesn't it feel good that nothing dangerous can see you?" Matil said one time when Khelya was fretting.

"No," came her emphatic reply.

Just now, she looked the same. If only there were some way to help. Fading had saved their lives several times, but it *was* the magic that had 'cursed' Khelya.

Dewdrop's antennae twitched again, and she slowed in her six-legged gait.

"What is it, girl?" Matil said.

"*Latuam!*" roared a stranger's voice from the undergrowth. A bird startled out of a bush to their left.

The forest abruptly rushed downward. Or was Matil going *up*? The forceful motion knocked her head against Dewdrop's shell and pressed her down. She cried out in pain and surprise. Dask's sharp yell and Khelya's bellow were near, a fact that comforted Matil until she realized that it meant the same terrible thing was happening to all of them. Nychta had finally caught up with them. She'd captured them and there was no way out—

But Matil didn't sense her presence. She didn't hear Crell's voice or the telltale buzz of Skorgon wings.

The sharp ascent stopped, and the air grew thick with a disgusting stench. Matil cringed. Dask told her about the smell that the beetles might give off when threatened, but she hadn't yet had the…pleasure of witnessing it. She pinched her nose shut and assessed what had happened. Fear seized her.

A flower had closed around Dewdrop, who jerked her six legs, trying to free herself from the broad, pink petals. Yellow-topped stalks brushed Matil's legs and Dewdrop with sticky pollen. The petals twisted tighter to resist Dewdrop. An unstable feeling led Matil to look down. The ground was very far beneath Dewdrop and her.

"Hey!" Dask said. "What are you doing? Leave us alo— ow!"

"Uhf!" came Khelya's voice.

A heavy green net dropped on Matil's head, restricting her movement, and chatter in some unknown language fleeted past her ears. No matter which way she turned, she couldn't see the source of the voices. She could see her friends, however, and they didn't look injured.

Just below to the left, Khelya was sprawled on her back across the spiny center of a sturdy flower with four large, light blue petals. She struggled against a net, but its corners hung down past the flower head, weighted with stones. A big yellow flower with many layers of inwardly-curved petals had sprung up to Matil's right, and only Dask's head could be seen over the walls of that lovely prison. Matil's flower swayed dangerously with Dewdrop's movement.

"Outsiders!" a man shouted with a heavy accent. "Who are you?"

Matil looked up and stared, wondering if she had dozed on the beetle and was now dreaming. Above them hovered a kind of alva that she had never seen before. They were light-skinned and hearty like Khelya, but as short as Ranycht. In almost every hand was a wooden staff, and they wore sleeveless robes together with leggings, both made from foliage and rough fabric. Intertwining symbols and geometric designs were painted in white on their bodies and clothes.

They fluttered like butterflies, but their airy and vibrant wings were more flora than fauna. The wings resembled petals that could have fallen from the flowers all around, and several alva appeared to have leaves for wings instead. Their hair was untamed and richly colored. Straw-yellow hair framed some mischievous faces, jet-black flopped over others, and Matil glimpsed manes red as raspberries. Their ears had a rippled triangular shape; they curved forward and then backward again at the upper ear tips, and both the earlobes and the tips came to points. They looked like what Khelya and Dask had described to Matil.

These alva were the Eletsol.

The man who had shouted hovered in the center, facing the three confining flowers. He wore a sleeveless dark blue robe and was lean-bodied, with tawny brown hair and eyes. Lines of white paint went down the center of his face, punctuated by a many-pointed star on his chin and another on his forehead. His jagged elm leaf wings flapped quickly while he glowered at the prisoners. "Answer!" he said.

The Eletsol lowered their staves toward Matil, Khelya, and Dask. The end of every staff sharpened to a point instantly. Matil blinked.

"We're, uh, we're just humble travelers," Dask said, voice squeaking at the end. "If you let us go, we'll be out of your territory very soon."

"Why is the giant…" The man waved his hand. "Why is she not whole?"

Dask smiled weakly. "No reason."

Some of the Eletsol were examining Khelya's transparency, poking her with blunt staves. She grabbed one stick through the net to stop it. Its tip suddenly became sharp. Khelya yelped and let go.

Matil cocked her head. How did they change the staves?

The leaf-winged man scowled. "You'll speak the truth later." He shouted something in his language to the warriors. Was he the leader of these Eletsol?

All the warriors focused as they held their staves against themselves, where the wood began to curl. In a moment they relaxed, and the staves had become wooden belts and sashes. They turned to the flower prisons and waved their arms expansively. The flower stems responded to the Eletsol's magic by shifting around and then surging forward. Matil clung to Dewdrop in panic as her flower sagged backwards and almost tipped over. Dirt flew up around its base and the flower's trailing roots left a furrow in the ground.

The prisoners traveled in this manner for some time while the rest of the group flew above, below, and all around in an ever-changing swarm. The beetles calmed down as the flowers settled into a more stable motion. Occasionally, the strange magicians had quick spats in their sharp language. The leader was silent except when the arguments grew too loud, and then he intervened. But they didn't stop until a different man, with blue wings and golden-yellow hair, barked out words that quieted the others right away.

Matil checked on Khelya and Dask again. Khelya looked disgruntled, pinned against her flower, and Dask was trying to communicate with his captors in a friendly way. They responded with not-so-friendly words and gestures.

Another Eletsol burst out from the forest with a scrap of orange cloth in his hand. He headed straight to the leader and the yellow-haired man. As all of the magicians took notice of the cloth, they began moving the flowers faster. The two men briefly conferred, and then the yellow-haired man gave muted orders that spread through the party in a babble of soft voices. Some magicians broke away to fly around the group, watching the forest and readying their staves.

Matil's ears lowered as the tension affected her. She looked up at the trees casting shadows across the under-growth. Shadows. She imagined the cool touch of shade spreading across her whole form, the shadows growing to envelop her. Just how she pictured it in her mind, her body faded out of sight.

Savage cries and twanging strings rent the air, and a few of the Eletsol magicians dropped to the forest floor. The flowers halted. The stem of Matil's flower rocked to one side, tipping her backward. Shocked out of her faded state, Matil abruptly became visible. Her fingers scrabbled at Dewdrop's back. She found the edges of the beetle's shell and gripped it until her knuckles turned white. The beetle tried in vain to lift her spindly legs out of the flower, then the two lurched as the flower swung in the other direction. When Matil felt the motion slowing, she stretched to look over the pink petals. Something stuck out from the body of a fallen Eletsol. She nearly let go of Dewdrop.

Arrows. The Eletsol had been shot.

2

The Bonds of War

The rest of the Eletsol drew together around Matil and her friends and coiled their staves into oval shields. Arrows continued to fly, but now the shields blocked many of them. Matil's heart clenched when the projectiles whizzed past. Another Eletsol fell. An arrow grazed Khelya's flower.

The leader and two others flew down to the ground and then back up, appearing to pull at the air with their hands. Plant tendrils and grass twisted upward, forming a barrier around the flower prisons and the Eletsol. The whir of incoming arrows diminished as they stuck in the plant wall. Matil kept her head low against Dewdrop's back. She peeked past the petals of her flower and tried to spot the enemy through the gaps in the grass and plants. The attackers were nowhere to be seen. The Eletsol inside the encircling wall waited, quiet and still, until long after the sounds of bowstrings had stopped.

The yellow-haired man finally said something, pointing toward the arrows' source. The Eletsol turned their shields back into spears and began to peel back the plant wall with their magic. The leader cut in sharply, causing them to freeze and look at him. The two men glared at each other before launching into a heated exchange. Matil met the eyes of Khelya and then Dask, whose head was still the only visible part of him. It looked like he was trying to pry his flower open under the net.

The leader gave one final shout that sent the other into dour silence. Things moved hastily afterward. The Eletsol let the plant wall fall to the ground and then retrieved their four fallen companions, piling them in a larger moving flower taken from the wayside. Wind blew Matil's hair back as they traveled at a newly urgent pace. The Eletsol moved in an odd way while they propelled the flowers onward; they rocked back and forth in the air and let the currents determine their flight paths. They looked like falling petals. Matil wondered why they would travel like that, but then she imagined the staggered movement helping them to evade a sudden barrage of arrows.

At the mushroom-ringed base of a huge, gnarled tree, someone gave an order and the party came to a halt. Trilling calls echoed down from the branches, to which the leader responded entreatingly. He seemed to reach an agreement with the unseen alva. The yellow-haired man began directing the Eletsol in forming plant walls, fortifying an area among the extensive roots of the tree. One side of the area was already walled in by immense rocks that rose out of the roots. Gravel lay scattered on the ground. While the Eletsol worked, they left the flower prisons off to the rocky side with a guard. The guard stood between the prisoners and the tree on a squat tree stump with a flat top.

Matil looked around to make sure the leader was out of earshot. He was the only one who had spoken the common language so far. Hopefully the guard couldn't understand it. "Can either of you move the nets? Mine's too heavy."

The guard looked at her without much interest.

"Same," Dask said. "I'd suggest we cut the nets, but that's obviously out of the question."

Khelya grunted, pushed off from the flower as much as she could, and fell back down. The guard flew over and smacked her with his staff.

"Why, you—git back 'ere!" She again struggled at the net, drawing another smack. "Ow!" Now Khelya settled down, grumbling.

What would the Eletsol do to their prisoners? And would it take a long time? Matil couldn't help but picture the Skorgon marauding through Eventyr. She would make the leader understand that he had to let the group go. What if Nychtfal was devastated and war-torn because it had taken so long to journey north on this search? Still, if Matil, Khelya, and Dask wanted to stop *her* – Matil wasn't sure whether *her* meant Nychta Olsta, Matil herself, or both – they didn't know how else to do it. Which was why they must get free soon and find the human, Mr. Korsen.

When the Eletsol finished setting up their fortifications, the forest was darker. Matil could see snatches of heavy clouds through the trees.

"Looks like we'll have some rain," Khelya said. In her position, she was unable to do much besides look upward.

"Looks like it," Dask said.

Khelya pursed her lips. "Think we'll have any trouble?"

"Trouble?" He smiled, the round flower making him appear to be a yellow fruit with a Ranycht head. "Nah."

Even Matil could detect his sarcasm.

The hum of wings alerted them to the leader's approach from the camp. He landed beside the guard on the stump and his wings flicked down into a rest position. "Outsiders. I am Ansi the Smart of the Taina Eletsol."

Dask coughed to stifle a laugh. "The Smart, huh? Nice name. Puts it all out there. I should be Dask the Incredible."

Khelya snorted. "Dask the Incredibly Full of Himself."

"Ouch."

"How about Dask the Smart?" Matil said. "Smart-mouth, that is."

"Ooh, you guys are hurting me."

Ansi stared, unamused. "This is not the time to joke."

"I know," Dask sighed. "But somehow that's when things are the funniest."

"I am the son of the chief who ruled our tribe." He stepped forward, taking his wooden staff from around his chest. It uncurled in his hand to its full height. "You will respect me."

Dask bowed his head to Ansi, coming across as very oily. "Of course, sir prince, of course. We're at your service."

Matil bowed her head, too, and Khelya could only nod.

"Good. The giant, what's wrong with her?"

"Magic," Dask said nonchalantly. "We used ours on her too much and she's been stuck that way since."

Ansi looked at each of them in fascination.

"Now," Dask said, "let's do business. If you promise to let us go, we'll owe you one."

"What is this 'one' that you would owe me?" Ansi said.

"Oh, anything you want – within reason, of course. We can put you in connection with merchants of rare goods, provide building and farming advice, perform at feasts and festivals, and a lot of other things. The only price is our freedom. We keep tips."

Ansi turned his attention to cleaning his fingernails.

"Or- or *you* could keep our tips," Dask said. "If that's what it takes."

"You are bound for captivity unless you tell all," Ansi said, looking up from his hands. "Maybe it's different where you come from, but spies are not welcome here."

"Spies?" Khelya said. "We ain't spies!"

Matil patted Dewdrop's head, partly to calm herself. "Sir, have you heard about the Skorgon and Nychta Olsta?"

"Only some. We Eletsol…we have our own problems." Ansi looked down in distraction. A moment later, he lifted his chin sharply. "Talk."

"Basically, we think Olsta's trying to take over Eventyr," Dask said.

"With the Saikyr," Khelya added. "We're on our way to ask Mr. Korsen how to wake up the Elders from the Hibernation."

Ansi burst into laughter. "You speak of tatuvar! Baby stories!"

"You're…you're an Eletsol," Khelya said. "Haven't you seen Mr. Korsen?"

"Yes. The Watcher is real enough. But to talk with him? The Watcher watches. He doesn't speak. And to 'wake up the Elders'? They can't be woken. The Elders have been dead for a thousand years."

3

Such Is Death

Khelya's mouth hung open and Matil stared. The Elders were everything. Without them, Nychta may already have won.

"Dead?" said Dask. He leaned toward Ansi. "How do you know?"

Ansi chuckled. "Dyndal of the Green told our ancestors so as he laid himself down for the last time."

"That's a lie!" Khelya said. She grappled briefly with the net and then gave up. "Calo made a speech about the Hibernation an' everything! How can you say the leader of the Elders is wrong?"

Matil looked with apprehension between Khelya and Ansi.

Ansi folded his hands behind his back. "Have you ever seen an Elder?"

"'Course not," Khelya said.

"I *have*," he said. "The body of Lord Dyndal."

The three prisoners stared, even more astounded.

"Slow down," Dask said. "A body? A dead guy? There's no way he'd last a thousand years. I think you've been conned, my friend."

Ansi shook his head. "You won't understand, not unless you've seen him. And as outsiders, you will never see him."

The barest amount of color rose in Khelya's translucent cheeks. "Why not?"

"Dyndal trusted us enough to give us the truth," he said. "He told us to guard his body for the rest of time, because it has much power still. He spoke, 'Those outside of the Eletsol clans may not enter, save he who bears my sign.' But the sign has never been seen."

"What if *we* have the sign?" Matil said a little desperately.

He looked at her. "Then show it to me."

"Um…" She thought about everything they had in their packs. An Elder's sign, whatever that meant, would probably be mystical and ancient. None of their food scraps or cheap supplies fit that description.

"Don't waste time showing me a fake," Ansi said. "Even Eletsol children know what the sign is. We can't be fooled by outsiders."

"You're makin' all this up," Khelya said. "You gotta be."

Ansi gestured at the camp. "Each one here has looked upon Dyndal. According to his instructions, passed down through the generations, every Eletsol visits his tomb after Thrualrest, for our greatest festival." Ansi's expression darkened. "This year's Velana Festival has passed, but Tain Fridda did not allow our clan to go. She only listens to her pride." He glanced behind him. "I shouldn't let such things slip from my tongue."

The guard on the stump stood idly, showing no signs of comprehension.

"We didn't hear a word," Dask said, grinning.

"Good." Ansi strode across the stump as if distancing himself from his own words.

"Then, um, now that you know what we're doing here," Matil said, "can you let us go?"

"You are no longer prisoners, but guests," he replied.

"Then we can leave!" Dask said.

"You're our *guests*." Ansi maintained a level gaze. "You may leave, but it is…a bad plan. First, you're still under suspicion. You appeared right before we were attacked."

"We didn't have nothin' to do with that attack!" Khelya said.

"I believe you," he said. "For now. But how will it look if you continue northwest toward the Watcher, straight into the territory of our enemies? And you saw that they didn't care whether you three were hurt. When they capture you, I doubt they will treat you better than we have."

Dask's ears lowered in frustration. "Okay, Your Smartness, we get it."

"You will stay with us, then, ensuring everyone's safety. Yes?"

Matil and Khelya nodded reluctantly. Ansi said something to the guard, who frowned with clear disapproval.

But together they moved their arms, tilted Khelya's flower until it touched the ground, and peeled back the net. Khelya rolled out with a yelp. They did the same for Matil and Dask, putting the nets aside in a heap.

The beetles and supplies fell in disorder, so Matil, Khelya, and Dask helped them flip right-side-up. Matil rubbed both of the beetles on the head. Olnar shuffled sideways rather grumpily, but Dewdrop wiggled her antennae.

On the stump above, Ansi looked out into the forest with a troubled gaze.

Matil watched him curiously. "Is something wrong?" she called.

"Yes, as always." He floated to the ground, the guard following him. "Is it not the way of life?"

"But you look *really* worried," she said.

"I do not look worried!" His wings sprang back up, his frown deepened, and now it was true; he looked more offended than worried.

Seeing him, the guard crouched into a battle stance and glanced between Ansi and the outsiders.

"I definitely saw some worry," Dask said. He elbowed Khelya.

"*Ow!* Ow, uh…yeah," she said. "Some worry."

Ansi's wings fluttered before settling. He gestured at the guard to stand down and then walked closer to the outsiders. "I'm not worried, I am…puva. I have lost something that I never had."

"How does that work?" Khelya said.

"There is…a girl, but I can't approach her."

"That's it?" Dask stretched his legs. "Just go up and talk to her. Never fails."

"I cannot!"

"Of course you can, buddy."

"If I do," Ansi said, "I will be tortured by my own clan and locked up. Then, if I fail to publicly renounce the Vima daily for one year, I will be executed!"

The three outsiders exchanged glances.

Matil spoke for them. "What?"

Ansi turned to the side. "My father was chief of the Takkamakaini clan. My elder sisters, Fridda and Dag, are twins. One is a gifted magician, the other is not. Father wanted them to rule together, to share for once, but when he died, they fought to the point that it split the Takkamakaini. Two years ago, Fridda gathered around her the Taina, the strong in magic. Dag led away the Vima, the strong in arm. Since then we have been at war, a war you have already seen. It is the Vima who ambushed us earlier. So do you understand?" He lowered his voice. "I am Taina, and the beautiful lady is Vima."

"Oh…" Matil said. "I wish we could help somehow."

He looked at her in surprise and then narrowed his gaze. "Do you really?"

"Count on it," Dask said. "Most alva would be more concerned with their own problems in this situation. But Matil's a contrarian."

She blinked a few times, embarrassed. "I just like it when

things are right, and- and what he told us doesn't sound right." She turned to Ansi. "Can't you leave to find her?"

"No!" he said. "No, it would be unthinkable. Just as Father gave to my sisters the clan, so he gave to me the responsibility of the clan. I will not leave."

Dask casually tugged on one ear. "Why not get rid of your sisters?"

"Dask," Khelya warned.

"Hey, I don't mean what you think I mean. Just, you know, put someone else in charge. Someone smart." He gestured at Ansi.

The Eletsol appeared shaken. "I…have not thought that way. It is against Father's wishes also."

"What do the Taina want?" Matil said. "Do they really want to be at war with the Vima?"

"When it first began, they wanted very much to fight. For them it was good sport. It was important to show the Vima that magic was the most powerful and that Fridda was more fit to rule. But alva died on both sides in the battles. My alva no longer desire war. I have heard the same of some Vima."

"Then why are they still fighting?"

"The clan loves my sister," he said. "I am smart, but they call her Tain Fridda the Smartest. They trust her. They don't see her making mistakes or losing control. She and her closest advisors make certain that they don't."

"Thiffen," said Dask. "Sounds bad."

"It's more than bad, you dense Ranycht," Ansi groaned.

Dask opened his mouth indignantly, but Matil caught his eye with a shake of her head. A covert glare at Ansi seemed to settle his conscience. "Look," he said, "I think we can help each other."

"You can't help me," Ansi said. "You are outsiders in this land."

Khelya put her hands on her hips. "You said you were given responsibility of the clan. But I don't think it's all that responsible for these chief ladies to keep fightin' a war when nobody else wants to."

Ansi paused, then paced back and forth, muttering to himself in his own language. "Alalat…"

Dask held up an encouraging fist to Khelya.

"What can I do?" Ansi said. "You've shown me that I am failing my father with each flight of the sun." He dropped to his knees and struck the ground. "But I cannot take control from my sister!"

"Ferra?" the guard said, looking alarmed.

Ansi held up a hand. "Alatinnen."

"Taking control won't be easy," Dask said, "though it's not impossible. Buddy, what you need is power."

He glared up at Dask. "Buddy is not a respectful word."

"Sure it is!"

"Quiet." Ansi stood, taking on his previous morose state. "I can't get power. I lost what I had, because I assumed my sister would listen to me. She listened instead to the Maati, her council of friends, and now I merely lead scouts through the wilds."

Dask put a hand on his chin thoughtfully.

"What about the alva of your clan?" said Matil. "You could show them the truth about your sister. If you don't give up, there's still a…"

The blue-winged, yellow-haired Eletsol flew over from the camp and landed. The guard thumped his chest in a salute.

Ansi spoke smoothly to the other man, who responded with a short sentence and much hard staring at the outsiders. A sharper pronouncement from Ansi got the yellow-haired man to leave.

"Who's he?" Dask said.

"Kirra, the leader of this force," Ansi said. "I've explained to him that you are not spies."

"Leader? I thought you were in charge."

Ansi pointed at the guard and the camp. "These men belong to Kirra. I am the chief's son and higher in rank, so Kirra belongs to me. Even so, he doesn't submit to my authority because he knows I hold little influence. I believe he wishes me gone, out of his way. He would have a better chance of joining the Maati then." He opened his spiny wings and shut them again with a downward slice of his hand. "It would seem that I'm falling without wings. May the ancestors have mercy on me."

Matil stepped forward. "You don't have to——"

"Not now. I must leave and do my duty." A gleam of life entered his eyes. "That ambush should not have happened in this part of our territory. I'll speak with the clan living here to see what's gone wrong. I will return tomorrow." He gazed at the outsiders a moment, nodded, and took off into the branches above.

"He didn't mean it," Khelya said. "'Bout the Elders. He's wrong, anyway. They're the strongest beings in Eventyr. Once they wake up, everything…everything'll be…" Her half-faded face looked wobbly. "He said they had Dyndal's t-tomb."

"It could be a mistake," Matil said. "Besides, I'm certain that Myrkhar is alive."

"That's *comforting*. What if the Heilar are dead, but Myrkhar's still alive?" Khelya covered her eyes with her hands. "We wouldn't have a chance."

"Don't be so sure about Myrkhar just because Nychta's using the Book," said Dask. "If the other Elders are dead, it's more than likely that Myrkhar is, too."

"Oh, you don't even believe in them," Khelya said.

He smiled. "Who knows? My mind could change."

Matil perked up her ears.

"I'm a logical guy," Dask said, squatting down to pat Olnar's head, "and my new theory makes perfect sense. Try this: The Elders were real alva a thousand years ago. Powerful magicians worshiped as gods by the other alva. Some 'Elders' got mad at the others, and they fought until they all died, either from the war or from old age. Most of the forest preferred to think of their deaths as a 'Hibernation' while the Eletsol had the real story the entire time. I saw the same thing in my orphanage. The nurses would tell really young kids that their parents were just asleep."

Khelya looked sternly down at him. "That's not what the Chivishi says about the Elders."

The Chivishi. It was a scroll Matil had seen in Khelya's home that recorded laws, history, and songs from past ages, from before the Hibernation.

Dask looked right back at Khelya. "The Chivishi was written by alva. You don't think alva can lie?"

"'Course I know they lie," she said. "But why would they lie about somethin' so...so..."

His smile returned, small and bitter. "Depends. Some alva lie to make power for themselves. Like Ansi's sister. Other alva lie because they're afraid of the truth."

"And what's the truth?" Matil asked. Day after day, Khelya believed Thosten and the Chivishi were true while Dask called them lies. Matil was getting frustrated. "Is there any way to know for sure?"

"Great question," Dask said. "As far as I can tell, there's one sure way to know the truth. It's by looking at the world around us. You see those flowers they put us in?" The yellow, white, and pink flowers still stood over the three outsiders and the guard. "Those things live and then they die. Same with everything here. *That's* the real truth."

He was right. But when she looked at the world around her, Matil got the feeling that there was more to it than could be seen.

"Anyway, Khel," Dask went on, "all I meant is that we're better off if the Elders are gone for good. We'd have a chance against Nychta, and we wouldn't need to go hunting for a human. I didn't say it to make you feel bad."

Khelya paused. "Sometimes it's good to feel bad. You think harder about things then."

The three of them gathered their scattered supply packs into one pile as light rain began dripping from the tree canopy. Khelya moved closer to one of the flowers for extra cover, but it looked like they would stay dry under this tree.

Matil scrutinized Dask. He rarely talked about his orphanage. He had no problem telling harrowing stories of growing up in Ecker's Brug and racing all over Nychtfal on jobs for his gang. But he deflected questions about his childhood, saying he didn't remember it very well. Maybe he remembered better than he let on.

4

Darkness in the Light

The Council Herald's voice echoed through the gilded circular hall of the Ambermeet. "…and, as it should be, the Obrigi reacted to this latest rise in taxes with unwavering loyalty." His wings glowed, shafts of light spilling outward from his back. He read from a parchment. "Construction of the Fortification has taken farmers from the field, resulting in a late planting season for many. The reduced crop yield is expected to hollow our coffers further."

"Understood." Golden-bearded Lord Councilman Owynth stood in front of his grand chair at the head of the assembly, his many-branched staff in hand. Beside him was an empty but even grander throne adorned with two butterfly wings.

The soaring walls of this place were made from ancient amber that encased fragments of the past – torn leaves, pebbles, huge insects. Raised wooden stands surrounded a beautiful sun mural on the floor. Sangriga with wings like sunlight and delicate purple robes sat in chairs on the stands. This was the Council of Tyrlis, where decisions were made for two nations of alva bound by alliance: the Sangriga and the Obrigi.

"What news, then, from Nychtfal?" Lord Owynth said.

A woman at today's meeting stuck out from the other lavishly-styled Council members due to her plainness; she wore no jewelry, used sparse cosmetics, and tied her dark blonde hair in a simple bun. She held her own wooden staff, which ended at the tip in an upside-down iron triangle. It looked like a weapon, destructive and without subtlety. Councilwoman Lyria's appearance fed the wary talk that she didn't deserve her title, that she was a brazen commoner, an interloper making fools of the rest of them. In Lyria's humble opinion, they didn't need help with the last bit.

Her greenish-blue eyes were locked on the stout herald and she realized that, without thinking, she had leaned forward in her chair and tilted her head as though it would enhance the hearing of her long, tapered Sangriga ears. She wasn't the only one with an interest in the alarming events taking place in the dusky realm of Nychtfal. Wise alva took heed of them.

The Council Herald was already unrolling another scroll. "When the eastern township of Goska was taken without bloodshed by Nychta Olsta," he read, "many nearby villages surrendered themselves. Shortly thereafter, Nychtfal's government entered into negotiations with her, learning that she had named her captured territory the 'Ranycht Dominion'. The result of their diplomacy was a treaty, the details of which are unknown save for the knowledge that the High Court of Nychtfal has ordered its subjects not to resist the Dominion.

"What has been seen of the Skorgon armies puts their number at roughly three thousand soldiers in total. Some Ranycht from the threatened townships in eastern Nychtfal have fled southward and are preparing for resistance. There are also claims that the Dominion worships the Elder of Night, Myrkhar."

Mutters and whispers swept through the Council.

None of these details were new to Lyria. She had heard much the same from her spies. Unfortunately, with the tenuous situation in eastern Nychtfal and the Nychtfal-Obrigi Fortification in place, it would now be very difficult to glean information from those parts.

"Three outlaws have been seen traveling through Nychtfal, one of whom is a Ranycht woman *without wings*... however, no reports of them have surfaced since the sixty-third."

Lyria felt a glimmer of satisfaction, but carefully arranged her expression into one of frustration. If Councilman Nider looked her way, she must not appear to be the one who had freed those three outlaws, for he had made it clear that he suspected.

The herald rattled off some things about trade, and then he mentioned the ongoing dispute with the High Courts of Nychtfal. The Book of Myrkhar had been stolen five weeks ago from its Vault here in Corwyna and carried to Nycht-fal, where the governing powers refused to permit entry for Sangriga investigators. That refusal angered many Council members, particularly the older ones who recalled the last time the Book's magic had been unleashed. Lyria was just a child when it happened.

As soon as the herald rolled up his scroll, the sturdy and short-haired Commander Dalen stood at attention. He was not an appointed member of the Council and, lacking the traditional purple robe, he looked out of place. Dalen, though young, was a senior military officer and wore a stunning deep bronze cuirass and heavy leather belt over a long white robe. He thumped the end of his bladed, tasseled staff on the floor in preparation to speak. Several Council members snickered. Only the Lord Councilman stamped his staff. Lyria knew, however, that Dalen was more used to shows of authority over his soldiers than he was to Council etiquette.

"Order," Owynth said, and that was enough to quiet the Council. "Speak, Dalen." He nodded encouragingly at the man to whom his daughter was betrothed.

Dalen hesitated, looking like a boar amidst deer. He drew up his chest. "I advise the Council to fully mobilize our forces. With what we've just heard, I'm convinced that being caught unprepared would be fatal."

One Councilman with his hair in a curled tail floated upward out of his seat, legs dangling but crossed at the ankles. His bearing looked casual, but Lyria knew he was carefully replicating a fashionable pose she had seen in paintings. With no sign of outward effort, he caused his wings to pulse with bright light. Now all eyes were on him. "Forgive me, Commander," he said, "but…caught unprepared by whom?"

"By this Nychta Olsta," said Dalen.

"And you think she is a threat…why?" The Councilman lifted an eyebrow.

"How do you suppose she managed a treaty with Nychtfal? Intimidation? A dangerous possibility. A promise? Even more dangerous. If they've allied with designs to acquire more territory – if they're confident enough for that – then we had best be ready."

The Councilman looked unconvinced even as he shut his mouth and descended into his chair.

"If what you say is true," said another Councilman in a calm voice, "we oughtn't use it as an excuse to fight." A few Council members expressed their assent.

The voice belonged to Councilman Nider Vyng, who sat relaxed in his chair, tracing circles on the floor with the end of his emerald-studded staff. He had a handsome face, piercing yellow eyes, and a tasteful sleekness about him. His reddish-blond hair was pulled back at the crown and the rest fell silkily down his neck. Among the others he was popular and respected – not always present at meetings, but certainly there when the most important decisions were to be made.

"At the first sign of aggression," he went on, "our diplomats can work out an agreement that will make violence unnecessary."

"I said nothing about violence, or fighting," Dalen assured. "I meant only that we have got to be ready for it. And in the case of diplomacy, the suggestion of force will help us to argue our cause."

"Once you have your army, Commander, then what? Will you think of some clever excuse for a war? No disrespect meant, but I don't believe that this is a prudent path."

Alva all around the Ambermeet nodded. Owynth's head bobbed thoughtfully.

Lyria's wings and thick staff propelled her upright. "Lord Councilman."

"Speak, Lyria."

"Nychta Olsta is the one who stole the Book of Myrkhar."

Voices gasped and exclaimed. She knew what some of the Council members must be thinking: *How did she discover it? Whom did she pay?*

"Those of you who do not believe my words," Lyria continued, "search the histories. Skorgon armies? A nation folding like parchment? The Book's magic has returned."

Nider and Lyria met eyes briefly. He winked.

Despair washed over her as firmly-buried memories emerged. The last time he winked at her, she had been living a nightmare engineered by him. She refocused on the proceedings, determined not to let him put her off-balance.

"If you are correct," Owynth said, "this changes much."

"Indeed," Lyria said, pushing the past to the back of her mind. "We have a right to demand answers from Olsta. I propose we send a diplomat to do just that. In addition, I second Commander Dalen's proposition of mobilizing the army."

Owynth glanced around the Ambermeet. "Has anyone more to say?"

"I counter the proposals." Nider drifted upright out of his chair.

The sparring would go on for as long as he was willing to fight, but it was only a matter of time until the proposals gained enough support. Common sense and the deals Lyria had struck would win today, at least. She allowed herself a grim smile.

5

Matters of the Heart

The rain picked up and the scent of moist soil filled the atmosphere. More water made it past the tree branches. Matil liked rain – but only when she and her friends stayed dry.

Atop the tree stump, the Eletsol guard flicked his yellow wings to shake out raindrops. He squinched his eyes in concentration while he carefully motioned with his hands around a protrusion of ivy on the tree trunk beside him. Part of the ivy twisted away from the trunk toward the guard, new leaves sprouting until the plant covered his head. The guard's magic protected him from the weather, but he didn't seem to care one bit about the outsiders. The other Eletsol in the camp had formed thick roofs out of leaves and living grass. Wind rode through the camp and shook the flowers from side to side. Matil jumped backward when she felt spray from a splash of water. Khelya squeaked. Her boots had gotten drenched.

"I think this rain is out to get us," Dask said. "C'mon, let's find some better cover."

As they left their place under the flowers, Matil caught the yellow-haired Eletsol, Kirra, staring at them from the edge of the camp.

The three, pulling Dewdrop and Olnar behind them, dodged streams of rain pouring from leaves and droplets hitting the rocky ground. Finding no better place, they huddled together with their beetles and supply packs under a strong-smelling red mushroom. The beetles climbed up on the mushroom stalk and went into a state of rest. It was cold enough that no one was in the mood to speak. Matil rubbed her arms and stamped her feet. She noticed another problem with taking shelter under a mushroom; the stalk didn't leave enough space for them to lie down.

"This mushroom…" she began.

"Is terrible," Khelya finished. The Obrigi stood with her head hunched to avoid sticking it in the gills on the underside of the mushroom cap.

Dask pointed to the gravel strewn throughout the roots. "Can we make a shelter with those rocks?"

Khelya considered them. "Yeah."

"It'll be hard to build in the rain," Matil said.

"It'll be easy with Khel's help," he said, leaning his elbow on Khelya.

She frowned down at him. "Whenever you say 'with Khel's help', I end up doin' all the work."

"That's because you get upset when we do things 'the wrong way', and then you take over."

"There's a right way and a wrong way," Khelya said indignantly. "I've *tried* showing you guys the difference. Maybe this time you'll learn."

Dask wiped his wet hair out of his eyes and twitched his large ears. "All right, then. How do we start?"

"Get some rocks," she said.

Matil and Dask hurried through the steady onslaught of rain to gather big rocks and pebbles in their arms, while Khelya began moving dirt. The guard leaned down from his stump to better watch them. A flat-topped mound of dirt grew, upon which Khelya built three-quarters of a circle with the stones, a high wall that looked like it shouldn't even be able to stand. Next, she went among the mushrooms, tore off the top of the largest one, and placed it upon the stone wall as a roof. It was dark enough to be night when she finished, and the only light in the area came from the sheltered Eletsol campfires.

They shuttled their supplies into the shelter and lined it with their blankets. The inside was small, and once they had dried off and sat down, the extra space would have been enough for only one more alva. Their warmth filled the cave-like structure. By now the three of them were famished. They took out some of the food stored in their bags: strips of pea pod and dried meat.

"If you noticed, I did a lot of that work on my own," Khelya said. Her spectral face was turned toward the ground, probably because she couldn't see the two Ranycht in the dark like they could see her.

Dask held up his hands. "We tried."

"C'mon." She crunched down on a slice of pea pod. "It's not hard to stack rocks."

"We don't have your freakish ability to stack them just right so they won't tip over," he said.

"It's a very nice freakish ability," Matil said, "but it's harder for us since we're not builders like you."

"I'm not a builder," said Khelya. "I'm a farmer."

Dask poked her with his foot. "What's that got to do with anything?"

"I-I'm a farmer."

"I mean, farmers farm," he said, "and you didn't get much time to do that. You've probably done more building than farming by now."

She looked up blindly. "Does that mean…I'm a builder?"

"I wouldn't call you a builder either." Dask tore a bite from his chunk of meat.

"Then what am I?"

"Hm. You're a lotta different things, aren't you?" He finished chewing and swallowed. "Right now we're travelers."

Khelya smiled. "Khelya…Epalen."

"Ehpullen?" Dask repeated.

"Well, when Obrigi make their work choice, they get a name. Epalen means traveler in the older language. I was called Dylsen, farmer, before I met you two. Never expected it to change."

"Never? You get a job and you're always that job?"

She scratched her head. "You know somethin'? Everyone I knew, old or young, was the same thing they'd been since they got out of school. My pa was all turned up an' yelling when I worried if I'd regret being a farmer. So over and over I told myself I wanted it. 'Cept…now the farm's long gone and the world's turned wilder than a vole with fleas. And I'm kinda—I dunno. I think I'm ready for a new line of work."

"I'm just glad that doesn't mean another gang is gonna have it out for us." Dask snickered and then cleared his throat. "Sorry, that wasn't funny."

"It was," Matil said. "Kind of." She tilted her head to listen to the patter of rain on the mushroom cap roof. Her mind turned to their travels in the past weeks, especially to what Khelya had been teaching her: stories about the Elders, and what the Chivishi said. Dask tried not to be around when Khelya talked about those things, but even when he was and then inevitably argued with her, Matil found it interesting to hear what both of them believed. She just wished she could settle on her own beliefs.

"Would it be all right for Khelya to tell a story?" she said.

"Yeah," said Khelya. "I could tell a short one."

Dask waved his hand. "Go right ahead."

Matil grinned at him and, swallowing any hesitance about her next words, turned to Khelya. "I'd like to know more about Myrkhar."

"Myrkhar, huh? Scary choice." After a moment of thought, Khelya snapped her fingers. "I've got a story. It's really important, too."

"Wait, how'd you do that?" Dask said.

"What?"

He rubbed his fingers together. "How'd you snap?"

"You don't know how to snap?" Khelya said in disbelief. "Look, let me tell the story first. One thing at a time." She sat up straight and cleared her throat. "Ready? Okay. When Thosten made Eventyr, it had no magic. So he made a pool of water called the Heart, which held all magic."

"The Heart?" said Matil. "But…what about the Heart of Myrkhar?" She'd seen Myrkhar's round symbol in a dream and had never forgotten it.

"Myrkhar made his own 'Heart' later—hey, that's a different story."

Now Matil wanted to hear *that* story, but she nodded. "Sorry."

"So," Khelya continued, "Thosten made the Heart, the pool of magical water, and then he made the first Elders… along with us, the first alva of the eight races. At the start, Eventyr was a place where no one got hurt, but no one was really awake, either. They flew around like they were dreaming. To wake his new creations, Thosten said to them, 'C'mere. I've got one rule that you are never to break.'" Khelya held up her thumb. "'Don't drink the Heart's water. If you do, you'll die.'"

Dask snorted.

"After layin' it down like that, Thosten made the Elders guardians over the alva and the Heart. He put the Elder Calo in charge of the others because Calo cared the most for Eventyr. But Wuren of Day was the strongest Elder, an' he thought that Thosten was wrong. As the strongest, Wuren should rule. Time went on, and he started to suspect Calo of drinkin' from the Heart. Must be fair to let the other Elders in on it, too, so Wuren decided to try it for himself first. He had two Elders loyal to him draw away the guards at the Heart Sanctum, an' then he went in. The inside was a maze that no one could get through unless the Heart let them pass. Even so, he used the sun to light the true path and pushed his way through the enchantment. Finally he got to the Heart. When he kneeled next to it and tried to cup the water in his hands, it burned them something awful, so much that he had to let go."

"Let me guess," Dask said. "He didn't get the message that maybe, you know, the stuff wasn't good for him?"

"No, he did not," Khelya said. "With his power he made a stone bowl from the floor of the Sanctum and then used it to lift out some water. Calo, showin' up and finding the Sanctum unguarded, ran in after Wuren. 'You can't drink it!' he said. Wuren was still convinced that Calo'd already tasted the water, and if he drank, he'd be able to challenge Calo for leadership. He downed the whole bowl. From the first swallow his throat felt like it was bein' torn apart. He'd never been in pain before that day. Now it was all through his insides. It took everything he had – his magic, his strength, and his jealousy – to keep 'imself from burning into bits. Calo just watched in fear for his fellow Elder."

Matil's mouth had opened in a tiny grimace. Dask seemed impressed.

"Something happened to Wuren as the water filled him. His body changed. It turned cold as death, and he didn't hurt as much. Soon, he didn't hurt at all. He felt much more awake than before. Calo couldn't believe his eyes and asked, 'How're you still alive?' But Wuren felt something else growin' inside and itchin' at his fingertips. It was power. He finally realized exactly what it meant to break the rule.

"Calo attacked him and Wuren held him back with magic. The Heart was beginning to shine brighter and brighter, so Wuren carved a big urn outta the stone floor. He filled it with water until the light made him blind. Then there was a sound so loud his head felt pierced through. Finally he could see again, but he wasn't standing beside the Heart anymore. He stood alone in the wilderness with the cup, the urn, and the water he had stolen. And he didn't show himself to the others for a year.

"The Elders loyal to him waited and waited. When he came back, his eyes were pure white. His friends said, 'Wuren, where've you been?' He smiled at that. 'I am Myrkhar,' he told 'em. 'Don't y'all wonder, like I do, why Calo has the crown? It's because of the Heart. He broke the rule.'"

Matil had suspected who Wuren would turn out to be. She nested farther into her blanket. "Did Calo really drink from the Heart?"

"Naw," Khelya said. "Myrkhar lied to get the others to follow 'im. But hold on now, I'm almost done." She deepened her voice to imitate Myrkhar again. "'I brought back the Heart's water so we can all drink and be like Calo. Here, use this cup.' Each one of his followers drank a cupful of water, and they felt the terrible pain, but at the end of it they were stronger and their minds were sharper.

"The Mekydra Time started when Myrkhar's Elders, who called themselves the Saikyr, went to the alva and said that it was good to break Thosten's rule. They said that the rule was a test given by Thosten and Calo to see who in Eventyr could discover the goodness of the water. Myrkhar told them he just wanted to share it with everyone else, 'cause that was fair. He gave the first alva a drop of water each. They seemed to wake up even more. The world looked scarier to them, and now they knew pain, but the water tasted so good that they told the rest of the Elders what they'd done. The Elders who hadn't taken the water yet were confused. The alva they loved and watched over had done what Thosten said not to. So they listened to the alva, even though they knew it was wrong, and they went to Myrkhar to drink from the urn.

"Again, Calo found out too late to stop 'em, but the good Elders saw more clearly now, and they were sorry. They went straight to the Heart and begged Thosten to kill them. Thosten was angry, but he saw into them and knew that even though they were corrupted, they would do what was right. He let them live. Their punishment was that they must battle the Saikyr and keep the laws. Speakin' of which, he gave 'em a new set of rules called the Great Vishi, and that's what we follow in the Chivishi." Khelya folded her arms. "There. Crazy, huh?"

"Crazy," said Matil. "So the Elders all used to be on the same side?"

"There weren't any sides back then. Myrkhar made his own side by drinkin' the water."

Dask rubbed at his chin, frowning. "I get the entertainment value, but it's creepy the way you alva talk about dusty old stories like they're so profound and real."

"Thanks," Khelya said.

"Just—alva write books night in and night out. The Chivishi is your average book-scroll-thing, but someone thought it was super special and now we've got insane cultists trying to summon thokiri because of some make-believe bad guy in said book. There's something wrong with that situation, don't ya think? Maybe if we all stopped believing in bedtales, we'd forget about evil spirits, too. Maybe that's how this messed-up forest can be fixed."

"But we do so many terrible things," Matil said. "What would happen if alva forgot the Chivishi? Wouldn't Eventyr be worse?"

Dask shrugged. "I think it might be better."

"That makes no sense at all," Khelya said forcefully. "The best alva I've ever known were Thosten-followers."

"The ones I've met were bottom-of-the-barrel, as far as alva go," said Dask. "Pretending they're goody-good niceynice while they dip into the funds they extort from honest dupes who believe every word."

"Says the gangster," she retorted.

"Don't call me that," he said.

"Well," said Khelya, "aren't you one?"

"He quit," Matil said. "Look at what he's done on his own. He even bought supplies and beetles for us with his last bit of money."

Dask stared at her and then nodded. "Yeah. I quit my gang, Obrigi. I crack jokes about it, sure, but that part of my life is…is over. Got it?"

Khelya's tone gentled. "I get it. But you can't assume the Chivishi is bad just 'cause some Thostenics do bad things. Read it, you'll see."

"I got enough of that stuff when I was a flightling in the orphanage," he said. "'No lying. No cheating. No sweets unless you work real hard, no laughing except on festival days, and definitely no pretending to be the nurse or she'll make you sweep the floor until your eyes fall out from boredom. Follow *all* the rules to get into a magical land filled with Elders and good spirits and special white robes for especially good children!' Yeah, I think I'll pass."

Matil giggled.

"That's not what it's like," Khelya said.

"Khel." Dask's voice took on a serious tone. "That's what it's like for a lot of alva."

"But…" Khelya trailed off with a sigh. "I see what you mean. I'm tired. Night."

"Good night," Matil said, nervous about the mood in the shelter.

"G'night," Dask mumbled. "I got first watch. Thanks for the story."

At Dask's words, she blinked. Then she lay down and pulled the blanket over her ears. Her friends were changing, weren't they?

* * *

Matil stood on a rooftop, shivering and looking out over the city. She couldn't believe how far it spread and how deep its streets ran. Under clouded moon and dark leaves, Ranycht flew from perch to perch at frantic paces. They pushed, jostled, griped, and still had a good word to say about each other. Strong smells – pungent and delicious, rotting and growing – coiled up from the labyrinth of bridges and platforms all over the trees.

"Hey, stay focused."

Her eyes snapped to the man in front of her. Short strands of dark brown hair hung around his face, with the rest fastened back in a tail. He had a skulking demeanor and a prowling walk. Matil was beginning to realize that in the back-ways of the city, there were two types of Ranycht who survived: birds of prey and scavengers. This man was a scavenger, and he would teach her how to become like him.

"Sorry." She bit her lip nervously. For the first time since coming here, she had hope, and she couldn't afford to let it slip away. "I'm listening."

"Before we get started with the pointy objects," the man said, "you'll learn how to fight."

"Don't I need a weapon to fight with?"

"Everything is a weapon, Manners, remember that." He held out his hands. "These are some of your most important tools. With 'em, you can eat food, handle your money, hold a dagger, and give someone a North Side Kiss." He punched one hand into the other.

Matil nodded and looked down at her own small hands.

The man continued, "Feet and wings are important, too. They get you where you need to be. And feet, along with the rest of the legs? Great weapons. Now, you never wanna root down like a tree. Be ready to go in *any* direction. Which brings me to eyes and ears. Eyes need to watch, ears need to hear. If those two are on full alert, no one can sneak up on you. You see each opening for attack and escape and can act on 'em. Now tell me the tools you got."

"Uh, hands," she said. "Feet…wings. Eyes and ears."

He looked pleased. "And of course you can use your whole body in a fight. We'll get to that later. I wanna focus on how to feel, see, hear, and move when you're scrapping." He laughed. "For all this trouble, you better save my life someday."

6

The Exiles

The rain had stopped by morning and the plants were an invigorated green. Rays of sunlight stretched between the leaves. Matil noticed Khelya sitting on one side of the hut's opening, keeping watch on the forest.

Matil yawned and then stopped midway when she remembered her dream. That man...

Her dreams were memories from her old life, resurfacing while she slept. At first she had only guessed so, but one fateful night confirmed it. She had seen Crell, her orange-eyed childhood friend, in the flesh. She had met the alva she used to be, Nychta. And she had heard the Book of Myrkhar speak in her mind, its voice deeper than a well.

Pursue your revenge however you see fit, but it will not be complete. Not until you have summoned and harnessed the full power of Myrkhar and the Saikyr.

Matil hated recalling those words, yet she latched on to them. They told her what to race against.

This is only the beginning.

"Whazzer breakfast?" Dask said. He had sat up from his blankets with green eyes half-closed and black hair fanned out around his head.

Matil held back her laughter. Now she felt better. "A delicious meal of dried apple chunks and dried meat."

"…Yum." He rubbed his eyes. "Do we still have water, or is that dried, too?"

She passed him a waterskin.

Now that the three of them were awake, they ate before leaving the shelter. A different guard was posted on the stump. The other Eletsol scouts milled around the camp a few lengths away. Ansi caught sight of the outsiders and began flying over to them.

"Dask's leafy friend doesn't look too happy," Khelya said.

"He looks the same as he did yesterday," Matil said. "Do you think he's ever happy?"

"Probably not." Dask smiled at the approaching Eletsol. "Hey there, how's it going?"

"I thought about what you said." Ansi landed and lowered his voice. "And I have an idea to show my sister's true nature. The problem is that my alva don't know me well. Amongst my clan, I am…restrained."

"Sour," Khelya muttered.

"Sour?" Ansi said. "Have you eaten something sour?"

Dask nodded quickly. "Apples. We ate sour apples." He stepped in front of Khelya. "So, you're not exactly a full moon in your clan, huh? Don't worry. I knew a guy who was very good at his job, and he told me, 'Apply charisma, build trust.' You just need to become charming. How about it?"

Ansi looked dubious.

"We'll give you a few tips," Dask went on, "train you a little until we can get outta here safely."

"It may be some time until it's safe." Ansi strolled toward the shelter. "The forces of this territory's tribe appear much weakened."

"My advice? Leave Kirra and his guys here, go home – bringing us with you so we can get supplies, of course – and be a man."

"A dead man. My sister would take my head for abandoning this mission." Ansi poked one of the rocks in the shelter wall. "How do these stay in place?"

"I dunno," Khelya said, eyeing him uncharitably.

Ansi poked a different rock. This time the shelter wobbled and all the stones crashed down. He fluttered away with a yelp.

"Look at 'im, knockin' down our stuff!" Khelya's voice sounded upset but, to Matil's confusion, she seemed to be hiding a smirk.

Dask sighed and put his fingers together. "That took us a while to build, Mr. the Smart."

"You mean it took *me* a while to build," Khelya said.

Ansi stomped up to them indignantly. "I didn't knock it down. I only touched it and—"

"We still helped build it," Dask told Khelya.

"You are the most irritating foreigners I've ever met." Ansi put up a hand. "Give me your teachings now and I will see if you speak rightly or wrongly."

"I'd love to," Dask said, "but if we're not getting anything in return…"

Matil tugged on his sleeve. "Let's just help. We might be able to do something for his clan." She cupped her hands and whispered, "And we'll get on his good side."

"You make a decent point. All right, sir prince, first things first." Dask stepped on top of a fallen rock, using his wings to balance. "You gotta have the right outlook. That means—"

"*Ansi!*" a woman snapped.

Ansi spun around. The woman headed from the camp toward the group, flapping her daisy petal-like wings. She was followed by a retinue of Eletsol, each one with a painted white stripe down the left side of their face. They wore robes like Ansi and the scouts, but strips of bright cloth hung from the armholes and tied together at the wrists to make slashed sleeves.

"Tain- Tain Fridda!" Ansi said, bowing his head and raising his palms to her.

Fridda had a wide physique and wore a loose, sleeveless white dress. Silky, ash-blonde hair ran limply down her head, and her eyebrows arched in surliness. At Fridda's command, two men broke away from the retinue and stood on either side of Ansi. Kirra hovered nearby, looking pleased with Ansi's misfortune. Four men came and surrounded the outsiders.

Fridda addressed Ansi with clipped, abrasive words. Ansi then spoke quietly. One of his responses caused Fridda's features to curdle with venom. She flew into a rant that jabbed at Matil's ears like a prickly twig. Ansi's eyes remained downcast while the group of Eletsol stared at him in varying shades of disgust. Kirra spoke up from time to time. At last, Fridda gestured violently at Ansi and the outsiders.

Matil's face pinched with worry. Maybe imprisonment wasn't so bad. It was better than being crushed to death by a flower – which was what Fridda's gestures seemed to convey. One of the men used his staff to prod Ansi to stand with the outsiders. Matil tensed up.

Ansi lifted his head. "Follow the soldiers."

"What's going on?" Dask said.

"We are banished," he said in a monotone. "I'm sure you're glad of it."

Matil stared at him. "You too?"

"Kirra told my sister I was too lenient with you three, and he was able to convince my sister that I was plotting against her. Fair enough, I suppose."

Fridda began to leave.

"Wait!" Matil said. "What about our beetles and our packs? We have to take them with us."

"Tain Fridda," Ansi called, and then he said something in a gentle tone. Wistfulness grew in his voice as he spoke.

Fridda neither turned around nor unfolded her arms. After a moment, she said something to Kirra. His smug expression turned to annoyance, but he gave the guard a command. The guard untied the beetles and brought them to the group. Two other Eletsol rummaged through the rubble of the shelter, found the supply packs, and threw them on Dewdrop's and Olnar's shells. Two of the men guarding the outsiders took the beetles' reins.

The Taina led the outsiders far away from the camp. At last they stopped and, after a chorus of rude noises directed toward Ansi, vanished into the forest. A tiny rock launched from the undergrowth and pelted Khelya's arm.

"Ow!" She scowled.

"Are you hurt?" Matil said.

Khelya rubbed at her arm. "Not really, it's just…just…"

Dask went over to Olnar and began setting the beetle up to take two passengers.

To help, Matil transferred some supplies from Olnar to Dewdrop. "How are you, girl?" She rubbed Dewdrop's shell, and the beetle bumped her head against Matil's legs. "Did the rain scare you? Oh, you weren't scared at all."

"I've just had enough of Eletsol," Khelya blurted. "They're like those kids in school who went around in a group and picked on the other students."

Matil, Dask, and Ansi looked at her blankly.

Ansi then looked away with a sniff. "*I* don't do such things."

"Yeah?" said Khelya. "Well, you're the one who ruins everyone's fun on purpose."

"Your Obrigi is very disrespectful," he said.

Khelya kicked at the ground. "I'm not *their* Obrigi."

"That's the spirit," said Dask. "Anyway, thanks for getting our things back to us, Ansi."

Ansi shook his head. "I didn't expect Fridda to grant my request, but she still cares for her brother. The good memories of my youth counted for something in the end. You, outsiders. Where will you go?"

Matil stood up straighter. She knew what he believed. "To find Mr. Korsen."

"Ah." Ansi glanced at each of them. "Do you realize how dangerous it is?"

"We figured there was some danger involved," Dask said. "'Specially now that we've experienced Eletsol hospitality."

"If you go directly toward the Watcher's land from here, you will be made into slaves or dinner by tomorrow evening at the latest."

Dask froze for a moment and then turned to Matil and Khelya. "Well, ladies, looks like we've got a lost cause on our hands. Let's give up. There's gotta be another way to do this."

"But—" Matil and Khelya began at the same time.

"Give up if you'd like," Ansi said. "But I can guide you to the Watcher through the clans' territories. I'm offering my service, like you did for me."

"Yeah, and look at how that turned out," Dask said.

Matil coiled Dewdrop's reins around her hand, remembering the gigantic eye they had seen and the laughter they had heard down by the southern border. "Ansi says that Mr. Korsen exists. Please, Dask, let's go find out." She looked down. "Or if you'd like to leave for Nychtfal, we could… split up and meet somewhere afterward—"

"We're going, we're going." He shook his head. "I guess Ansi'll keep us safe."

Khelya shot Ansi a look. "Do we *have* to go with 'im?"

Ansi folded his arms and returned the look.

"Yes, we do," Dask said. "I dunno about you, but I'm not keen on either slavery or cannibalism."

"Which way are we going?" Matil said.

"We'll travel due north for a time," Ansi said.

Dask flared his wings. "I'll find out which direction's north."

"That is north." Ansi pointed.

"Oh." Dask's wings flopped back into place. "See, Khel, this guy'll make it easy for us." He hopped onto Olnar and patted the saddlebags.

Matil's sensitive ears picked up Khelya's mumbled response, but she hoped that Ansi's smaller Eletsol ears had not. She climbed over Dewdrop's shell into the saddle and watched their new companion from the corner of her eye.

He had turned back toward his homeland. For an Eletsol he was tall, yet at the moment he stooped with his head lowered. It made Matil think of the dreams she had of her life before, especially the dreams about her family's house near the ground. Why did alva have to leave their homes so quickly and on such bad terms? She blinked. Did she… remember something?

No. Of course not.

"Take us away, flower boy," Dask said.

Ansi glared. "Very well, bird boy."

They proceeded with caution, watching the forest around them, and then slowly they settled into the rhythm of travel. Khelya walked and Matil rode Dewdrop with most of their supplies. Dask and Ansi rode back-to-back on Olnar.

"Matil." Khelya motioned with her transparent hand, a gesture that Matil nearly missed.

She pulled on the reins, slowing Dewdrop's pace. She and Khelya fell behind the others.

"Let's say the Elders are gone…for good," the Obrigi said quietly. "Shouldn't it make Ansi sad?"

"He could be wrong," Matil said. "We don't know yet."

"But he acts like he doesn't care!"

She reached out to pat Khelya on the arm. "He's had all his life to get used to it, whether or not it's true. Let's just ask Mr. Korsen and find out."

It was past noon when they stopped to rest and let the beetles crawl over nearby plants in search of a meal. Ansi concentrated on a pair of green strawberries, which turned plump and red as he moved his hands in quick little gestures. They sliced pieces off of the newly-ripened strawberries and started to eat.

"Where'd you learn how to speak Alvishu?" Dask seemed glad to talk to another man for a change and had been chatting with Ansi since they left.

"When I was young," Ansi said, "I stayed in Vangara City with King Eldos of the Nervoda."

He whistled. "Fancy, aren't ya?"

"I *am* the chief's son."

"You've been to Vangara City?" Matil asked excitedly. "Dask told me that it's underwater." Dask had once described the Nervoda home, Lake Vangara. Despite his impression that Nervoda in general were "snoozy waterbugs", he had grudging respect for those that lived under the lake.

"U-underwater…" Khelya shuddered. "Alva can't live underwater!"

Ansi rolled his eyes. "They use their magic." He spat out a seed. "It is very interesting to live with water all around and fish flying by. Once, I was nearly eaten by an eel."

"Huh," Dask said. "Gotta agree with Khel on this one. Sounds terrifying."

They set out again and, while they traveled, Dask reminded Khelya to teach him how to snap his fingers. Once he got the hang of it, he wouldn't stop snapping. Khelya and Ansi soon grew annoyed, but Matil was having too much fun encouraging him. A few snapping wars later, even Dask had to admit that it was getting old.

Ansi monitored the forest constantly to make sure he knew where they were. "A new tree," he said as they skirted a ramble of tree roots.

"New?" Khelya squinted at the tree's rough bark. "Looks like it's been here a good long time."

"It is certainly new. See? There is no moss and no ivy. One of the reasons outsider maps are so pathetic is that the clans often change the forest."

Matil blinked. "*Change* the forest?"

"Kal. I mean—yes. Sometimes we grow things and move them around. Because of territory disputes, building projects, festivals, or just…for the fun of it." Ansi's mouth lifted in a small smile. "That tree was not here when I visited this area two weeks ago. The Ivainen clan is a vassal of the Takkamakaini—ah, the Taina clan. We let them stay among the tree branches while we live nearer the ground. I suspect that they grew the tree over many days in order to build a new village. It must have taken all of their magicians. I am impressed, but they should know better than to do so without permission. Maat Enna will have a shout at their chief, I think."

Later on, the group was thrown into alarm at shrieks coming from the undergrowth. Ansi spoke quickly in his own language, drawing a few fur-cloak-wearing Eletsol out of the forest. Their hostility was calmed by Ansi's words. After they left, Dask asked who they were.

"They are from a small clan," Ansi said. "I've visited them before to mark territory lines. I acted very stern with them that day, but later I was more generous with territory than they expected. Their leaders became my friends."

"Hm, I see why they call you 'the Smart'," Dask said.

Night rolled in and the four of them built a little campfire in a patch of red clover. Khelya tied the plants back to keep them from catching sparks. For dinner, the group had watery clover blossom soup with slices of mushroom – except Khelya, who filled her stomach with the raw pinkish blossoms. There were bilberry shrubs close by, so they finished up by picking and eating the tart blue berries.

"Let's set up watch," Dask said, wiping the purple juice from his hands on a clover leaf. "Khelya goes first, so we don't have to try waking her up in the middle of the night. Matil, second watch?"

"Of course," Matil said.

"Great," Dask said. "I go next and Ansi gets last watch."

Ansi frowned at Dask. "Watch what?"

"Keeping watch, you know? You're a lookout. A guard."

"Guard?" he said. "I'm no guard."

"But you're gonna help us keep watch tonight," Dask said firmly. "Right?"

"I'd rather not."

"Too bad, 'cause you've fallen in with us. Everyone does their part, whether they're a chief's son or a normal alva."

Ansi rolled his eyes. "Tch. I will watch, then."

They all settled by the fire on their blankets, but Matil didn't feel like going to sleep right away.

"Does anyone have a story to tell?" she asked.

"Let's change things up." Dask looked at the Eletsol. "You got a story, Ansi?"

For a moment, he stared into the fire. "I do have one. It's more history than story."

"That works," Dask said.

Ansi took a deep breath. "In the far past, there lived an Eletsol who conquered the clans and united Fainfal. His name was Emperor Ivu. He was not a merciful ruler, but he was powerful. Traditions that we take as timeless began in his time, with his commands. His reign lasted long and brought him wealth beyond imagining. Yet when he died, he left behind a spirit of disharmony. His chosen heir was weaker than he, and his sons fought between themselves for the throne. Not ten years after Ivu's death, his empire had broken into warring clans once again. Since then, no other empire has been as mighty as Ivu's."

The fire crackled in the following silence.

"Is that it?" Dask said.

"Yes. It was an important time in our history. Ivu is also the subject of much debate. He was ruthless and lived as a brigand, but he's also seen as the perfect warrior and chief. Does he have a place among the elders in the treetops? Or not?"

Khelya tilted her head. "Treetops?"

"The Elders?" said Matil.

"Ah, I've confused you," Ansi said, smiling. "The treetops aren't the tops of those trees," he gestured upward, "but an after-death place. The great Elders, such as Dyndal, have ruled the treetops since their deaths. They are high chiefs over the lesser elders, our ancestors. And those who were chiefs, or those with the blood of chiefs in them, rule over the other ancestors. In this life, I…I try to honor both the Elders and my own deceased family, for they will judge me when I rise to the treetops."

"Do you believe in Thosten?" Matil said.

He nodded. "He formed the world."

Matil glanced uncertainly at Khelya. "He also judges the dead, doesn't he?"

"Right," Khelya said.

"No, that is the realm of the great Elders and our ancestors," Ansi said. "They decide whether someone becomes a lesser elder or whether they fall from the treetops in shame."

Khelya frowned at the fire. "The Chivishi says that since Thosten made us, he's the only one who can judge us when we die."

"The Chivishi is not an Eletsol work," Ansi said. "Though some clans in the far east of Fainfal dishonor the elders by holding to the Chivishi, and by believing that the Elders are merely asleep. They're kept from visiting Dyndal's tomb because of their dishonor."

"That's terrible," Khelya said in dismay.

Dask put his hands behind his head with a yawn. "It's all make-believe anyway."

"Make what believe?" said Ansi.

"It's just pretend. Bedtales. Baby stories, like you said yesterday."

"Ah." He smoothed down his leaf wings before lying down. "Then what do you believe in?"

"What do *I* believe in?" Dask laughed. "I guess I believe in…right here and right now."

"Here and now?" Ansi said. "I also believe in those."

Khelya nodded. "So do I."

"What we do right now matters," Matil said quietly.

"Well," Dask yawned again, "looks like we all agree. Sleep tight, everyone." He closed his eyes.

Khelya scooted closer to Dask and whispered, "I'll pray for you." She grinned at Matil.

He sat up, irritated. "Remember the last time you said that? I made breakfast for you. I actually *did* something instead of having a chat with the air. And I'm gonna do it again if you still don't…"

Matil and Khelya were both smiling now.

"Giant," Ansi proclaimed, "I give you my title. You are now Khelya the Smart."

"Really?" she said.

Dask pointed at her. "No more free breakfast."

7

Borderline

Matil, Khelya, Dask, and Ansi departed as soon as they were all awake. Ansi's route led them north and then west, past ragged villages in the trees and on the ground, or built into tree trunks and burrows. Equally ragged Eletsol sometimes emerged from these villages to gather around Ansi and learn who the strange outsiders were. Ansi told Matil and the others not to do anything more to draw attention to themselves. The chiefs in this area of Fainfal were cutthroat, rarely holding power for longer than a year at a time. The turmoil resulted in constant fighting between many different families vying for control. Even the smallest disturbance could cause a skirmish to erupt.

One time they rode past several scraggly children, all with hair down to their waists. Matil almost waved in greeting, but some women rushed up and herded the children back to their huts. A group of men buzzed down soon after, landed, and prowled past, carrying wickedly barbed spears, axes, and knives of wood and stone. Their hair was spiked up in ratty manes. Dask and Ansi gestured at Matil and Khelya to veer away from these sullen-eyed Eletsol.

Later on, when they were alone again, Matil remembered that Ansi had lived in Vangara. She moved Dewdrop behind Olnar in order to talk with him. "What do the Nervoda believe about the Elders?" she asked.

Ansi considered her question. "In Vangara, some believe in the Chivishi, but many more believe that the Elders and Thosten are still alive in some distant realm, ruling our world from there. Those Nervoda say the Elder Eset created their race."

"Eset, lady of water," Khelya told Matil.

"We talked about Elder stuff last night," Dask said. "And the night before. Ansi, what about your girl? How do you know her if she's in the other clan?"

Ansi seemed to turn inward. "Her brother was a captain of the guard in our capital city. He attended the great feasts we held, sometimes with his family. At those feasts I saw her and became enchanted, but I, ah…never learned her name."

"You've thought of her for how long?" Khelya said. "Two years?"

He cleared his throat. "Kal. Yes. I should have forgotten her a long time ago."

Dask whistled. "And you don't even know her name."

"It never came up," Ansi said defensively. "I was busy. I had to look after two sisters ready to tear each other to scraps."

Dask tipped his head from one side to the other as if weighing it out. "I'll give you that."

"Yes, you will." His expression softened. "Her family was loyal, and they didn't leave with Dag and the Vima at the start of it. But they were not skilled in magic. Fridda drove them out, and all like them."

"What happened to them?" Matil said.

"The Vima accepted the exiles. I'm glad that at least my alva had a place to go."

Ansi fell silent as everyone's ears picked up harsh-throated yells and helpless screams somewhere in the forest. It sounded like many alva fighting. Khelya lowered her head fearfully.

"The war-chiefs I spoke of," Ansi said in a low voice. "They have no lines of highborn families to rule them, so… there is chaos."

"You don't need a 'highborn' family to keep things together," Dask said. "I mean, sure, Nychtfal's got it's problems, but it's doing fine without a king or a chief. No, something else is missing here. Can't say I know what."

Matil looked toward the noises. Knotty trees and thick flower bushes concealed what lay beyond. "Can we help and…stop it somehow?"

"Helping is a quick way to die," Ansi said. "I don't encourage it."

Dask nodded. "We have to keep going, Matil."

Though she knew they were right, leaving the terrified cries behind felt like stepping on her own heart.

The villages came less frequently, and then they disappeared altogether. Ansi again directed the group northward. As sunset approached, a long and powerful weasel slipped by them with a hiss. The beetles shied away from the lithe beast and scuttled off course.

"Talrach," Dask said. "The Kyndelin are great, you know that? Without their magic…"

"We'd be weasel supper," Khelya said.

"I haven't met a Kyndelin yet, besides the mouse-alva who stole from us." Matil reined in Dewdrop and rode back up to Khelya. "Have any of you?"

"Nope," said Khelya.

"I've met some," Ansi said from behind Dask as Olnar returned to the group. "They are a cold-tempered sort of alva."

"Seems that way," Dask said. "I've talked with two. The reason you don't usually see them around for a chat is 'cause they hate interference. They hate it so much they built a secret city away from the rest of the alva. Pretty uptight, huh?"

Ansi shrugged. "I rather like the idea of a secret city."

"Oh, look!" Matil pointed ahead of them at a boulder sitting on a low hill. The boulder was splashed with weathered blue paint and nestled among weeds and wildflowers. Ansi had told them about these. "It's one of the markers, right?"

"It is," Ansi said.

Dask angled Olnar toward the boulder. "The Barrier's just a few lengths past that rock, then."

"The Wall," Khelya corrected. "Can't believe it's right there. I was always too scared to go near it when I had my farm down south."

"I don't blame you." Dask rubbed his arms and glanced around. "I can already feel it. The end of the world."

Matil fixed her eyes on the darkening forest that loomed beyond the boulder. It didn't look any different from the wilderness around them, and the Wall was nowhere to be seen, but she knew what he meant. She remembered back to the first time she had been this close to Eventyr's border, when they had seen – or thought they'd seen – Mr. Korsen. That time and now, she felt a heaviness engulf her. She sensed finality. The end of the world.

Khelya climbed the hill, Matil, Dask, and Ansi following on the beetles. She stopped, leaned on the boulder, and untied her headband to smooth down her hair. They caught up to her.

"Setting up camp is our next step, I guess," Dask said.

Matil slid off of Dewdrop's back and stretched. "What happens if you keep walking? Do you hit the Wall?"

"Barrier." Dask eyed the trees and bushes just ahead. "You'd have to go there to find out. I sure as wasps don't know. I don't really want to know."

"Many young Eletsol go right up to the border, to Ilmasenna," Ansi said. "I went with my sisters when I was a boy. It's nothing to fear."

Khelya patted the two beetles absentmindedly. "Hear that, Dask? Nothing to fear."

"Not afraid," Dask muttered.

They tied Dewdrop and Olnar to a hardy root sticking out of the ground. Ansi fluttered to the top of the boulder.

"Should we go over there together?" Matil said. "See what it's like for ourselves?"

"Well…" Dask squared his shoulders. "Okay. Let's go. Ansi? You coming with?"

"One visit is enough for most alva." Ansi sat down. "Including me. But you go on."

The three of them went north from the boulder as night closed over the forest, hobbled by their own caution. Khelya lightly rested her right hand on Matil's head as a guide.

As Matil moved forward through the underbrush, her steps slowed. Some invisible presence was waiting. She reached out, expecting to walk straight into it, yet she wasn't stopped. Everything simply continued to slow down. The forest's sounds vanished and were replaced by strange, soft noises that Matil could barely grasp, even with her bat-like ears. First, a deep tone hummed. Then a high tone joined, sighing above its counterpart. It sounded like music, but a tune could not be pieced together from the snatches that Matil heard.

Eventually, she wondered if she was moving at all. Then she saw the light. There, right in front of her, it flickered and flowed. It wasn't like any light she'd seen. It had no color of its own, taking on aspects of its surroundings as it swirled through the air and played among the leaves. Matil's outstretched hand met an uneven resistance, like strong wind silently pushing back. The light bloomed under her splayed fingers and then danced away. Her ears lowered in awe.

She remembered her friends and turned to the right. As if he were her reflection, Dask stood with his hand against the light. He looked at her and in his wide-open expression she saw fear and wonder. She knew he was asking a question, because she was asking the same thing of herself.

What is this?

With no proper answer to give, Matil offered a small smile. The fear in Dask's gaze abated. He looked up at the lights flying into the dark canopy of trees.

Now she turned to her left, where Khelya had placed both hands on the unseen Wall. The Obrigi's eyes darted back and forth, enthralled by the twisting lights. And then…her see-through figure became more solid. She became more herself. Matil watched and willed her to cast off the Ranycht illusion entirely, but the change stopped short. Khelya hadn't noticed.

A few minutes later, the three of them stumbled backward and took very deep breaths. The light vanished with distance, and the forest's chirruping night sounds returned. A few lengths away, Ansi crouched by the boulder, struggling to start a fire.

"Khelya, you…" Matil tried to say. Words didn't want to come out of her throat.

Khelya stared at the empty space where they had stood. "I swear…I felt like…"

"Camp," Dask said. "Let's…make camp."

Matil and Khelya could only nod.

* * *

The house, built of twigs slightly elevated from the ground on wooden posts, was nestled between two slender tree trunks. A leafy herb garden thrived to the left and a rose bush formed a dark green background to the right, its pink buds adding splashes of brightness. Matil could see every feature of her home in breathtaking detail. She took a step forward and the dirt crunched softly beneath her feet. To her astonishment, she *knew* that she was dreaming.

The knotty front door opened. There was Father with his deep brown beard and dark purple eyes. "What are you doing out here, little rose?"

Mother walked up to the doorway from inside the house and stood beside Father. Bechel was in her arms, his own little arms reaching around her neck. Their eyes almost matched in color, though Mother's were dusty red and Bechel's sparkled like cherries.

"Dinner won't stay hot forever," Mother said.

"I'm honey," Bechel added with great seriousness.

She touched his nose. "You're not honey, child, you're 'hungry'."

Father beckoned Matil toward the house. "Carrot, cabbage, and vole tonight, with Mother's special brown bread. It might be the best food you've ever tasted."

Matil went nearer, drawn to her family but afraid that they would disappear if she came too close.

Mother narrowed her eyes. "Did those boys hurt you again?" She nudged Father. "If their families won't do anything about it, you have to tell the magistrate."

Matil shook her head. "It's...it's okay. Nothing happened, Mother." She finally made it onto the porch and closed the gap to her parents.

Father put his hand on her right shoulder, and Mother laid a hand on the left. The pressure on Matil's shoulders felt...real. She reached up and stroked Bechel's soft brown hair.

He blinked at her. "Hungry?"

"I think so," Matil whispered.

"Then hurry up," Father said. He pinched her arm lightly. "We're waiting for you."

Even their love felt real. Maybe it was. Matil entered the comfortable, dim warmth of home, and the door shut behind them.

8

Fighting Form

Ansi stirred Matil and Dask out of their sleep, having taken last watch again. Khelya was harder to wake, and eventually Ansi bent a fluffy dandelion down with his magic to bounce against her head a few times.

While the group dragged themselves around the camp, Matil thought about her dream. For a short time, she had been able to control herself within it. She felt like kicking herself for not trying to fly or even checking to see if she had wings. But at least she remembered the beginning, with her parents and brother. That wonderful beginning.

After a while, Matil saw that no one else was speaking. The four of them sat eating sweet roasted hazelnut pieces in silence. "How did everyone sleep?" she asked.

Khelya and Dask nodded and grunted.

"I had excellent rest," Ansi said. He scratched at the peeling white paint that still marked his face. "But one terrible dream. I dreamed that Fridda found me here and began to shout, louder and louder and louder…and then I awoke. I nearly feel glad about being exiled." He kicked a pebble by his foot. "Nearly."

"What will you do after we find Korsen?" Dask said.

Ansi leaned forward energetically. "Since we left, I've been wondering what to do and have now decided on action. I see why you alva keep watches. It is a great time to plan."

"That's not the point of keeping watch, but I know what you mean. What'd you decide?" he asked.

"I must seek refuge with a neighboring clan," Ansi said. "Find a place in their courts. I will also take your words to my heart and use charisma. With influence, I will do whatever is needed to unite the Taina and Vima."

"I hope it works," Matil said.

After eating, the group went west along the invisible Wall. They saw one old Eletsol man that day, his head encased in frizzy gray hair, his feet stained with dirt, and crinkled tulip-petal wings hanging from his back. He gave them an empty stare as he ambled past. Ansi explained that most Eletsol stayed away from the Wall due to strongly-held superstitions.

Khelya told Matil – and Ansi confirmed – that Mr. Korsen's home was said to be past the Wall bordering the northwest part of Eventyr, the very farthest someone could go in that direction. Nobody had ever *seen* his home, but some alva witnessed him walking away from Eventyr near that section of the border. Ansi led them toward it, thinking that they'd have the best chance of finding Mr. Korsen if they waited there.

Before nightfall, they found a clearing in an area thick with bushes where they made a fire and put down their blankets. Dewdrop and Olnar wandered toward some tall flowers to hunt bugs. Ansi followed them.

"We're a little out of practice," Dask said to Matil. "Wanna spar?"

She brightened. "Sure."

From a stick, Dask broke two pieces of wood the size of their knives. The two of them whittled the sticks down to smoothness and rounded the points, to avoid injuries.

"Y'all are gonna lose an eye sparring," Khelya said. She sat by the fire, watching them. "I could make a couple training dummies instead."

Dask got a feel for his practice weapon and spun the stick-knife around his nimble fingers. "Thanks, Khel, but no thanks. Dummies don't fight back."

While the two of them got into position, Matil factored in everything she noticed. The ground was mostly rough dirt veined with thin weeds, and the air was cooling down from a hot day. The fire cast its orange light only so far before it was choked by the maze of darkness that the bushes created.

"Okay," Dask said. "Let's...go!"

He flew up, going in circles over Matil's head. It was a ploy to make her spin trying to keep him in sight. He had held back his strength and ability the first couple of times they'd sparred, but their fights had soon become more serious. It was a way to keep their skills sharp. Matil knew that Dask could overpower her in a fair fight, so she came up with ways to cover her weaknesses. Like smoke, a hazy thought rose from her mind: *Live fair…don't fight fair.*

She moved carefully toward a bush with prickly leaves, keeping her guard up and relying on her ears to tell her where Dask was. A whoosh came in from her left. She slipped farther into the bush, feeling the breeze as he whipped past her. Thorny shadows fell across her skin, and she welcomed them, drawing them close. Her body faded into the surroundings. She crouched underneath a branch and observed Dask.

His green eyes seemed to glow as he peered through the bush. He crept in, ducking a branch and sidestepping sharp leaves. One leaf scraped his hand. He sucked in a breath and stopped. "Come on, Matil. Hiding?" He gestured at a branch by his midsection. "That's pretty low."

Unable to contain herself, Matil snickered. She quickly covered her mouth and nose and began slinking away.

Dask's ears swiveled. He headed in her direction, climbing and shoving through the bush at a frightening speed. Matil scrambled out of the way just as he barreled past her. Her heart thudded and she found it difficult to regain the fading that she lost by her sudden movements. If he turned around and saw her, that would be it. She pulled herself three branches above the ground. A large green caterpillar sat peacefully on the third one. In Matil's mind, she begged Dask not to turn.

He turned. His eyes focused on the vibrating branches that she had climbed. Matil looked at the caterpillar and immediately shoved it off the branch with her foot. It smacked the ground with only half of its legs under it, but it was able to start getting its body back upright.

With a frown, Dask surged forward. "Matil?" he said. There was too much foliage for him to see the caterpillar.

Matil raised herself slightly from the branch. A little closer…there! She sprang off and slammed into Dask's shoulders. They both crumpled. A branch blocked Matil – painfully – from tumbling farther. She hopped to her feet, turning aside Dask's sudden stab and beginning their clash.

They burst out of the bush in a furious scuffle, thrusting their stick-knives through the air and slashing at each other. Dask swiped his knife just past Matil, overextending his reach. She grabbed his arm and then swung behind him, using his arm as a pivot. She almost stabbed the back of his neck, but he recovered in time to whack her across the stomach. She doubled over in pain. His hand shot out in front of her and she found the wherewithal to grab his wrist, stabbing it at its most vulnerable point. At the same moment, Dask stabbed Matil in the gut.

They saw their stalemate, looked at each other, and then let out short, breathless laughs. Dask dropped his stick-knife and sat on the ground beside Matil.

"You okay?" he gasped.

She swallowed past her sandy-feeling throat and nodded. "It only…hurts…everywhere. Good ma…match."

He winced. "Sorry about that." Waving at Khelya, he said, "Can ya get us water?"

Khelya stomped over with two waterskins, handed them to Matil and Dask, and squatted down to pat Matil on the back. "Go easy on her," she said, glaring at Dask. "Lookit how tiny she is."

"She *asked* me not to go easy," Dask said.

Matil took a refreshing swig of water and wiped the sweat from her forehead. "We're trying to stay in practice for a real fight. And Dask got hurt, too."

He stretched out lying down. "When I'm rich and famous, none of us will ever have to fight again. I'll hire fifteen bodyguards for each of us. Maybe five extra for Matil, since she's tiny. How's that?"

Khelya tilted her head back in thought. "All right. That's good."

Ansi fluttered out to them. "Khelya, will you help me with something?"

"I guess," she said, standing up. "What is it?"

"I've grown some flowers very large and I need you to cut them down. They may help attract the Watcher's notice."

"Good idea," Matil said.

Khelya followed Ansi away while Matil and Dask rested.

"Hey, I've been wanting to know who trained you," Dask said. "Got any dreams about it?"

Matil pressed her lips together. Something in her mind drifted into view, but when she tried to grasp it, it slipped back into a darkness she couldn't penetrate. *Don't fight fair.*

Now she could see a figure, someone familiar but barely known. "I think…I think his name was Etsel."

Dask sat up. "Etsel? Never heard of him. Do you know where he lives?"

She shook her head.

"Can you tell me if you find out?" he said. "I bet I could learn some tricks from him. You've always been more than good at street fighting."

Matil drained the last drop from her waterskin. "Street fighting?"

"I can tell by your style – how you get away, shove me around, and kick like a grasshopper. It throws me off, because you're nice until I say 'go'. Then you're not afraid to scrap."

Her ears drooped. "I'm sorry. When we start fighting, I stop thinking like myself."

"No, don't worry. I just meant that I think you're great. At it."

Maybe he was right. Her skills had saved her many times. "Thanks."

It always troubled her, though. Why had she learned to fight in the first place?

* * *

It wasn't her fault, it wasn't. It wasn't fair.

"*Where's the money?*" the man named Thorn bellowed. His wings unfurled, doubling his impressive bulk.

Matil cowered. "Someone st-stole it."

"*You're* the one who's supposed to steal!" He raised his arm.

Pain jarred Matil as he struck her. Everything seemed to float, silent, and then Matil's throbbing face landed on the splintery planks of the bridge.

"That's a day's worth of cash *lost!*"

A blow to the side winded her. "Please," she choked out.

"Hey, come on," said the easy voice of a stranger. "It's just a kid."

"A kid who lost fifty sgeldings!" Thorn said.

"She won't do it again. And if she does, you can throw her out."

"I'll *make sure* she doesn't do it again."

The stranger's voice grew serious. "Hit her one more time and you deal with me."

Thorn kicked, catching her in the arm, and she curled up with a wail. The bridge suddenly swayed.

"Rach!" Thorn spat.

Matil looked up.

A lanky figure darted and flapped around Thorn's wildly swinging fists. He revealed a dagger like a wasp stinger and stabbed Thorn in the shoulder. Thorn yelled, knocking the stranger to the planks. Seeing an opportunity, Matil grabbed his shins from behind as he lurched toward the stunned stranger. Thorn tore one leg out of her grasp before he overbalanced and toppled over the bridge's rope railing.

The stranger recovered and pulled himself to his feet. A

glaring Thorn rose above the bridge, huge wings pumping, and clutched his bleeding shoulder. He flew off.

The lanky stranger watched for a moment and then turned toward the bridge rail.

"Wait!" Matil said. "Mister?"

He glanced at her. "Go away, kid."

"Please teach me. I need to know how to fight."

"I…I don't have time for this. Buzz off."

Matil went closer. "But maybe if you teach me, I can help you."

"I don't need help." The man opened his wings.

She shouldn't have come to the city. Everything she brought had been stolen and she wanted to go back to Crell. But she had come here for a reason. Her determination burned stronger than her fear. "Then I'll teach myself," she said with a trembling voice. "Thank you for saving me, mister."

The man folded his wings, turned around, and pulled the dagger on her. Matil whimpered.

"Do you know what this is for?" he said.

She focused on the dagger's keen point. "K-killing alva."

He sheathed it. "Feeding 'em. Protecting 'em. Saving 'em. A weapon means life to someone who knows how to use it." His mottled brown wings spread out again. "Follow me."

Matil's heart zoomed around in her chest. "Are you—"

"Calm down, kid. Get those wings out."

She opened her wings obediently. "What's your name?"

"Um…Etsel."

"Pleased to meet you," she said.

Etsel leaned back. "You got real manners. Guess it hasn't been long enough for them to beat it outta ya. You know how to fade, right?"

Matil twisted her hands together. "Not yet."

"Wow," he said. "Great. I found a complete rookie. Fading is even more important than fighting, 'cause with the right skills, you'll avoid most fights. Just pay attention when I teach ya. I won't slow down." He pointed a thumb over his shoulder. "Let's go, Manners."

9

The Watcher

The distant crunch of a gigantic footstep woke Matil.

"It's him!" Khelya squeaked. She had been on the early morning watch, and now gray dawn was rolling in. "Wake up, you guys, *it's him!*"

Matil looked to the border as Dask and Ansi hauled themselves out of their blankets. Half-hidden by the trees and foliage, a figure of immense scale moved sedately rightward, to the east. Matil had never seen Mr. Korsen properly, and now…she was astounded.

The night before, Khelya and Ansi had pulled together a pile of bright flowers and petals. Matil, Dask, and Ansi now grabbed the closest ones and jumped up to wave them about. Hopefully it would help Mr. Korsen to notice the alva. Ansi had heard that it worked sometimes, drawing the human's attention for a moment before he moved on again.

Khelya held one of the flowers. "Mr. Korsen, sir," she bellowed. "Sir?"

He didn't seem to notice, so they ran to keep up while he took another massive step.

"Dask, Ansi, you could really help with those wings of yours!" Khelya said.

Dask launched into the air and unfurled his wings. "Hey! *Hey!* Slow down, ya big jerk!"

Ansi tried to keep up with Dask while shouting in his own language to Mr. Korsen.

Mr. Korsen continued forward, and Matil's heart beat faster in primal fear as she imagined being crushed by those boots. They needed to get his attention. She slackened her pace to look around. There were a lot of rocks. The small ones she couldn't imagine doing much, but the larger ones…

"Khelya!" Matil said. "What if you throw a really big rock? Right at the Barrier?"

"Okay!" The Obrigi threw down her flower and ran for a rock nearly the size of Matil. "Wall!" she said. She lifted it, hefted it a few times in her hands, and heaved it at the border with a grunt. It looked as if it would smash right into Mr. Korsen's leg, but—

The rock sprang off of thin air with an odd noise: *ffhe*. It arced back to the ground and rolled across the dirt.

Mr. Korsen came to a stop. He turned to the border and squinted down at the alva. Finally, the man bent down slowly, leaning and groaning like a toppling tree. Matil backed away even though she expected the Wall to protect them. As his face lowered, it became clear that his head was many times larger than any alva's. His bushy gray eyebrows drew together. Matil froze under his sharp blue-eyed gaze.

"Please," Khelya whispered.

He looked at each of them in turn.

She clasped her hands. "*Please.*"

He was so still that Matil could hardly tell he was breathing. The base of her ears itched. She scratched them and noticed that Ansi and then Dask were scratching their ears as well.

"Mr. Korsen," Khelya said, rubbing at her ears. "Plea—"

"Halsedys, alva." Mr. Korsen's voice was low and creaky. "Again our paths run parallel."

Ansi's and Khelya's jaws dropped. Matil's heart leaped. *He talked.*

Dask crossed his arms. "Again? You don't mean…"

"At the southern border of Eventyr, near the Jensym Grove." Mr. Korsen's wrinkled face was almost as tall as two alva. His nose and chin stuck out from the broad, stubbled countenance. Unlike pointed alva ears, his ears were rounded at the tips. Snowy white hair capped his head as though he were one of the great mountains.

"J-Jensym Grove?" Khelya said.

Mr. Korsen gave a little nod. "An old meeting place of the Heilar, I believe. You must have passed its entrance by."

"You were really, uh, down there?" Dask shifted uncomfortably.

"Yes. A little someone spoke confidently of my nonexistence." Mr. Korsen gave them a lopsided grin and then squinted at Ansi. "I see you have another companion. Such an unusual group of travelers."

Ansi knelt to the ground in a bow. "Great Watcher, I greet you on behalf of the Takkamakaini."

"I greet you, as well," Mr. Korsen said. "Please stand… yes, that's it. I *am* a watcher, but not a great one." He tipped his head toward Khelya. "Why is this Obrigi using Ranycht magic? Does she not want to be seen?"

"We're not sure why it's still there," Dask said. "She can't get it to stop."

"Hmm…there was a way, I'm sure," said Mr. Korsen. "It's been so long that I can't recall where I read it. But is that your only business with me?"

All at once thoughts crashed down into Matil's head. "We need your help, Mr. Korsen. There's an alva, N-Nychta Olsta, and she has the Book of Myrkhar, and we think she wants to summon the Saikyr. We- we traveled all this way to talk to you. Please, can you help us?"

Mr. Korsen nodded. "I don't know much, but it is enough. I—"

"Great Watcher," Ansi said, his shoulders raising in confusion and impatience. "*Why* are you speaking to us?"

Mr. Korsen's gigantic eyes focused on Ansi.

"Y-y-yes, sir," Khelya said. "Why don't you talk like you did in the past?"

He lowered himself heavily until he sat on the ground. "I myself have spoken to very few alva in my life. You may be thinking of my father, or my grandfather. Or any number of my forefathers. Some of them were chatty indeed. I am not the first Mr. Korsen."

Khelya dazedly pushed up her headband. "But the stories…"

"Time and distance can muddy the waters of reality," he said. "Mr. Korsen is not an Elder. We are merely men. My ancestors found this place, leaving journals that described all they saw. In the years since arriving here, I have watched and listened to Eventyr and have read my ancestors' notes. I learned Alvishu along with some of your other languages and grew to love the alva I observed. But I prefer quiet to conversation, and have rarely answered those who call out to me."

Dask pointed at himself and the others. "So why answer us?"

"One reason is very simple," Mr. Korsen said. "Eventyr makes its distress known in my dreams. Night and day fighting for the sky. Thorns choking the trees. Cities burnt to cinders, and a Ranycht without wings."

Matil rubbed her suddenly-cold arms. "I'm the Ranycht."

"Yes," he said. "And now that you are here, I know the dreams are true. Nature has been twisted and I hear rumblings of a great war in the making. The other reason I speak has to do with a particular Kyndelin man, a hermit. His name is Hasyl. He was born before the Hibernation, and he lives to this day."

"Sweet gherkin," Khelya breathed. "A normal alva livin' that long?"

Mr. Korsen nodded. "Hasyl told me that the Elders granted him his many years, along with some small sight-beyond-sight, an ability he could share. But to share it dilutes its power, so he chose just one other to share it with at a time. Thus, there have been generations of Korsens who accepted this ability from Hasyl, and they have used it to watch over the borders of your realm. He chose us because, being outside the border, we can do little harm to Eventyr. This sight we have is a way to read an alva's intentions, and I did use it on you. I hope you understand my caution."

"Understand? You mean that what I just felt," Dask touched his ears, "was you doing things to my head? What are you, some kinda demon?"

Ansi puffed up his chest. "I've nothing to hide," he said to Mr. Korsen, "but we are all due certain respect. You must request permission before trespassing so closely."

The human passed a hand before his face. "You shame me, alva. I apologize for invading."

Matil looked at Mr. Korsen's kind but piercing eyes and then darted away her gaze. "You saw…everything?"

"Be assured," he said. "I saw only a glimpse of the sum of your experiences. A being's mind is private and complex. Magic cannot steal its secrets." He paused. "Sorcery, the unnatural power, is a different story."

"Magic, sorcery, *whatever*," Dask said.

"Be respectful," Khelya said under her breath.

Mr. Korsen lowered his head farther to address Dask. "You are free to discard my words if you wish. Know that I can only speak to you or use the sight Hasyl gave me. Nothing of demonic origin will pass between us, because this border, Bo-Eventyr, abhors sorcery. It is formed entirely of Eventyr's own magic."

Dask folded his arms again. "I'm listening."

"Sir," Matil said, "what were you about to say earlier?"

"Hmm…" Mr. Korsen rubbed his chin. "You spoke of the Saikyr? The Book of Myrkhar?"

She met his eyes hopefully. "Yes."

"Then I must send you to Hasyl. He keeps the secret of the sleeping Elders."

"Sleeping?" Ansi said.

"Sleeping!" Khelya burst out. She smirked at Ansi. "So they're alive!"

Mr. Korsen moved his shoulders slightly in a shrug. "I don't know. Hasyl waits faithfully."

Ansi returned Khelya's look with an imperious one of his own.

"How long are alva gonna wait?" Dask said. "The Eletsol think they're dead, and all you've got is a guy who says the Elders made him immortal."

"I've seen many things in my time that I didn't believe, though they happened before my eyes. I have also believed what wasn't true, and," Mr. Korsen laughed, "I lost money that way. But I finally began to learn from my mistakes and from the stories of others. I sought words of wisdom and found that truth stands up to all scrutiny. Based on my experiences, then, and based on the records of my forefathers, I have come to believe what Hasyl says. Whether or not you believe, I ask you to meet him. This matter concerns all of Eventyr."

"I'll go, sir!" Khelya said.

"I'll go," Matil said. "Thank you."

Dask sighed. "Yeah, yeah. I'll go, too."

Mr. Korsen bowed his head low. "Do you have a map?"

Khelya held the map as close to the Wall as she could. Mr. Korsen pulled out a round glass that made his eye look even larger when he peered down through it at the map.

"Hasyl resides close to Bo-Eventyr and just north of the Tynsen River."

"Here?" Khelya said, pointing at the map.

"Farther south," said Mr. Korsen. "There."

They didn't have anything to write with, so Dask marked the spot with juice from a blade of grass.

"Mr. Korsen," Matil said. "What's it like outside of Eventyr?"

Mr. Korsen picked a leaf from a bush and rubbed it between his fingers. "We have a whole world, like yours. We have families and nations – and wars, just as you do. Magic is elusive outside of Eventyr. Many humans believe there's no such thing."

"I guess they don't have magic," Khelya said. "They'd know it was real if they did."

He folded the leaf into quarters as he thought. "True. Unlike alva, we don't have innate powers. Bending nature to your will is a part of you. Humans must fight nature. We are torn between disdain and longing for the thing you call magic." He set down the bent leaf – which was nearly big enough for Matil to use as a tent – and leaned toward the alva.

"Our world doesn't even know that *you* exist, yet they tell their children about you in bedtales."

"That's a laugh," said Dask. He nodded up at Mr. Korsen. "You're real. I can see that. Doesn't mean you're telling the truth. A bunch of humans swapping stories about alva? Show me, and then I'll believe it."

"All I am to you," Mr. Korsen said, "is an odd giant telling bedtales of his own. Is that right? Then let it be so. Once again, all I ask is that you find Hasyl."

Khelya smiled at him. "Well, *I* believe you. Why don't more humans live around Eventyr?"

"This place…it is protected. Bo-Eventyr's clearest function is to separate our worlds. Some of my forefathers tried to bring others here, and one of two things always happened. Those others had an excuse not to come, or they visited and maybe even stayed for a time, but never felt at home. Sometimes the feeling settles over me, as well, that there is a strangeness in the air. That I live a dream and must wake up one day. That I must leave. But such times are few."

"Seems unlikely that humans would catch sight of us and just leave," Dask said. "You're too big to be scared of us."

"It is odd," Mr. Korsen said. "However, those who looked did not see. Or so they said. I doubt if I would have had the eyes to see when I was younger and more obstinate."

Dask shook his head. "Humans must be blind."

"Says the alva who didn't see Mr. Korsen last time," Khelya whispered.

He winced.

Mr. Korsen looked around at the plants and trees. "The veil between our kinds may be for the best. Eventyr is protected from all but me, and I confess I do not mind the solitude." He stood up with a great effort. Dirt clumps dropped from his pants as he brushed himself off. Matil noticed a spider scuttling up his pant leg. Compared to him, it was tiny.

"I wish we didn't have to go," Khelya said. "Goodbye, sir."

Dask threw Mr. Korsen a casual salute. "It's been fun."

"Thank you again," Matil said.

Ansi lifted his palms and bowed from the waist. "Farewell, Watcher."

"Goodbye, alva," Mr. Korsen said with a small smile down at them. "Thosten fly with you."

* * *

The group packed up camp and passed another boulder that marked the Wall. Mr. Korsen had already gone on his way. Matil turned to Ansi, who rode behind Dask on Olnar.

"Are you coming with us?" she asked Ansi.

He looked at her and then looked in the direction of the Wall with an overwhelmed glance. "Strange things are happening, and for the sake of my alva I would learn the truth. But I can't leave them when they are in need. I'll offer myself again as a guide, this time to one of the clan courts that I spoke of."

"Is it on the way?" Dask said.

"Not entirely. It's a wealthy clan though, with strong ties to my family. I'll ask them to provide you supplies and an escort to the hermit's home."

Dask tapped Matil's arm. "Might delay us, but it beats bumbling our own way through the wilderness like before. I say we do it."

"Agreed," Matil said.

"I'm glad to travel with you farther," Ansi said. "You are better company than the Maati. And appearing at court with alva at my side will make me look more powerful. As soon as we arrive, I will work to get you the best treatment."

Khelya cleared her throat. "That's, uh…that's good of you."

* * *

The group rode southeast for the next two days. As the sun moved lower at the end of the second day, the colors of the forest blended into orange and red and then dimmed at twilight.

Dask's ears twitched. "I hear voices. Let's head away from them." He gestured to their right and urged Olnar in that direction.

Everyone went silently after him. Matil heard the hum of wings, which could have been some insects moving lazily through the air. After Dask's words, though, she worried they might be Eletsol. She didn't want to meet any more.

"You hear them, right?" Dask was frowning.

She nodded.

"We're in little danger," Ansi said. "This territory belongs to a clan that knows me. They are neutral in the Taina and Vima conflict."

The sounds came closer. Nearby ferns and bushes rustled.

Several beefy Eletsol painted in orange stripes rushed out of the forest to surround the group. They held spears with sharp stone heads and red beads tied up and down the shafts.

Ansi's body tensed. "Vima."

"Taina!" bellowed the one hovering above them.

Ansi jumped off of Olnar and dropped to the ground, where he scrubbed with dirt at the white paint on his face. Then he clambered back up, soil and flecks of paint on his cheeks, and covered his eyes with his palms. "Taina alat! Taina alat!" To Matil, Khelya, and Dask, he said, "If we fly, they will kill us! Cover your eyes like this and we should be safe."

Khelya and Dask hesitated briefly before putting their hands across their eyes. Matil waited as long as possible, but, intimidated by the advancing Vima, followed Ansi's example. She left a space below her hands so that Dewdrop's saddle was visible, and her ears swiveled, trying to catch and identify every sound. She nearly bolted when someone yanked her dagger from its sheath and further searched her for weapons. At last he grabbed her wrists, pulled them down from her face, and bound them behind her in scratchy fibers.

Now that she could see, she watched the others being restrained. One of the Vima tied a strip of cloth tightly around Ansi's eyes. Khelya pouted at the jagged spears as one of the Vima hovered behind her, binding her wrists, and others connected her ankles with a rope to shorten her steps. Before long, they finished and shoved everyone forward. The group of warriors strolled easily, laughed loudly, and pushed one another this way and that. As a stocky Vima crashed into Dewdrop, the beetle stumbled. Matil clung to the saddle and tried to calm her.

"I thought you'd know where your enemies are," Dask said to Ansi. "You're supposed to be smart!"

"I *am* smart!" Ansi said. "This is the territory of a smaller clan. These Vima scouts should not be here." He puckered his lips in thought. "What are they planning?"

"They've blindfolded you, but not us," Matil said. "Why?"

"Ah. Certain types of magic are very, very difficult to use without sight. Most Eletsol magicians are powerless when blindfolded."

Dask raised his ears. "Most…but not you?"

"No," Ansi said. "I am powerless, too."

"Great, great," said Dask. "Wonderful."

Ansi turned his head toward Dask. "Your voice is disrespectful. Must I remind you that I am the son of a chief?"

"Hey, chief guy," Dask said.

"Chief's *son*," Ansi said firmly.

"You're tied up and blindfolded. In your own words, powerless. You think I care about respecting you when I can't even respect myself right now?" Dask shook his head in disgust, and then noticed Matil's worried expression. He forced a small smile onto his face. "Let's never get caught again, okay?" he said to her. "If there's another time after this one…if we get that far, let's keep ourselves free. All right?"

She nodded faintly. "Good idea."

10

Strong in Arm

Daylight had gone completely by the time they came across more Vima. These Eletsol seemed thinner and quieter than the warriors who had captured Matil and her friends. They stared and bowed their heads as the warriors went past. The warriors stopped and shouted at the base of a small tree flanked by thick bushes. Matil realized that a gate made of bark was disguised in the tree's trunk. The gatekeeper wasted no time in pulling the gate open.

A smooth tunnel cut straight through the trunk, leading into a humble, cloistered village. Once inside, Matil could see a wall surrounded the village, a sturdy but flowing structure made out of woven plants that were still green and alive. The plants abounded with five-pointed leaves and purple flowers, but in a few places brown sticks revealed themselves as the framework on which the plants grew. The round wall curved farther inward the higher it went, leaving an opening at the top that was roughly half the size of its base. The village felt enclosed yet still open to the air. Dome-shaped huts covered in bright cloths clustered against the wall, built upon each other in staggered piles about four huts tall. To the right, beside the entrance tunnel, was a squat stone watchtower. Moths flitted in circles over the torchlit town.

Almost as soon as the warriors entered, the noise of the village quieted to murmurs. The villagers going about their evening business moved well out of the way of the group, keeping their heads low. Matil watched sadly as the beetles were led away, deeper into the village. A young boy flew down from one hut carrying a tray and timidly offered bowls of diced nuts and berries to the warriors. The group stopped to gather around the tray. Each man grabbed a bowl, downed its contents, and tossed it to the ground. The boy gathered up the fallen bowls and dodged the other ones being thrown, while the tallest warrior barked orders at him.

"Kal, ferra," the boy kept repeating, until he had gathered all of the bowls and sped back to the hut.

The tallest warrior then pointed at some of his men, who took the prisoners from the group and toward a low, gray structure in the dusty village square. The structure was rectangular, built with heavy stone blocks that left small square openings all over the walls. One of the warriors unlocked its metal door and then went inside to shake a bony Eletsol on the cell's floor. The Eletsol didn't move. He was taken out of the cell and left on the ground, where frightened-looking villagers carried him away. Matil, Khelya, and Dask shared uneasy glances.

Brandishing curved stone daggers, the warriors grabbed the four of them. Khelya was forced into the cell and she bumped her head on the doorway with a loud yell. After the warriors pushed Dask forward, he walked in on his own. Matil hurried in after him. Blindfolded Ansi was shoved even more roughly and stumbled across the threshold. A warrior tore the bindings from Matil's hands and left the cell. The metal door grated against the stone as it closed.

It was dark inside the cell, but the openings in the walls provided vision of the outside. The floor was also stone, padded with dry grass and set slightly below the ground. Matil started untying Ansi's hands. After she freed him and Dask, she went to Khelya, who had sat down in the corner to nurse her head, and started with the ropes binding her feet.

Dask rubbed his wrists. "Food, blankets, weapons, mounts. They took everything this time. Got any Eletsol tricks you can use?"

Ansi untied his blindfold. Right away he searched the cell, felt the grass on the floor, and looked through the holes. He finally sat cross-legged on the ground in a huff. "I can do nothing with rock and dead grass."

The creaky cell door opened. The same boy from earlier threw their blankets inside and followed them up with a large tray shoved along on the floor. Matil saw the guards standing outside, spears at the ready, and then the door closed.

Ansi's eyes were large as he stared at the tray, which was loaded down with greasy strips of meat, several leaf scraps, and a jar of water. "So much meat," he said. "They may be snake-food cuts, but…*koi-kirra-dal.* This is a lot of meat. I eat leaves and berries, as the Maati do. They said that meat was for peasants, so my sister always grew angry if she saw me eating it." He bent down to smell the steam rising from the tray. "Rabbit. They must have just now cut it as it roasted."

The savory aroma spread around the cell, and Matil's stomach responded with a growl. "Let's eat before it gets cold, then."

Everyone scooted over to the tray and used the leaf scraps to pick up roast rabbit for themselves. While they chewed through the tough meat they talked about their new situation.

"What'll they do to us?" Khelya said.

"Only the ancestors can tell," he said. "The Vima are not as bad as the Salkai, but they *are* merciless."

"Salkai?" Dask said. "What do they—"

"Decorate their encampments with the heads and wings of all intruders." Ansi sighed. "Let's keep our expectations low."

* * *

The next day, Matil and her companions watched the village through the openings in the walls. The strong warriors were nowhere to be found, and now a lanky boy with a crude spear stood watch near their cell. Eventually Matil turned around and slumped against the wall. Ansi sat sideways by the adjacent wall, still observing the Vima villagers going about their day. Khelya was closely studying the construction of the cell and working out equations by arranging bits of grass on the floor. Matil opened her mouth to ask about them when Dask, sitting across from her, spoke up quietly.

"I've got a plan," he said.

Matil looked at him, but Ansi didn't seem to notice.

"Ahem." Dask used his foot to poke Ansi in the leg. "Plan."

Ansi shoved Dask's foot away and went back to staring out of the holes. "I'm listening."

"Fine. The plan is to pretend one of us is deathly sick. Coughing, crying, the works. When they send a doctor in, Khel knocks him out, gets whoever else is out there, and holds the door while we escape. Then we use the doctor as a hostage so they'll let us go. Good plan, huh? Ansi, you said you were listening, so what do you—"

Ansi turned his back to the cell wall with a sharp intake of breath.

Dask looked at him. "You weren't listening."

"What's going on?" Matil asked.

"It is she," Ansi said.

She looked through an opening. "Who?"

"*She*—her—my…the Vima woman I told you about."

"Oh!" Matil said. "Which one is she?"

Dask hopped up with a flutter of his wings. "Yeah, which one?"

"She has hair just the color of a horned beetle's shiny shell…wings deep and soft…and she is wearing a skirt of cloud-purple petals." He sighed and then realized Dask and Matil were both staring out of the cell. "Don't look so *obviously*."

"Hey!" Dask yelled. "You!" He pointed through the hole. "Yes, you!"

Ansi's mouth fell into horrified rictus. "Alat!" He shook his head. "N-no! Bad!"

"Dask, be careful," Matil said.

"Over here!" Dask winked at Matil and Khelya. "Relax, you two. It can't hurt."

The woman edged over with a suspicious look in her light green eyes. Her waist-length black hair shimmered in the low light, and her rounded petal wings were a dark magenta color.

"She's here. Turn around, Ansi."

Ansi clenched his eyes shut briefly before standing up and facing the woman, an unmistakable red creeping over his skin. "Elamys," he stammered.

The woman gave him a sweet smile and spoke at length in a rough but melodic voice.

At the end, he winced. "Can't hurt? *Pah*."

"What is it? What did she say?" Dask smiled back at the woman.

"She is…polite. And now I see I judged the Vima wrongly. They aren't merciless after all." Ansi flicked his disdainful gaze at Dask. "She asked if we would prefer to be executed and fed to their rodents *now*…or on a festival day!"

The smile disappeared from Dask's face. He threw his hands skyward. "Really?"

The woman tilted her head to the side and blinked benignly.

"Ask her name," Matil said. "Ask her about the Vima. Hey, Dask, let's wait over here." She went to the far corner of the cell, where Khelya was still absorbed in her calculations.

Dask followed with a sympathetic glance at Ansi.

"You must not leave me alone!" Ansi whispered urgently, and then calmed himself down. "You can stand beside me, to show that I have influence."

"Don't be a butterfly," Dask said. "We're just a few steps away if you get too scared."

"I'm not scared! She has threatened us and we shouldn't provoke her further! I—"

The woman snapped at him and began to walk away. Ansi froze. He twitched. Dask looked ready to slap him.

"Lyko!" he burst out. Her retreating form halted and he followed the word with a stuttering sentence in his language.

After a pause, she came back. "Vima," she said, lifting her chin.

"Alat," he said, looking frustrated. "Sin mennin." He pointed at himself. "Ansi." He gestured toward her.

She regarded him with new curiosity. "Vin mennin Teres."

"Teres," Ansi repeated softly.

Both seemed unsure as they began a conversation. Matil and Dask watched Teres's face carefully until Khelya looked up.

"I like the way they put this structure together," she said, gesturing at the cell's stacked blocks. Ansi's exchange with the stranger got her attention and she lowered her voice. "What's goin' on?"

"She's the Vima who caught Ansi's eye," Dask whispered, pointing at Teres. "Remember? If the dice are on our side, we'll soon have a little lady desperate to save her true love. See, he needs to bond with her, keep her talking for a good long—"

Teres walked off with a casual flip of her hair.

Dask froze, and then he mouthed *time* before turning to Ansi. The Eletsol looked like he was in a dream. "*What* did you do?" Dask said.

"She's different than I had guessed," Ansi said. "But even more wonderful..."

"Yeah? What'd you guys talk about? Flowers, right? You told her she looked like a nettle bush, huh?" Dask laughed acidly. "Bet she didn't like that."

Ansi sat down with his hands over his heart. "We mostly talked about the war between our clans."

He whistled. "Oh, that's romantic for sure. C'mon, smart guy, you're supposed to make a girl feel good, not depressed."

"No, she...I think she is planning something. I could see she dislikes what my sisters have done. She already knew who I am, so I told her what happened to me and that the Taina feel the same way."

"You trusted her?" Dask said incredulously. "Just like that?"

"She has the same war-weariness and fear in her eyes that many of my alva show. When she heard my story, she became very surprised. Very cautious." Ansi looked past Dask, out at the village. "Before she left, she said there were others."

"Others?" Khelya tugged anxiously on the ends of her blonde hair. "What kinda others?"

"Have you noticed that there are few men and those in the village are young? Teres told me that my sister, Dag, uses the men for her army and personal guard, and the weak as her servants and workers. The rest of the Vima are sent to hunt and gather to support the clan. They used to be loyal to the blood of the chief, trusting that Vim Dag would lead them to prosperity as she said she would.

"Recently, she has started new wars and conquered peaceful neighbors, and many men have fallen in battle. She has thrown western Fainfal into chaos. I am reminded of the Watcher's dreams. Alva are also dying every day building Dag's city, and half of what the villagers produce must be given to her in offering. The Vima are tired and want their families back. There is much secret talk of rebellion."

So that was what had happened to the village. Like Ansi, Matil gazed out of the cell and saw the bowed backs and heavy frowns on everyone who couldn't be distracted by games or small talk.

Dask narrowed his eyes. "This is a situation we want to avoid. Teres isn't trying to sign us up for a war, is she?"

"A war in the middle of a war…" Ansi said. "It's troubling. But it may be a swift path to peace."

"Can she get us out before it starts?" said Dask.

"She will come back tonight. I'll ask her then."

11

Captive Thoughts

Dusk fell and torches were lit around the village. Matil had stretched out on the ground with her blanket as a pillow. Thoughts drifted into her head – uneasy, half-formed thoughts from which she retreated. Khelya sat against the wall next to her. Dask reclined on the other side of the cell, and Ansi sat quietly with a glance out of the cell now and then.

The cell door opened and a woman slid the dinner tray inside. Hope filled Matil when she saw who it was.

Ansi stood quickly. "Teres!"

Teres patted her throat, backed out of the cell, and shut the door. The tray once again held a single bowl, this time piled high with chopped flower stalks and yellow petals.

Dask picked up a handful of the salad and tossed it in his mouth. "Is your friend here to talk?" he said through his food.

"I don't know," Ansi said. "She wants us to be quiet."

Teres appeared on the opposite side of the cell, where light from the torches didn't reach. She whispered and Ansi crept over to listen.

"The local scouting parties are loyal to Vim Dag," he relayed to the others in a low voice. "Though they are gone now, they always return without notice. That is why we must be alert."

Dask crawled closer. "See if she can let us go."

Ansi nodded and spoke to Teres. After her reply he turned back with an apologetic look. "She could help you leave the village, but you won't avoid capture in Vima territory." A few words from Teres changed his expression. "Wait, she has more to discuss."

Ansi and Teres talked for a while – strategizing, he told them, though half the time the two Eletsol were laughing and smiling. At the end of their conversation, Teres gave a small bow to the prisoners and flew away.

"Kal," Ansi said with a sigh. He turned to the other three. "She is gone."

"We can see that," Dask said.

"But she has a plan."

Dask looked relieved. "Good. A plan that gets us out of here?"

"If all goes well," Ansi said. "Teres told me of a plot to seize power from Dag. She and her brother, among others, have barely been able to hold back those who demand an uprising. She said they were waiting for the right time, when Dag is weakened somehow. But now, hearing that I am imprisoned may draw my sister out of her city.

"Teres will make it known that I am in this village await-
ing judgment. She will also suggest that Dag attend a feast
here in her honor – Dag should be quick to accept such
flattery – and come to see me as well as you outsiders, since
you are curiosities. Teres's brother and other soldiers from
this village will most likely be chosen as Dag's escort on the
journey. They share our desire for peace. Once in the village,
Dag will be overwhelmed by her own guards…and on the
same day, her city will be taken by the Vima who long for
freedom." He puffed out his chest briefly before becoming
downcast. "May my father forgive me when I rise to the
treetops."

"When will they show up?" Matil said.

"Teres is sending someone now," Ansi said. "I think Dag
will come in the next couple of days."

"A couple of days isn't too bad," said Dask. "As long as
it works."

* * *

"Ah, ben, cen," Matil said.

"Ah, ben, cen," Bechel's small voice repeated.

She sat across from a toddler who had large eyes with
deep red irises. Dark stems formed the walls of their playhouse, and the smell of roses floated around them. Father
had sawed away the thorns until only smooth bumps were
left.

"Chah, du, eh," she continued.

Bechel bounced from side to side. "Chah, du, eh."

"Yee, fen—"

A girl with ruffled black wings peeked into the playhouse. Her eyes were intensely blue. "Nychta! Bel!"

Bechel's furrow of concentration lifted. "Arla!" He stood up, wobbling, and barreled into her. "Let's play!"

Matil folded her arms. "We have to finish your letters. Mother said so."

"Sit down, Bel," Arla said sternly.

"Play!" Bechel protested.

"We can't play yet."

"You're mean," he said with a pout. "You're as mean as my sister."

"No, I'm meaner than her," Arla said.

"What?" Matil gasped. "Nobody's meaner than me."

Arla laughed. "You're lying. Not even Myrkhar?"

"Well, I guess *he's* meaner than me," said Matil.

"And Mr. Rochen?" Arla said.

"Oh, he's definitely meaner than Myrkhar."

"Misser Roken is meaner than Myrkhar," Bechel sang.

Matil tried to cover her grin. "Shhh! Don't let anyone hear that!"

* * *

Matil slept that night until Khelya, yawning, woke her for the next watch. She sat against the cell wall, alert and concealed where light from the torches didn't reach. A painful thought flashed across her mind and she huddled closer to the wall, taking comfort in the shadow.

"*Matil.*"

Nat's dark face appeared, made vague by time. No, Amacht. That was his real name, the name of the spy who had died saving Matil. He gazed up at her. "*Run.*"

"*Do you know who you are?*" Wings…purple eyes covered with a pale sheen, like a layer of ice… "*You're Nychta Olsta, too.*"

Matil shook herself and pinched her ears until they hurt. It hadn't happened for so long that she'd hoped it was over. When things were quiet like they were now, she supposed that she couldn't hide the past from herself. She dried her wet eyes and sat up straight to watch the village twice as vigilantly.

A while later, there was noise at the gate. The watchmen were speaking with someone on the other side. As Matil looked, one of them flew up to Teres's hut. The alva outside the gate raised their voices impatiently.

Teres left her hut and flittered over to the cell, black hair in disarray. "Saino," she whispered loudly. "Saino!"

Matil climbed around Khelya to the wall. "What is it? Mi? Mi onla?"

"Dagin tevem Dag alat!" Teres waved her hands with frustration. "Ansi, saino!"

Matil located Ansi, who lay sleeping against the back wall. "Teres is here!" she said. "Something's happening."

He looked around, disoriented, before rushing to the cell wall. He and Teres began to talk urgently. "Wake the others," he told Matil.

The commotion had already woken Dask, and Matil went to Khelya to use a combination of talking and shaking to get her at least half-awake. After the three gathered next to Ansi, Teres nodded and made for the gate.

Ansi turned with a determined expression. "Ten of Dag's elite warriors are outside the gates. My sister is not with them. They've come to take us to her city."

"What?" Khelya said. "Why?"

"Teres believes that when we arrived here, someone recognized me and took word to Dag," Ansi said. "We have no choice but to go with them. Teres and her alva will travel ahead of us and prepare things in the city. What happens then is unknowable. We must do our best."

Dask hit the wall with his hand. "We won't be able to get out of a city. Have Teres sneak us out *now*. We can do more if we're not locked up."

"We don't have time," Ansi said.

"Get her over here." He ran both hands through his hair. "I knew it, I knew it!"

"Trust Teres. Trust my alva. When the rebellion starts, they'll see that there is a way out of the wrong that has been done, and they will follow it. As I did when you showed me a way."

Dask shook his head. "*It won't—*"

A group of burly men with orange designs covering their arms and legs filed into the village from the entry tunnel. They crossed the square, surrounded the cell, and leveled jagged, stone-tipped spears at the prisoners while one of the village women unlocked the door. She entered with a coil of cords and began to tie Ansi's hands. Noticing the woman's fearful look and feeling sorry for her, Matil held her hands out willingly to be tied.

Dask tensed up and his ears lowered like he was getting ready to fight.

"Dask, please," Matil whispered.

His ears fell and he let the woman bind his hands. She finished tying the prisoners and blindfolded Ansi. Soon they left the village to the stares of alva who had come out to see what was going on.

12

Workers Divided

They walked until morning, took a rest, and kept moving. Along the path, Vima Eletsol chopped and hauled hefty branches. By midday the prisoners could see in the distance a wooden wall so high that, even from where they stood on a ridge, nothing of the inside was visible. Trees stood outside the wall, their branches laden with stout houses and towers. As the group came closer, the wall seemed to soar up like one of the massive trees beside it. Matil was in awe of how tall the unbroken planks were. It must have taken a hundred alva to handle them.

The group entered a sea of squalid huts and lean-tos just outside the wall. The Eletsol among the shelters, mostly children, stared and laughed at the prisoners. The children's laughter hushed into susurration as they paid careful attention to blindfolded Ansi. Many lengths ahead, a gate set in the wall and painted with animal designs was open just enough for two lines of wagons to enter and exit. The wagons were pulled mainly by ground squirrels and rats. Some Eletsol pulled wagons themselves or led scuttling beetles strapped up with supplies. Wood and stone filled the entering wagons, and the exiting ones were empty. The prisoners and their escorts joined the shuffling entrance line. It took some time before they made it past the front gate, but then they stepped into the busiest city Matil had ever seen.

The air was heavy with smoke, the thunder of timbers falling into place, and crash after boom from many hammers striking stone and wood. Everything was moving – the alva, the work animals, and even the buildings. Roofs were hoisted and walls raised before Matil's eyes. Helmeted soldiers drove the workers hard, but some seemed to be helping the workers as best they could. The encompassing wall cast cool shade over the city.

Dask gave a low whistle. "These guys could put the Obrigi to shame, huh, Khel?"

"They're fast," Khelya said with distaste, "but they're takin' a lot of shortcuts. Look, they even left some of their construction behind without finishing."

Teetering skeletons of buildings were scattered haphazardly throughout the city. The throngs of bent-backed workers gave each abandoned structure a wide berth. The guards led the prisoners down a broad main road of hard dirt, and Matil looked nervously up at one of the unfinished buildings as they walked close beside it.

The road split in two. Between the new roads was an imposing wooden statue. It depicted a woman, similar in appearance to Fridda but more muscular. With her chin lifted and bare feet solidly planted, her posture communicated ownership of the land and its alva. Workers went back and forth by the statue with their heads low, carting loads of lumber and plant material. The group took the left road and, with the guards shoving people out of the way, they made quick progress through busy crossings and under wooden sky-bridges. Smaller statues of the same woman glared down from pedestals and building facades.

Dask looked up at one statue's fierce visage and elbowed Ansi. "Hey, there are statues of your sister *everywhere*."

"Don't say out loud that she is my sister," he spat. "I don't care if no one can understand you. It is embarrassing."

At last Matil saw that the road ended in the distance at a grand stone hall. Its walls were old and overgrown with vines, bolstered by what appeared to be newly-crafted buttresses. Nearer to the group, down the road, grimy young men jeered at several children who were tied to a post.

Matil grabbed Ansi's arm with her bound hands. "Ansi, they tied up some children. They're blindfolded, like you."

"Ah, Teres told me about the children," he said. "Their magic is too strong, so they cannot be Vima. She says that they are separated from their families, put on display, and then exiled." He frowned. "Likewise the Taina are not kind to children with weak magic."

Matil watched the children until they were out of view. When she faced forward, it took her a moment to understand what she saw ahead of her. From the point where the prisoners stood to the front of the great hall, a rowdy mob of Eletsol had gathered. They talked loudly to each other and some surged toward the building, only to be repelled by guards. An escort's irritated grunt got Matil moving faster.

"Are we approaching the palace?" Ansi said. "It sounds like something is happening."

Dask's eyebrows were halfway up his forehead. "Um, yeah. Something's happening."

"Teres is doing her part, then."

"Ansi Palikunika!" a nearby voice cried.

Another voice yelled from the crowd. "Ansi Palikunika! Takkamakaini!"

Ansi's mouth fell open.

"Takkamakaini!" The shouts continued. "Ansi Palikunika! Takkamakaini!"

Many in the crowd turned around to see the prisoners, and the chants spread.

"Takkamakaini!" Ansi shouted. Matil and Dask looked at him in alarm.

The crowd was growing. The escort guards had difficulty pushing their way through, but the threat of their spears cleared a path. The air was hot and dusty, and raw throats spoke clamorously all around, hurting Matil's ears. She tripped when they reached broad steps leading to a terrace along the front of the great hall; a man from the crowd caught her, nodded, and helped her up. It was heartening to know that they had allies in the rowdy throng, but she wondered whether they could resist trained warriors.

At the top of the stairs and across the terrace, one of the large double doors was opened to let the guards and prisoners inside and was quickly closed. The sound dampened immediately. They stood in a foyer that continued into a long passage with wooden walls, closed doors, and a ceiling of woven plants strung with flowers. The escort guards led the prisoners straight down the passage. Khelya had to lower her head for the ceiling, but her face still brushed the flowers, resulting in a few explosive sneezes. Open windows along the passage looked out on lush courtyards filled with berry bushes.

The group came to the end of the passage and entered a large room. A few paces in front of them, a low table stretched to the right and left down the length of the room. Several Eletsol sat on cushions around the table. They looked up at the prisoners walking in. Old murals decorated the walls, showing scenes of building and living, as well as hunting parties facing off against wildcats and weasels.

"Busaino," a woman said. The voice drew Matil's attention toward the left end of the room, where this woman sat – comfortably, if her pillows were as fluffy as they looked – in a wide wooden throne. After the woman spoke, the Eletsol at the table grumbled to each other, stood with a flutter of wings, and walked out of the room. The escorts brought the prisoners before the throne. One of them untied Ansi's blindfold.

This was the same woman depicted in the statues outside: Dag. She resembled her sister even more in reality, though her hair was dark russet brown instead of blonde, and her wings had the appearance of fire lily petals, as flaming orange as the paint covering her arms and splashed across half her face.

She wore an ample skirt of green leaves and a sleeveless vest of fine leather with fur around the collar. Her throne was encircled by upright spears, some with heads that were narrow and made of stone, others with barbed, metal tips, several decorated with flamboyant beads and carvings, and one spear entirely carved from rock. By her arm, a small table bore a bowl filled with chunks of berries and nuts.

Dag smiled so that her eyes pressed into slits. "Veli."

Ansi stepped forward with a hostile look. "Tuko."

She gestured at the bowl beside her. He didn't move. A hint of something unpleasant twisted her smile, and she asked a question.

Ansi responded steadily. As he spoke, Dag's smile evaporated into a resentful glare. She snapped back at him, grabbed a piece of walnut from the bowl, and shoved it past her lips. Before Ansi could say anything else, frenzied yells carried through the passage.

Dag leapt to her feet and pulled a spear from the collection decorating her throne. At her strident call, more soldiers filed into the room. She led them marching down the passage. The escorts blindfolded Ansi again, pushed the other prisoners into line, and followed the soldiers. Dask jumped up to see what was happening in the front, earning himself a wallop from one of the escorts.

At the far end of the passage, the door opened, and it sounded like the uproar outside was even louder than it had been earlier. Matil could hear the humming of countless wings. She stayed close by her friends as they passed through the open doors to the terrace.

The whole city seemed to have gathered in front of the great hall. Half of the crowd hovered in the air, forming a shifting, colorful cloud of Eletsol. Dag stared out at them, her face coloring red and knuckles turning white against the spear shaft. While there were soldiers arrayed in defensive positions around her and the hall, other soldiers could be seen protesting within the crowd.

Dag finally burst out with a screeching reprimand. The alva quieted to hear her, but with each word their faces grew wilder. Their renewed shouts arose to drown her voice. She raised her spear and stood as proudly as her statues. On her twitching face, however, was the beginning of desperation.

Matil and Khelya scrambled back toward the wall. Dask dragged Ansi over. The escorts no longer guarded them, but now engaged in yelling, shaking their thick broadaxes and spears, and generally returning the threats of the crowd.

Dask picked up a sharp stone fragment someone had thrown, used it to cut through the group's bindings, and then tore away Ansi's blindfold. "They were yelling your name earlier," he said. "What do we do?"

Ansi took in the scene, his eyes wide open. Dag's guards thrust their spears into the crowd, felling Eletsol and tearing alva's wings. Many in the crowd fought back, armed with the tools of their labor. At the back of the mob, swarms of Eletsol broke off and attacked the half-built dwellings, temples, and markets. They pulled the structures apart from top and from bottom. A tall hive of huts shuddered and shook before toppling with a mighty crash. Voices rose in panic.

Ansi took a step backward. "Teres was supposed to—this is—"

"If only the good guys would just calm down and plan," Khelya said, her voice high with fear. "Or maybe there aren't any good guys." She looked around. "Ansi, can you stop this with magic?"

"I could use these vines from the palace, but they are too large. I don't have enough strength." Ansi raised his hand, making the leaves on a vine rustle. "And there are no other magicians to lend their power. There must be something we can do…"

Other magicians?

Matil hopped up and down. "The children, the children!"

"What?"

She forced herself to stand still. "Can the children I saw earlier help you?"

"Ah, the Taina children!" Ansi said. "Where are they?"

"On the side of the road as we came in." Matil pointed.

Ansi stared through the tangle of brawling alva that surrounded the palace.

Dask nudged him. "Follow me."

"Be careful," Matil said.

He smiled and unfolded his wings. "You two watch out." Straight upward he went, blasting air in his wake, followed closely by Ansi and his humming leaf-wings.

Matil and Khelya pressed closer to the wall of the palace, away from the brutal scene. Khelya put her large fists up in a fighting position and Matil covered her ears to give them some relief from the onslaught of noise. To their shock, a thick-armed old man fell at Matil's feet. His eyes were closed. A trickle of blood traversed his face from forehead to chin. Matil and Khelya jumped when he opened his eyes and struggled to his feet, clutching a stone hammer. He gawked at the two of them only briefly and then threw himself into the fray, crying, "Latuaaam!"

After that Khelya began talking out loud to herself, or, as Matil listened, to Thosten. Matil didn't fully understand prayers – did they help or not? – but sometimes she silently joined Khelya in reaching out for the mysterious Thosten. It was comforting to have a way to ask for help when alva were kicking in each other's teeth just a few lengths away.

Yet Matil couldn't shake the wretched feeling that…she didn't deserve anyone's help.

"Watch out!" came a shout from above.

Matil and Khelya moved over to let Dask, Ansi, and eight Eletsol children land on the terrace. Ansi spoke kindly but hurriedly to the children, who gaped at the riot with pale, tear-stained faces. Though they seemed uncertain, they nodded as he took his place amidst them.

He continued to talk in Eleti. One by one they turned from the riot to look up at him. He pointed toward the palace beside them and swept his hand through the air as though pulling at something. The children imitated his motion. They repeated it a few times, and then Ansi tensed his shoulders. He began the pulling motion in earnest. The children, now staring up at the plant-covered palace, moved their arms along with him. A tremor ran through vines as thick around as Khelya.

Several vines parted from the palace walls and threaded through the rioters, slowly enough that those who were hit only reeled out of the way. The green tendrils began to lengthen. Tiny leaves sprang out along their lengths, quickly growing to full size.

Ansi frowned deeply in concentration. The children's little flower petal wings quivered, and some of the children were squeezing their eyes shut. After several strained moments, Ansi exhaled. The vines stopped moving.

Dask prowled the terrace, watching to make sure no one got close to the magicians. As Matil cowered, she felt her mind shift. The din grew sharper and louder in her ears. The smell of dust and sweat filled her nostrils. Her hand went to her side, but there was no dagger.

"Come on," Khelya muttered. Her gaze flicked between Ansi, the children, and the motionless vines. "It ain't over."

She rested a hand on Ansi's shoulder. "It can work."

Ansi's mouth settled into a determined line. He straightened up and moved his hands again, pulling at the air. If it *didn't* work…Matil looked worriedly at the children. She and the others needed to keep the children safe, make an escape plan, and find Teres.

But the remaining vines on the palace responded to his gestures with even more speed than before. They grew out across the square in front of the palace, curling around the first ones and forming a web. From the ground to the air, the swarming crowd outside of the terrace was impeded by overtaking vines. Soon, Matil couldn't see far through the mass of alva and tendrils. She suddenly felt very small before such miraculous power.

Twisted vines shielded the terrace, casting shade and protection over the facade of the building. The fighting came to a standstill as Eletsol looked about in confusion, searching for the source of the unexpected magic. A few yelled at Ansi and the children when they noticed them. Sweat rolled down Ansi's neck. He gasped for air.

Alva began to squeeze themselves out from between the vines and climb through the overgrowth. The soldiers gathered together, drawing back from the rioters to slip into the palace. The prisoners were left on the terrace facing the crowd. Dag was nowhere to be seen.

Khelya recovered from her awe at the magical feat and took her hand off Ansi. "What now?"

"Teres is here somewhere, right?" Dask said. "Let's find her."

Ansi's face took on a hard cast as he saw bloodied bodies lying still in front of the terrace. He thanked the exhausted children and rose into the air past the thick vines and shouting alva. "Eletsol! Eletsol!"

Matil held back her impulse to reach out and stop him. The rioters didn't look pleased, but at least they were quiet and focused on him.

The impressive sternness departed from Ansi's brow, and he began haltingly with a few words in Eleti.

"Louder!" Dask said.

Ansi glanced down at Dask before continuing his speech more loudly. Now he grew more animated. His voice trembled with both nerves and zeal. At length he fell silent, eyes darting anxiously around at his audience's stormy faces.

"Takkamakaini!" Teres's voice rang out. Marred by scuffs and cuts, she flew in from the side to hover beside Ansi. She took a moment to catch her breath and share a hopeful glance with him before yelling a few words at the mob. Ansi's expression changed to surprise when she grabbed his hand and lifted it over their heads. "Takkamakaini dekossa!" She poked him in the side with her free hand.

"T-T-Takkamak-k-kaini!" he said. "Dekossa!"

The words were returned by some of the Eletsol extricating themselves from the vines, quietly at first and then lifting in volume. As before, it became a loud chant.

Khelya sat down heavily. Fatigue diluting her thoughts, Matil sat next to the Obrigi and leaned against her arm. Dask did the same, sprawling out at Khelya's other side.

A roof behind the buildings surrounding the palace was lit in a strange way. In moments, flames licked upward across the roof. Matil scrambled up in alarm. She found that she couldn't take deep breaths anymore.

"F-fire!" Matil shouted up to Ansi.

Khelya and Dask saw the fire too and sat up straighter.

Ansi looked across the city from where he and Teres were hovering. With a nod at Matil, he said, "We will contain it." He turned and spoke with Teres.

"*Why* would alva burn their own buildings down?" Khelya said.

"Letting off steam, I guess," Dask said. "Don't you wanna break things sometimes?"

"No!" She stretched up to see. "And especially not things I built myself. Ain't right."

There was a rolling crash as the roof sank behind the other buildings. The ground rumbled with the impact.

Khelya's shoulders lifted. "Ooh…that's what you get for treating buildings like dirt."

"Treating *alva* like dirt," Dask said.

"Right."

Matil wiped her forehead and sat back down beside them. "Alva and buildings."

13

Peace and Honor

Ansi and Teres rallied the rioters at the palace, sending alva through the city to stop looters and find Dag and her loyalists. They found a few soldiers, but most had fled the city. It seemed that Dag was still a threat.

Rebels supporting Ansi gathered in and around the palace. Matil and her friends helped however they could. The children who had lent their magic during the riot were brought into the palace to wait until their families could be found.

Ansi, Teres, her brother, and several elders of the clan disappeared into the throne room to plan their next move. After eating a small meal, Matil, Khelya, and Dask were given beds of loudly-patterned pillows in a hall that had become an infirmary and bunk room. The three fell fast asleep.

* * *

Matil woke with the darkness. Her ears stirred as she picked up distant sounds of alva bustling around the palace. She stretched and felt just how wrinkled and grimy her tunic and trousers were. Maybe someone outside could tell her where to wash them.

She left the restful infirmary without a sound and moved through the corridors of the palace, which became more populated the farther she went. The brawny Eletsol passersby didn't see her at first, but when they did, they squished to one side of the hallway to keep some distance from her. Matil's ears lowered a touch. She knew that without wings, she looked very small and odd indeed. A flash of Nychta entered her mind, leaning over and pointing the dagger, brown wings splayed and spiteful words on her lips.

Matil shook the vision away and once more noted the Eletsol edging past her, slowing down to watch while leaving most of the walkway bare around her. She was causing a disturbance; she should go back to the infirmary and wait.

"Ah! My friend." Ansi pushed through his fellows, dodged their shoulders and elbows, and crossed the empty part of the hallway to stop next to Matil. He looked tired and his hair was a mess, but there was a new strength in his posture. "Where are the others?"

"Asleep," Matil said. "I got up to find somewhere I could wash my clothes. Is the meeting over?"

He nodded. "It has just finished. I'll find help for you."

They began down the hallway. The other Eletsol, seeing Ansi beside Matil, walked on and behaved as if they hadn't been staring a moment ago.

"The city is nearly at peace," Ansi said as they walked. "Many of the Vima are free now. I – strange as it is – have been named chief of the old clan. The Takkamakaini."

"Chief?" Matil said. "That's wonderful!"

"But I- I fear I am doing wrong." He looked down and cleared his throat. "What I mean is…after what my sisters did, I see harshly that having the chief's blood does not make someone a good chief. Yet my father gave us instructions that we were meant to follow. To fight those instructions is high disobedience and dishonor, yes?" Ansi stopped. "I have something to confess." He pointed at a long bench by the wall. "Please sit."

Wondering what he wanted to say, Matil followed him and sat beneath one of the ceiling flowers, a delicate rosebud almost as large as her.

"Do you remember my tale of Emperor Ivu?" Ansi said. "How his empire turned on itself?"

"I think so…yes, I remember."

His wings flicked open and shut. "My father told me and my sisters to learn from Ivu, from his good and from his bad. That was the reason my father named both Fridda and Dag as heirs. He wished to leave a spirit of harmony in his clan, unlike Ivu." Ansi looked at his hands. "What happened today wasn't harmony. When I rise to the treetops… if I continue in this way…the Elders and my ancestors may judge me unworthy. My father might not accept me as his own son."

Matil frowned. She wanted to ease his conscience, but she didn't know much about the treetops. Somewhere in her mind, a soft murmur told her what she did know. "Why wouldn't he accept you?" she said. "Your father's plan brought chaos. And even though there was a fight today, it seems like it's brought harmony with it. If…if you do what's right, isn't it better than if you put the whole clan in danger by following his instructions?"

"Perhaps," said Ansi hesitantly.

"Then I think he'll have to accept you, otherwise he'll look bad."

Ansi gave a brief chuckle. "I miss him. He wanted us to be one family, but I have not brought us together."

Matil thought of her family, loving faces only revealed to her in dreams. She ached to know where they were – Bechel must be a young man now – and resolutely pushed away every possibility of their fates that occurred to her. Better not to consider anything until she knew the truth. She turned to the other side of the bench. It was empty.

In the middle of the hallway, Ansi stood speaking with a baggy-eyed Teres. He motioned down the hall, in the direction of the infirmary. Teres shook her head, but Ansi stepped behind to take hold of her shoulders and gently push her forward. She smiled up at him before walking away.

Ansi whirled back to Matil with a twitch of his leaf wings. "Kal, kal," he said. "Eten gil pai. I mean—this way."

* * *

Ansi and Teres accompanied the three travelers to the city's gate at noon the next day. They all wore new clothes, sturdy robes and leggings of leaves, petals, and leather. Khelya's clothes were baggy, made with various swathes of materials stitched together in haste. She held a heavy Eletsol spear while Matil and Dask had received wide-bladed knives. Several Eletsol were already at the gates, loading bags on two familiar-looking beetles.

"Dewdrop! Olnar!" Matil rushed up and hugged Dewdrop just behind the head. Dewdrop felt Matil with her antennae.

"Teres's village was left undefended," Ansi said, "so our men secured it last night. Your beetles were still there."

Dask took Ansi's shoulder in a friendly grip. "Thanks for getting them back. And thanks for getting us free again."

Khelya knelt to be on the others' level. "What was it you said to the mob the other day that made them like you so much?" she asked Ansi.

His cheeks turned pink. "I asked them why we still fight. I said that our clans were one, so why is it that we fight now? Because my sisters are angry with each other? Because we must prove whether strength or magic is better? I said that we were at our best when we were together."

Khelya eyed him and nodded in approval.

"Ansi?" Dask said. "Is that you?"

His wings fanned out defensively. "Of course it's me. What do you mean?"

"You've changed over the past few days." Dask nudged him. "Trying to impress a girl really made you a hero."

"I don't understand." Ansi primly folded his wings. "I have always been courageous and intelligent."

"And charming?" Dask added.

"Charming, yes," Ansi said.

"Uh-huh," he said. "Right."

Ansi began to fiddle with his hands. "In…in truth, it was the plight of my alva that drove me, and it was all of your guidance that gave me strength. Thank you, outsiders." He bowed to them. Teres did the same. Straightening, he said, "After the Taina hear of these events, I hope they will not stand for Fridda to keep power. I will strive to reunite the clan."

Matil was eager to hop on the beetles and move out, but she slowed herself down to savor the warm feeling of having taken part in helping these alva win back their land. All across the city, Eletsol rested and celebrated. They no longer trudged wearily, nor flew like they would fall out of the sky. Some had returned to working on construction already, vigorous purpose in their movements.

"Together we heard the voice of the Watcher," Ansi said. "Such an occasion will be rejoiced in, and I'd hoped you would stay to enjoy it. Although…even more, I had hoped I could help you with your mission."

"You *have* helped," Matil said. "We're very grateful for it. Thank you for the maps and supplies, too."

"It's pretty nice, being friends with a chief's son," Dask said. "And, uh," he winked, "invite us to the wedding."

Ansi tilted his head. "What? I don't know that word."

"Yes, you do."

"Way-deen?" The corners of his mouth lifted slightly. "Is it a kind of bread?"

Dask shook his head. "A man shouldn't be this shy."

"*I'm* shy?" said Ansi. "Then what about you?"

"Ha ha ha. But really, invite us to the wedding or I'll come after you." Dask shook Ansi's hand. "Take care of yourself, buddy." He tipped his head to Teres. "And you take care. Ansi's a good guy. Don't make him start too many wars."

Teres spoke to Ansi, keeping her eyes on Dask.

Ansi snorted. "She doesn't doubt your spirit, but you look like one who cheats in games. She thinks you should change that."

Matil looked down, straightening her dark green jerkin and yellow flower petal robe to hide her chuckles, but Khelya burst into snickering.

Dask smiled. "Sure. Anything you say, lady."

When Khelya recovered, she dipped her head to Ansi. "I'm sorry I was in a foul mood toward you."

"And I'm glad that I was wrong about the Watcher," Ansi said. "Colthal, friends."

"Colthal," Teres said.

Matil waved at them as Dewdrop and Olnar trundled them off into the wild forest of Fainfal. The three travelers were on their way once again.

* * *

Through rotting doors and down curving steps, Lyria found a dungeon cell that held a single prisoner. The cell was painted with shadows and soft yellow light from the torch orb on the ceiling and the guttering wings of the long-haired Sangriga man inside. He shifted and fussed, his chains scraping the floor. He was someone Lyria had wished never to see again. Her accursed curiosity had overcome her and here she was, looking upon a man whose past held horrific atrocities. Despite the wall of bars that acted as a large window in and out of the cell, he hadn't noticed her.

"When will they let you play with the charcoal?" he said to himself. "You've been getting good at portraiture." He yawned. "Mmm, finally getting tired, are you?"

Lyria watched from the dark passage with a cloak drawn tightly around herself. She had dimmed her bright wings before setting off on this excursion, and the strange feeling it gave her – of holding her breath without actually holding her breath – was finally bothering her. She relaxed her shoulders. Her wings radiated farther and farther until they were back to normal.

The man in the cell stood.

Few alva knew of Verys Ila Saikyr, as he liked to be called. Lyria had stumbled across his cell one night on an unrelated investigation and at first had thought him merely mad. She'd soon understood the truth.

"Lookity-look, she's backity-back," Verys muttered. "Don't you remember? She's the one who hates you." His head snapped up with a wide grin. "Why, hello! Come to cry again?" He held out his arms and rattled their chains. "Closer, closer, so this'un can hold you tight."

Lyria could barely contain her fury at the sight of his hunched form and pale eyes like a green forest pond frozen over. "I've come to ask you a question," she said, voice wavering.

"Question? Ooh, a question. This'un *likes* questions. Can't say he likes answers quite as much, though. Hmm."

It was as she expected. When they captured him all those years ago, the magicians hadn't been able to extract answers from him. Though he'd lost the Book of Myrkhar, his mind and body were still protected by its dark power.

She must stomach his grating words in order to get anywhere. "What happened on the day of the Myrkharen Invasion? How did you summon the Skorgon? Why can't you die?"

"Quite a private matter, you know," Verys said. "He didn't tell aaanyone else. But after all, this'un owes you a favor for his rude behavior that day. It's only fair he tells you." He let out a chuckle.

Lyria couldn't do it. "Never mind," she said through her teeth, and she turned toward the door.

"You want to know very badly or you wouldn't be here."

She whirled back around to face him. "I'll send someone else and you tell *them* all about it, how does that sound?"

"Not nice at all. He wants to tell you in particular."

"Why?"

Verys smirked. "Because you're pretty. Pretty girls get pretty words."

How dare he, knowing whose blood was on his hands?

"You are the lowest of scum," she said.

"Lowest? *Scum?* This'un wouldn't deign to touch the lowest of scum with his boot heel. His body may be locked away, but in essence he is greater than the greatest king in Eventyr! Why? Why?" He grandly raised his arms as high as they could go in their restraints. "He did what it told him to do. He killed himself…and became…an Elder."

Lyria frowned. She had learned about the man's Elder delusion when researching his records, but the first part was new. "How did you kill yourself? You're clearly alive."

"He was crying, you know. He didn't want to die, didn't want to hurt all those alva, but this'un had the Book and the dagger. What was he to do? He could only wait and cry while this'un spoke the words."

"It sounds as though you're talking about two different men."

"That would be because he *is*. He speaks of the being you see in the flesh," Verys laid his hands delicately on his chest, "and the man created in order to be destroyed. When the second man died, it was the most wonderful feeling. Yes, it was. His fear died, too."

Lyria leaned against the cold stone wall. "One man is you, and the other was created…how? With a spell from the Book? Why?"

Amusement glittered in Verys's icy eyes. "Have the doctors ever bled you? Drained the illness and impurities from your blood? The two were one flawed man before. An Elder and a half-man after."

"Are you saying…that you were split in two? And then you *killed* the other half?"

He yawned loudly and sat down. "This'un is entirely spent. Leave him in peace now."

The concept amazed and disgusted her. Nychta Olsta might have cast the same spell as Verys. The ghost of a thought occurred to Lyria. "I promise to leave after one last question."

"Oh, very well," Verys said. "It *was* your mother."

Her fists clenched, and, noticing them, Verys smiled.

"Your question?" he said.

She shut her eyes in order to regain control. "What would have happened if, instead of dying, he escaped?"

"Escaped? The Book wouldn't like it. This'un would hate it. Because everything he hated in himself would still live."

"Would you be able to die, then?" Lyria prodded.

Verys stared at her, mirth tugging at the corners of his mouth. "You promised to leave, and we mustn't break promises." He flopped on the ground and giggled as though he had told quite a joke.

Suddenly taken with the urgent desire to silence him, Lyria shook herself and hurried away down the passage. Echoes of his laughter followed her. If her guess was correct, then Matil…

Did the wingless girl know who she was?

14

Old Enemies

Matil, Khelya, and Dask traveled southwest for two days. The third morning, Matil lay rolled up in her blanket with her eyes closed and back wedged under a curving tree root. She fuzzily wondered if she should get up and then decided that she wasn't ready yet to begin another dull day of travel.

Dask shrieked.

Matil flailed into a sitting position and struggled out of her blankets, but Dask was nowhere to be seen in their small camp encircled by roots.

"That *tickles*, you nach-tickering—*ah!* Help! Khelya! Matil!" His voice was coming from the other side of the roots.

She crawled onto a root to find out what was going on, and her heart skipped a beat at the sight of Dask's adversary.

He was grappling with a slithery Skorgon. The insect-like alva had two short legs and four short arms along its slender length. Its back was shielded by natural armor, brown plates that bent easily with its movement and protruded at the base of its crystalline wings. While it climbed on Dask, he stabbed its shell without effect. The face came into view, a gaunt, gray face with endlessly-champing mouthparts and glistening black eyes. The Skorgon lashed out with its own knife, slicing through Dask's jerkin and forearm. He grunted in pain but was able to parry its follow-up strikes.

Draped on a pack behind Matil was her belt; she yanked her dagger from it and bounded over the root. Where should she go in? It looked like the underbelly was its weak spot. She sprinted forward, grabbed both edges of the Skorgon's shell as she passed, and threw herself to the side. With a thin *skreeee*, the Skorgon separated from Dask and crashed onto her, buzzing, wriggling and waving its limbs. Matil's face was smothered by the shiny shell. As she turned her head to get air, the Skorgon bashed her with the back of its head. The world seemed to blink out of existence and her grip on the shell loosened.

The Skorgon started to roll off of her and then suddenly stilled. Matil's vision cleared, though a budding pain throbbed in her temple. She looked up to see Dask holding his long knife at the Skorgon's throat. Puffing with effort, she slid out from under its shell and readied herself again with the dagger. There was only uneven breathing as they all looked at one another.

Khelya poked her ghostly head above the roots, blonde hair straggling over her face. "Why're y'all makin' so much—" Her sleepy eyes got big when she noticed the Skorgon. "Hey!" She frowned. "You two *know* I don't like eatin' bugs."

The Skorgon's eyes, despite being wide already, grew larger. "Naaa!" he said in his wheezy voice. "Do not eat! Skorgon, not bug! Na, blednuv. Do not eat!"

"Wha…uh, yeah, that's right!" Dask said. He licked his lips. "This one would be great basted in oil, sizzled up, and served with cider. And then afterward we could have those little cookies the Sangriga eat, you know?"

"But I am Skorgon," he cried. "How can alva eat alva?"

Dask showed his teeth. "You think we care? Look at the Obrigi, look at her. She's too big to live on our measly Ranycht diet. She's gotta have *something* that'll fill her belly."

A shudder rippled the Skorgon's slippery length. Khelya stared at everyone in bewilderment.

"But let's say you answered some of our questions," Dask said. "We might, just might, be willing to take you off the menu."

The Skorgon folded both pairs of hands together pleadingly.

* * *

In their camp, Dask reclined against a root while Matil tended the shallow wound in his left arm with a wet cloth. They had tied the Skorgon's feet, four hands, and the bases of his wings, and the beetles were curiously tracing him out with their antennae. He clacked his mandibles at them.

"So…" Khelya looked at Dask, who encouraged her with a 'go on' gesture. She turned back to the unblinking Skorgon. "You'll tell us what we wanna know, right?"

"Khel," Dask said. "Khelya, my dear child—ow!"

Matil winced. "Sorry." She approached his sliced arm even more carefully. At this point she was barely touching it.

"Ah!" Dask coughed. "No, keep going, it didn't hurt. Khel, you have to *tell* him he wants to tell us. Give him something to fear."

Khelya edged closer, reached out, and shook the Skorgon violently by the shoulders.

"Naaa." His plated head flopped forward. "I talk. I will."

"Is Nychta Olsta nearby?" said Dask.

"She is southeast, in Nychtfalnia. Lady Nychta sent my company to loathhh-ful bright land under command of General Crell."

Crell? At least Nychta wasn't here. Matil believed she would sense her double's presence, but she still felt better knowing without a doubt. "Why were you sent here?" she asked as she wrapped Dask's forearm in a bandage.

The Skorgon's mouthparts clicked when he spoke. "For finding Kyndelin wise man."

"Have you found him yet?" she said.

"No."

"How far away are your buddies?" Dask said.

The Skorgon gave them a shifty glance. "They will be here soon to ssslice your necks." His laughter whistled around the enclosure.

"Then we gotta leave," Khelya said, alarmed. "What'll we do with this guy?"

Dask reached into one of the bags. "Gag him and drag him. Where's the map?"

Matil looked in another bag, pushing everything to the side. "Not here."

"Who used it last?" he said irritably.

Khelya busied herself rolling up her blanket. "I might've—I dunno."

"Do you remember where you put it?"

"I don't even remember using it," Khelya said.

"Here it is!" Matil said. She pulled out the crinkled roll of parchment and held it aloft.

The Skorgon sprang to his hobbled feet and leaped over her, snatching the map in two free fingers. Khelya climbed on a root and jumped after him, but he was already buzzing into the air so erratically that she couldn't grab him. Dask whipped open his wings and hurtled up into the Skorgon's midsection. They tumbled through the air far from the enclosure.

Matil took up her dagger and dashed out once again, looking for Dask. He and his opponent rolled down the roots of another tree and onto the ground. The Skorgon grabbed his throat with one pair of bound hands. As Dask choked, flailed, and bashed him, the Skorgon shot the other pair of hands out to clamp down on Dask's bandaged arm. Dask shut his eyes in pain, his mouth still open and gasping like a fish.

Coldness fell over Matil. She pumped her legs faster. As soon as she got within reach, she wrapped her left arm around the Skorgon and sunk the dagger in sideways, just under his shell. Screeching, he let go of Dask, who gulped in air and followed up with a punch to the Skorgon's jaw. Matil held on to the struggling Skorgon long enough to stab higher on his torso before he shook her off. But after that effort he could only crawl away and collapse. Matil sat up, breathing hard.

Dask staggered past her. He kicked the Skorgon over, revealing a frozen expression and abdominal scales drenched with green blood. For a moment he waited to see if the Skorgon would move. All was still, so Dask took back their map. Matil shuddered as she realized that her dagger and right hand were also covered in the Skorgon's blood. She wiped them on a blade of grass next to her. It had been weeks since they'd last fought Skorgon. Her ears lowered at the memory of fighting beside Nat…beside Amacht.

They went back to the enclosure.

"Typical," Dask said loudly but hoarsely as they entered. "Let the little guys do the fight—Khel? Khel, what's wrong?"

The Obrigi was lying face down and now looked up. Soil stuck to her nose, already turning transparent like her skin. "You're okay," she said in relief. "Sorry I missed the fight."

"What happened?" Matil said. "Are *you* okay?"

Khelya pushed herself up. "Yeah. Nothing hurts, anyway. Couldn't see my idiot feet and tripped over a root."

"You have to fix that," Dask said, beginning to roll up his blanket.

She hit the ground with a faded fist. "I *can't!* How many times do I have to tell you?"

"Maybe…" Matil knelt next to her own blanket. "Maybe the Elders can put you back to normal." She remembered how Khelya had solidified slightly next to the Wall. If Elders were real, Matil thought they might use the same kind of powerful magic she had felt at Eventyr's border.

"And that's if they pay any attention to a dirt-walker like me." But Khelya looked away with a dreamy smile.

They packed up camp and led the beetles through the undergrowth, Khelya crouching beside them. The map indicated that they were close to Hasyl's place. Here and there a Skorgon scout searched the forest. When one rustled a bush or flew overhead, the group froze. However, all soon became peaceful. It seemed that there were no more Skorgon around.

"Wait," Dask spoke at last. "Maybe Captain Crell's grub club hasn't made it any farther than we have. If I go on alone, I can bring the hermit back here quick, so he's safe."

Matil and Khelya nodded. He burst upward in a rush of air and feathers and tore away through the forest with the velvet sound of beating wings. They didn't wait for long. Dask returned, wiping sweat from his forehead.

"Two of 'em," he panted. "There were two Skorgon outside the hermit's house. I flew through the area, but didn't see anyone else. I guess they're keeping the hermit inside."

They stole onward with their hands on Dewdrop's and Olnar's heads. Past a spectacularly fat tree and under a bush of star-shaped flowers, they stopped. Matil lifted her head to see through the leaves.

As Mr. Korsen had described, the hermit's home was a huge, twisted log, nestled in earth and tufts of grass. Dull lacquer covered its age-pitted bark. The end of the log closest to the group was filled with interlocking stones. Between the log and the group was a circular brown hut, wide and dominated by a pointed roof made of dry grass. Two Skorgon stood by the hut's door. Matil and Dask tied the beetles to a thick dandelion stem.

"So we take the bugs out," Dask said. "Easy."

Matil touched the handle of her dagger. "It was hard enough fighting just one earlier. I think these are stronger than the ones we fought in Valdingfal."

"Okay, we'll need a distraction while you and I sneak up."

She nodded. "Khelya can be the distraction."

"They'd see her and shout. Anyone inside would hear." He ran his eyes over the scene before them. "Maybe she can throw something to get them away from the hut."

"I've got an idea," Khelya said abruptly. She paused and then shook her head. "Feels strange saying that…maybe you guys are rubbin' off on me. Anyway, let's say I sit here in the bush and let one of the beetles out by its reins, with a pack or two on top to look suspicious. The Skorgon would come over to see. There." For a moment she thought about it, and then her matter-of-fact air slipped away. "Nah, it's- it's too simple. Any more ideas?"

"Well…" Dask looked at Matil. "Khel's idea could work."

"Let's use it," Matil said.

Khelya gave them a surprised look.

They soon set up Dewdrop, the more compliant of the two beetles, with some packs on her shell. Matil took her place to Khelya's left while Dask went to her right. The shadow beneath the leaves was enough to surround Matil comfortably, allowing her to fade. She turned her dagger in a reverse grip and breathed out to slow her pounding heart. At the feeling of the dagger's hilt in her hand and at the tension of uncertainty, her state of mind changed. It grew detached and prepared, searching for advantages in her surroundings. She stepped to the side, onto higher ground. Just like Etsel had taught her.

"Now, Khel," came a whisper from where Dask was faded.

Khelya slackened Dewdrop's reins and tapped the beetle out of the bush with the butt of her Eletsol spear. It took a bit for Dewdrop to get far enough out that the Skorgon noticed. One Skorgon pushed the other's lower shoulder – most Skorgon seemed to have four arms – and then they both approached the beetle with lowered spears. Khelya gently drew Dewdrop back toward the bush until the two Skorgon were close.

The one near Dask was tall and pale, with feathery antennae. White fur covered his head and otherwise bare chest. The other one, of short stature with a round, bald head, bulging eyes, and pointy mandibles, crept around Dewdrop into Matil's range. Besides the worn brown tunic and pants he wore, he resembled a black ant. Dask's target looked like a moth. At first Matil had been relieved that the smaller one went in her direction, but now she felt uneasy.

She didn't have time to think about her feeling. Just then, Dask stepped out of the shadows, clamped his hand over the moth Skorgon's mouth, and stabbed him in the side. The Skorgon clawed at Dask with his four hands. Dask pulled out the blade and stabbed his neck, green blood staining the white fur on his chest. The moth Skorgon's arms grew weak, and then he fell to the ground, lifeless.

Just as the ant Skorgon was turning to look at his partner, Matil grabbed him and went for the stomach. Her knife cut through his tunic, but slid across his tough skin. Before she could stab again with more force, he moved all four of his arms and twisted out of her grip with shocking strength.

He began a scratchy yell. "*Shalakad bleyaaa—*"

Dask tackled him to the ground, and they grappled with each other. The Skorgon soon threw Dask off. Wings flapping, Dask hurtled into the dirt a few steps away. The Skorgon's spear fell nearby. Khelya got to her knees to help Dask up while Matil grabbed one of the ant Skorgon's arms. She pulled herself toward him, using the extra momentum to sink her blade into one of his upper armpits. He hissed, lashed out with a lower arm, and smacked her in the gut. Her legs buckled. She choked and collapsed.

Things would be worse the longer she was down, so she hurriedly struggled to get up. When she'd regained her senses, she saw Khelya rush the Skorgon with her Eletsol spear, but the Skorgon sidestepped and tore the spear from her hands, sending it hurtling over Matil. Khelya yelled in shock as she stumbled. The Skorgon grabbed her by the leg and then pulled her along, finally letting go with a mighty heave. Though he was a third of her height, his throw sent her scraping across the ground. Now Matil was afraid to go near him. Dask circled at a distance, too, flying between the bush branches. Khelya grunted as she got back up.

The Skorgon grimaced around his mandibles and spewed at them what sounded like the vilest curses in his language. He was loud, but his battle cry must have already alerted whoever was in the house. Matil cleared her mind and watched the Skorgon more closely. From the way he stood and fought, she could tell that he put more strength than was necessary into each movement. Not each attack, but each movement. Once he made up his mind to focus and do something, he would do it.

"You'd better not be talking about my mother," Dask called down. "If you are, this fight'll turn as ugly as *your* mother!"

The Skorgon doubled his stream of chatter.

"Yeah, that's right, your—" Dask cut himself off and dove at the Skorgon. His speed allowed him to drive his knife into the Skorgon's belly. Again he was flung away.

Matil sprinted in from the side and slashed the vulnerable crook of the Skorgon's lower arm. His rattling roars of pain carried around them. Before he could turn all the way, Matil went for an arm on the opposite side, causing him to change directions. But she switched back and sliced the crook of the arm above the first one. The Skorgon swayed and reached for her. She darted beneath his two good arms to twist and pull out Dask's knife. Green blood quickly stained the Skorgon's tunic. He fell.

Khelya stomped over with her spear and thrust it downward. When his struggling ended, she pulled out the spear and stepped away with a cringe. Dask picked himself up off the ground. The three of them looked toward the hermit's house, but apparently it was far enough that no one inside had heard.

"You two okay?" Dask said.

Matil nodded, catching her breath, and handed him his knife.

"Didja see 'im pick me up?" Khelya said incredulously. "He's smaller than Matil!"

"Sorry about that." Dask wiped his blade on a leaf by his shoulder. "I should have seen it coming. Skorgon are like different kinds of bugs. That one looked like an ant and, whaddaya know, he was kind of strong."

They tied Dewdrop next to Olnar.

"I'll check it out first," Dask whispered.

Matil and Khelya waited under cover, neither one moving their eyes from the hut as Dask entered. They stayed that way in tense stillness, listening for any noise.

A short time later, he walked out wearing a bleak expression. "No one's there," he said.

"We're- we're too late?" Khelya said.

He pressed his lips together and nodded.

15

Workshop in the Woods

Matil looked between Khelya and Dask, her ears lowering. Then she ran to the hut's door and flung it open.

"Matil?" Dask said.

Beyond the door, the dirt floor descended into the ground at a steep angle, forming a spacious tunnel. Furrows scored the dirt, like something had been dragged through it. Khelya and Dask came up behind her.

"They turned the place upside-down," he said. "We might as well start making a backup plan."

Khelya narrowed her eyes. "I'll find 'im."

"I already checked the forest around here, Khel. No trace."

She turned and bolted away, her long legs carrying her straight across the clearing.

Dask stared after her. "What is it with you ladies?"

"If Hasyl knew the secret," Matil said, "wouldn't he keep a…a record of it?"

"I'm telling ya, it's bad. If there was anything, the Skorgon probably got it."

Her heart fluttered, nearing panic as she saw their hope disappearing with the hermit. "Let's look anyway."

He shrugged and Matil stepped down the tunnel. It led them deeper in an underground path, where rooms led off from the tunnel through earthen archways. She stopped at the first one. It was a storeroom. Chopped roots and other edible plants covered the floor, large wooden containers and a stack of carrots had fallen over, and the air was thick with herbal scents. Dried earthworms spilled out of one tall container. Matil looked in the other rooms briefly. They were also storage, all in a state of chaos.

At the end of the tunnel was another door, hanging open so that a shaft of faint light spilled out. The dirt was especially churned up there, and deep lines marred the wood door, as if a large animal had clawed it. Warding off dread, Matil pushed the door open. Just through the doorway was a wood plank floor spattered with dark red blood.

She tore her eyes from the floor and looked around. She and Dask stood on the threshold of a great room with a high ceiling all the way up to the top of the log, where sections of the log had been cut out to let in rays of daylight from the outside. Flaps of bark were propped up in lean-to fashion over the cutouts, attached to a system of ropes and poles that would allow someone on the ground floor to pull them closed and push them open. To Matil's right, the room ended in the wall of stones she had seen outside sealing shut the end of the log. A fireplace in the wall yawned out of a pile of stones that appeared to have fallen into place and frozen together. To Matil's left, large ramps made from woven twigs gave access to three stories of rooms. It was an airy and well-cared-for place – except for the destruction waged throughout.

Clouds of dust threw a haze over the house and tickled Matil's nose. Two roomy wicker chairs faced the hearth, but they lay sideways with caning snapped, their dark blue cushions torn apart beside them, and all of it covered in soot disgorged from the fireplace. A low table was cracked in two, half of it butted up against the wall. Separating the fireplace area from the rest of the house was part of a hefty tree branch that rested on the floor, its sub-branches mere knots on its smooth surface. Ten thick candles of various colors studded the upper side at the height of Matil's head. The larger portion of the room on the left was nearly inaccessible, covered in a storm of abused books and smashed-up frameworks of metal and wood. Gears and pipes cluttered the ground, along with some more complete mechanisms, such as numerous clocks. There were hooks all over the walls where things had hung before someone had strewn them across the floor. In the center of the hooks was a clear wall space where Hasyl had painted some numbers.

Matil and Dask stepped farther in.

Dask picked up a metal knob from the floor. "From the looks of it, this guy's a tinker," he said, inspecting the piece. "Tinkers are nutty, but they're usually all right."

At the loud scrape of a foot, Matil whirled around.

It was Khelya entering the room, her transparent face wet with sweat. She tugged off her brown headband and gazed at the mess. "They wrecked up his home somethin' awful," she said heavily.

"Look where you're standing," Dask said.

Khelya looked down, squeaking when she noticed the blood splotches. She took a big stride away from them.

He set the knob down on a table. "They wrecked up more than just the house."

"Thiffen," she said. "Oh, thiffen."

Matil breathed slowly to calm herself. "There has to be a way."

"Any ideas?" Dask said.

"Nothing specific," she said. "Hasyl might have hidden the information in case something like this happened. It's about the Elders. There has to be something."

"Yeah," Khelya said. "It's too important."

"Oh, so he might have made a backup plan?" Dask leaned against the candle branch. "Backup plans are nice. In fact, they're so nice that I made one for us."

"You don't think he left anything behind?" Matil said, losing confidence again.

He thought for a moment. "I guess I could see a tinker hiding something in a secret cupboard, or putting a false bottom in a drawer. My gang hired 'em sometimes to squirrel away big money merchandise so the guards wouldn't find anything in a raid."

Matil's spirits lifted at his words. "Let's look around, then."

She began to pick through the intricate mechanisms on the floor. Whether large or tiny, the pieces were carved with precise, artistic details; symbols flowed into faces, which flowed into forms, and again into symbols. In one corner she found interlocking gears stuck to a board, though some empty pins showed that a few gears had popped off. Enough of it remained to fascinate Matil. In the center, the largest gear showed a man with his hand held out, toward the right side. The surrounding, smaller gears each portrayed something different, like a mouse, an ant, or a flower. Each of these had its own adjacent gears with more images. Matil carefully turned the center gear with her finger and the man slid into place beside one of the other images, appearing to pet a mouse's nose. The gear below it, the ant, touched a leaf with its antennae. As Matil kept turning, the man met the ant, and the mouse above them nuzzled a baby mouse before sniffing at a strawberry on another gear. All of the gears moved as one to create new scenes.

"Dask," she said, "look at this one!"

He picked his way over, watched her demonstrate the gears, and then nodded in appreciation.

Khelya was especially taken with the gadgets. She broke from studying a tall frame that held bowls and tubes to say, "This whole place is as good as an apprenticeship! If I had a season to spare…" Looking around the house and again at the bloodstains by the door, her face fell.

Matil shook her head. It wouldn't do to get distracted and narrow her focus before she could check everything out. Dask had flown up to the ceiling and begun prodding at the wall of stones. She gazed over the living area to see if there was anything else to investigate. The candle branch – that was something.

Each of the ten candles was tinted a different color and carved to depict some alva or creature – a creamy orange candle on the close end had claws and a big belly. Matil stepped beside a purple candle. It was in the shape of a long-snouted animal with thick, curling horns and a man's body. Was it a Kyndelin? A light green candle seemed to be an Eletsol, by his many-leafed wings and the backward curve of his ears. But another candle, dark gray, had a flat face, holes for ears, and jagged skin. It didn't look like any alva or animal Matil had seen. She made her way down the row. Sleek antlers spreading around the surface of the far end candle lured her over. It was a black stag with gaping white eyes. Horrible and familiar eyes.

The outer two candles, the black and the orange, were the tallest. Each next candle was shorter, with the inner two, light green and restrained blue, being the shortest.

"What kinda candles're these?" Khelya said. She put her headband back on and walked over from where she had been staring at numbers painted on the wall. "They remind me of—ohhh, I get it! You know the pictures in bedtale-books?"

Matil shook her head.

"'Course you wouldn't, sorry." She gestured at the candles. "They're like the pictures that go along with stories about the Elders an' other heroes."

Seeing the stag candle again, something clicked into place for Matil. "Are these supposed to be Elders, then? Is-is that one Myrkhar?"

"Yeah, I think so!" Khelya said. "How'd you guess?"

Matil could still taste the dank air from her long-ago dream, of a ritual in a cold chamber and a stag's head formed from smoke.

Khelya crouched to look at the candle. "It's pretty obvious he's a bad guy with those eyes, huh?" Then she went down the line, naming each candle so fast that Matil couldn't remember most of the names. "Falgar," she said, pointing out the purple half-man, half-animal. "An' Calo." She inclined her head slightly toward the large orange candle on the end.

Calo, leader of the Heilar. Matil stood on her toes to see his face all stylized with triangles and circles. His eyes were closed and a content smile broadened his beastly countenance. Bedtale-books. Stories for children. As far as Matil knew, Calo was just a smiling candle. She glanced around the ransacked house.

Dask slid along the walls, tapped them, and felt floorboards with his fingers. He saw Matil staring at him. "I'm checking for hidden doors and compartments. Anywhere he mighta put his important stuff."

"Good thinking," Matil said, trying to conjure some enthusiasm. She noticed the numbers on the wall again. Five – thirty-one – eight. They were painted with little flourishes. Did they mean something? "Khelya, did you find anything near those numbers?"

"Nope, just the numbers," Khelya said. "It's funny…I don't see a Chivishi scroll anywhere, but he must have one."

"Maybe he's not interested in reading that particular bedtale-book," Dask called over.

Khelya snorted. "Ooh, you know how to make me mad. I just think he has one 'cause he wrote down a line from it."

"Hm." Dask stomped on a floor plank. "Where?"

She pointed at the numbers. "He painted the reference numbers instead of the actual line."

"*Well*, then," he said. "I can't tell if it's smart or idiotic to disguise a lock combination in plain sight as a Chivishi reference. Least now we know we're searching for a lock."

Matil blinked at the numbers. "There's no Chivishi anywhere for us to see what the line is?"

"Maybe in one of those rooms," Khelya said, gesturing toward the ramps and platforms. "We don't need one, though. I know what it says."

"You do?" Dask said. "Did you memorize the whole Chivishi?"

She hesitated before nodding. "You make it sound like it's weird."

"It *is* weird. Weird, but impressive."

She wrinkled her nose. "Thanks."

"Impressive?" Matil said. "It's amazing. Can you tell us the line, Khelya?"

Khelya grinned. "Sure can. Five, thirty-one, eight. It goes, 'The branches of the Sanctum tree were filled with great flowers during the day and flames like lamps during the night, so that all of Eventyr could see the Heart.' It's talkin' about just before the Mekydra Time, back when everyone knew where the Heart Sanctum was. After the Elders drank the Heart's water, Thosten moved the Sanctum so Myrkhar couldn't find it an' drink more." She tugged on the knot of her headband. "Dunno why Hasyl would paint up that line out of all of 'em. I guess he thought it was pretty."

"Flames in a tree?" said Dask. "Flowers bloom the next day? That's proof the Chivishi's got nothing to do with reality. Khel?" He paced over to her. "Khel, tell me how you believe that junk."

"Well," Khelya said, her face turning red, "if Thosten made trees and fire, I think he can put fire in a tree without burnin' it up."

"That's assuming Thosten exists and made trees and fire."

'The branches of the Sanctum tree were filled with great flowers…'

The Heart, the Elders drinking the water…

Matil felt like Hasyl was speaking to them, speaking through a wall, and only muffled syllables were audible. Maybe it meant something and maybe it didn't. She began walking around the house with Khelya's words in her mind, up the ramps and through the thrashed rooms. The place was a jumble of ruined parts, fragile bits-and-bobs, and Hasyl's effects. Matil sped up, her eyes roving every surface and niche. Nothing fit with the Chivishi line. She stopped short at the sight of a small wooden flower carving that sat, untouched, on a shelf, and then she grabbed it. Smooth and simple. It didn't look like a 'great flower'. She set it down.

"*Delusional?*" Khelya said. "So that's what you *really* think of me? I should pull off those big ears of yours—"

"You called *me* a thief first!" Dask said.

"It's what you used to do, ain't it?"

Matil went back into the main room. "Please, you two. Let's keep looking."

They ignored her as their voices rose.

She stood in the center of the room and looked around with shoulders slumped. There was the candle-holding branch. It was so large that she wondered how Hasyl got it indoors.

The branches of the Sanctum tree...'

Matil's ears pricked up.

...and flames like lamps.'

She reached toward one of the candles slowly, a dark green candle that showed a snarling Elder with long claws. A fine layer of dust covered it and, underneath smudges of wax, the wick was clean white. Did Hasyl ever burn these candles?

"Khelya," she said. "*Dask.*"

"If Thosten's so good," Dask said to Khelya, "then why'd he make you so dumb?"

Khelya lunged down at him and took a swipe. He jumped back to avoid her, his wings stretching spastically and sweeping objects from the shelves behind him.

"Stop it!" Matil yelled.

Fist in the air, Khelya jerked to a halt. Dask stepped on a small cylinder, fell over, and landed on his wings.

"Talrach," he groaned.

Matil hurried over to kneel by him. "Are you okay?"

Dask lifted himself into a sitting position with an agonized expression. "There are less polite words I could use, but sure, let's go with 'okay'."

Khelya clasped her hands. "…Sorry."

He rubbed his nose and looked down. "Sorry, too."

Matil exhaled with relief. "Good. Look at those candles." She stood, holding her hand toward the branch. "If we lit them up, they'd be—"

"Flames like lamps!" Khelya said.

Dask scrutinized the branch. "Flames in a tree?"

"Should we try it?" Matil said. "It's just one idea."

"It's the only idea." Dask crossed his arms. "To be honest, I don't think we should stay here much longer. The moment they took Hasyl away, it became a waste of our time. We need to hurry up, try the candles, and move on if they don't work."

"All right," Matil said without looking at him.

Flapping his wings, he hopped over the candle-studded branch to the fireplace and then picked up a chunk of flint and a steel striker. After a moment's work, he started a small flame on one of the twigs from the fireplace. Khelya met him halfway across the room. She took the burning twig from him, carried it to the branch with a protective hand up – Matil winced to see the torch lick so close to Khelya's skin – and raised the flame to the first candle. It caught fire with a sound like a butterfly's wingbeat.

Khelya went down the row of candles, lighting them quickly and then blowing out the torch.

The three alva waited. The candles burned.

That Chivishi reference may not have been a secret code. The idea appeared sillier the longer Matil dwelt on it. Hasyl was a very important, very old man. For him to give the secret of the Elders to a few untested nobodies? There had to be someone else to succeed where Matil, Khelya, and Dask had failed. Otherwise, it was…Matil couldn't say silly anymore. It was scary. If they were all that was left…

They'd spent so much time, only to need another way. She looked down in disappointment.

Clink-clink.

Matil raised her head.

Clink.

The middle two candles had gone out. There was a chorus of *clinks* as the next two flames sputtered out as well. The next four died in the same fashion, and then… the Calo candle went out.

Ca-clink.

With a creak, a thin seam opened lengthwise in the branch beneath the Calo candle, revealing itself to be a secret panel. Myrkhar's candle, the final flame, wavered and spat its last breath.

Clink-clink.

The other end of the panel came loose, and the whole bottom quarter of the branch dropped outward on a hinge like a drawbridge. Ten short chains were attached along the top of the panel. Inside the branch, it was hollow, empty down its length except for a folded piece of parchment laid over a leather-bound book.

16

Stories and Sorcery

Matil's breath caught in her throat. She got to her knees and carefully slid the book out with the parchment on top. Khelya and Dask crouched around her as she unfolded the parchment. Hasyl had written a list in wide, loose handwriting.

'-Challenge the sorcerer near Lazmyr. He holds Jalt's glass hammer.

-Stal's fanged bow lies in the tomb of King Gedna.

-Locate a white mole in mid-Obrigi. Follow it to its den, where Shora's chalice is kept.

-Find the frog pendant in Icto Lan. Or toad, can't remember which. The Eletsol want it.

-One of General Suncloak's descendants is in possession of the Worthy Spear of Falgar.

-Look for the green stone at the...'

There were four more lines of instructions. Matil recognized a few of the names that Hasyl mentioned, but most of it read like gibberish to her.

"The Worthy Spear?" Khelya said wonderingly. "Shora's chalice? Those're…legends. Magic items from the old days."

Dask snapped his fingers. "I get it! See how these artifacts are connected to Elders? *This* is the secret Mr. Korsen was talking about. Hasyl knows their locations and that's why Nychta captured him. First, she stole the Book of Myrkhar. Now she wants the others, to collect up power."

Dask's theory fit Nychta perfectly. Maybe the secret wasn't really about…waking the Elders. Matil had let herself get excited for nothing.

"The pattern's off," Khelya said.

"Pattern?" Matil squinted down at the parchment.

"Mm-hm. All the lines mention an Elder's name. 'Cept this one." She pointed with her transparent little finger. "'Find the frog pendant in Icto Lan.' Or, uh, toad."

Dask scratched his chin. "'The Eletsol want it.'"

Matil ran her eyes over the list one more time. "Khelya, hold this." She handed the parchment to Khelya and then put a hand on the book's plain leather cover. It was large, almost the size of her torso. "There might be more information in here." She opened the book in her lap.

On the first page, the writer introduced the book – *'Being a record from the hand of Hasyl Koda,'* – noting that he would write only when something important happened. *'I am no scribbler of script,'* declared the faded ink. The next page held the journal's first entry.

"Look…" Khelya said. "Look at the date."

'42 Vana, Day 30 of the Time of Loss,' it read. *'That is what the priests named our despair.'*

Dask waved his hand. "It's gotta be fake. A thousand years old? Not a chance."

"A thousand years old?" Matil pricked up her ears. "What do you mean?"

"In my school," Khelya said, "they told us the Time of Loss was known nowadays as the Post-Imperial Span. But most folks still call it the Early Hibernation Age, 'cause it was the time directly after the Elders disappeared. So this date, day thirty, means that the hermit wrote it down just thirty days…*after the Hibernation started.*"

"Then the Elders have really been asleep for a thousand years?" Matil said.

"From what I've heard," Dask said, "alva counted up from the time that big Obrigi kingdom fell, and it's been a thousand years, give or take. Time of Loss and Post-Imperial Span? Those names have to do with the craziness going on when everyone tried to fill the hole the Obrigi left behind. Doesn't make sense to say 'Early Hibernation Age' when the Hibernation's just a myth."

Khelya jabbed the page. "What about Hasyl? The fact that he's a thousand years old—"

"Fact? Don't believe everything you read, Khel. All I see is a loo-loo inventor who knows where to find treasure. I mean, it's awful that we couldn't save him. I…" Dask sat on the floor. "I wish we'd made it, but that doesn't mean I trust this guy. Keep reading."

Khelya gave an offended huff and sat down as well.

The thick book's pages were packed with words and sketches. Skimming through, the three of them couldn't find anything related to their quest or the list of artifacts. Dask eventually lifted his head, prompting Matil to look for what had caught his attention. The light coming from the roof had started to wane.

"Let's get out of here before Crell sends more bugs," said Dask. "We can look at the journal later." He stood up. "I saw some things we should take with us."

"Isn't that stealing?" Matil said.

"I can't believe you're worried about stealing right now."

"Well," Khelya said, "what if he comes back?"

Dask pointed at the bloodstains on the floor and gave Matil and Khelya a meaningful look. "We're taking the journal and the list, anyway."

Matil frowned down at the journal.

Dask gave an exasperated sigh and hefted the journal out of her lap. "Besides this, we'll only take things that go bad. Things that can't be used later. How's that sound?"

Matil nodded uneasily.

"All right," Khelya said.

"We wanna be quick, then, so help me out. Khel? There's a nice slab of raw meat in one of the storerooms." He saw her holding the parchment. "You'll need two hands."

Khelya gave the parchment back to Matil and followed him to the front door.

"Matil," Dask said before he went through. "You got the other storerooms?"

"Yep," she said, walking toward the door after them. She stopped upon seeing the numbers on the wall again, the Chivishi reference numbers pointing the way to hidden information. It struck her that Hasyl had created the hiding place. Would he need such a clue to remind himself where it was? Or had he planned for someone else to find it?

Matil read the parchment list one more time. Pattern. Elders. How many artifacts listed? Ten. Elders, ten, Elders… ten Elders.

In a flash, she was pacing beside the candle branch, matching the ten candles to Elders on the list as best as she could remember from Khelya's explanation earlier. She couldn't place a couple of them, so she looked closely at the line on the list that broke the pattern by not naming an Elder. It said that the Eletsol wanted…

The light green candle resembled an Eletsol. Ansi's words poured back into Matil's mind. The Eletsol were guarding the Elder *Dyndal's* body, and they wanted to find his sign. They wanted the pendant. Khelya had said that this candle represented Dyndal, hadn't she?

A familiar restlessness itched at Matil's fingertips. She ran through the tunnel, out to where Dask was telling Khelya how to set the leaf-wrapped meat on Olnar.

"Khelya, Dask," Matil said breathlessly. "We need to go…" She looked at the parchment. "To Icto Lan!"

"Hold on, what?" Dask said.

She waved the parchment at them. "I realized something about the list." She explained her trail of logic, watching their faces to make sure she wasn't just seeing things that weren't there.

By the end of it, Khelya looked thrilled. "*Dyndal's sign*," she said.

"Sounds like it," Dask said, scratching his sideburn with his thumb. "Where's Icto Lan?"

"In northern Tyrlis. It's one of the Sangriga universities."

He blew out through his mouth. "Nearsighted book-worshipers. *And* they're Sangriga! The Ranycht universities are scary enough."

The three of them moved back and forth between Hasyl's home and the beetles, salvaging more fresh food and herbs. Finally, Matil stood outside with Dask, putting away the last of it.

"Is Khelya still in there?" Dask said.

"I'll look." Matil entered the little hut and wandered down the tunnel. "Khelya?" She stepped through the clawed-up door. "Khelya?"

It took a moment for Matil to find the see-through Obrigi blending in among all of Hasyl's devices. With delicate hands, Khelya was examining the ropes that hung from the ceiling. She tugged on one rope, but nothing happened.

"Oh!" She took two other ropes and pulled those at the same time. One of the rooftop flaps smacked shut. Khelya beamed. "Just wouldn't do, leavin' this place open to the elements," she said. "Help me with the rest, 'kay?"

Khelya told Matil which ropes to pull, and they closed the remaining three flaps. Matil led Khelya by the hand through the now-dark maze of debris and then the storage tunnel, up into the hut. In the clearing outside, Dask was securing buckles and knots on Olnar.

Matil looked over Dewdrop, climbed onto the saddle, and set her feet in the stirrups. "Ready to go?"

Khelya lifted and put down one knee and then the other, preparing to walk. "Ready."

"Wait." Dask squinted and held a hand by his forehead to block the low light that reached the forest floor. "You know those Skorgon we dropped?"

"What about 'em?" Khelya said.

"Something's…happening to them."

Matil reluctantly dismounted and drew her dagger as Dask already had. The three of them edged across the clearing to see the bodies.

"What're they *doin'?*" Khelya said when she was close enough.

"Whatever it is," Dask said, "it's not normal."

The Skorgon's lifeless bodies were changing. The moth-like Skorgon that died first had been larger in life, but was clearly smaller than its ant-like comrade now. Its long antennae were simply gone, as were its hands and its legs up to the knees. The ant Skorgon had just begun to lose the tips of its spiny feet. A small cloud of dust surrounded both corpses, though on closer inspection, the dust came from the bodies themselves. They were crumbling, tiny bits floating down into the earth. A stale smell invaded the fresh air as the two dead Skorgon withered before Matil's eyes.

* * *

Together with his scouting force and their unconscious prisoner, Crell had returned to their base in northern Nychtfal, hidden in a network of caves. Nychta spent most of her days summoning more Skorgon with the Book, but she didn't think that their army was strong enough to stay out in the open.

The soldiers reported seven missing – larger scouting groups checked those locations but found nothing – and two other soldiers were witnessed to have been killed by a rat. The missing ones had probably died in similar ways. The Book's Skorgon didn't seem to share the Kyndelin protection from wild beasts that other alva took for granted. Crell had seen it happen right in front of him; a songbird descended on a lone Skorgon, held it down with its talons, and pecked the alva to death before flying away. When such things occurred, the other Skorgon showed no emotion at all. They would say, if they said anything about it, "That fate will not be mine, General."

Crell leaned against a rocky chamber's entrance, keeping watch on their prisoner. He wasn't afraid to go in…just understandably cautious. A badger three times his size that might wake up at any moment was best left to the four muscular Skorgon who stood by. Each of them had four arms, and two of them held ropes looped around the badger's neck and limbs.

The badger stirred, his head stripes muddied by blood.

As he opened his eyes, his body shrank and transformed smoothly into an alva now only twice Crell's size, wearing a simple robe of brown cloth. The two Skorgon pulled on the ropes to tighten them around the groaning Kyndelin. Hasyl, the Book called him. Hasyl was heavily built and had big hands, a big nose, and small, round ears. On one side, his thin, white hair was matted with blood.

"Let me up, if you please," Hasyl said, blinking at Crell and the Skorgon guards. "I'd appreciate an opportunity to whip the lot of you." He struggled to his knees.

Crell stepped into the chamber. "Where did you hide it?"

Hasyl's expression was blank. "What?"

"Dyndal's velanach." He hoped he was pronouncing it correctly. Nychta had told him about the object this hermit supposedly had. According to the Book, it would bring the Elder Dyndal back to life. Having it under their control would be a huge advantage.

"Now, now, now," said Hasyl. "You interrupted my reading and bopped me on the head to ask about a *children's rhyme?*"

"We're going to hurt you if you don't talk," Crell said. "Pretending you don't know won't change anything. So please…please talk."

The Kyndelin tilted his head at those last words.

Crell narrowed his eyes. "Where is it?" He felt a twinge by his ears, so he reached up to scratch.

"May I tell you a story?" Hasyl said.

He hesitated. "What are you talking about? I asked *you* a question. Answer it!"

"My answer is that I will never tell you where it is. Now answer *my* question. May I?"

Crell wanted to be upset for what seemed like flippancy, but there was no trace of humor in the old man's eyes. Maybe the story would provide some information. What did he have to lose by hearing the hermit out? "Make it fast." He sat down against the dirt wall.

Hasyl nodded gratefully. "In the Age of Elders, that age long past," he said, "lived a poor, widowed miner and his daughter. Though the miner mined all day to provide for their needs, he worked also at night making baskets to pay for the whatnots and trifles his daughter desired. She was his heart, his dearest one. So it was that whenever she fought her playfellows or demanded a gift, the miner took her side. Yet despite his indulgence, the girl found fault with him at every turn."

The story seemed pointless, though Crell had no urge to stop Hasyl. It reminded him of hours spent listening to the old village men talk. Their tales had been the only good parts of that time without Nychta.

"One day," Hasyl said. He paused to itch his jaw on his shoulder. "One day, the miner traveled through the woods on his way to market, with baskets stacked high on his back. He heard a desperate cry and searched for the source. The voice came from a close-by pond. There in the water was a man thrashing and splashing so the pond looked like a boiling cauldron. The miner took off his basket stack and put two in the water, climbing into one. With the other basket in hand, he paddled over to the man. That basket helped the man float, so the two got to the side and out of the water.

"Now this man, even drenched like a half-drowned squirrel, was clearly someone special. His shoulders were broad, his skin a ruddy brown, and his ears forward-pointing like those of a Brandur, though he was no Brandur. After staring for a short time, the miner saw that the man had become dry. The miner asked if he was an Elder, and the man laughed. 'Well met,' he said, 'and great thanks for saving me. I am Elder Vogyn. My domain is warmth, which that pool leeched from me most audaciously. Allow me to repay you, sir. Request anything within reason.'

"The miner was pleased and wanted time to think about what to request, so he invited the Elder into his home for a meal. They set off together, arrived at home, and for once the miner and his daughter ate a meal that didn't grow cold. At last the miner asked his daughter what she wanted.

"'I want a different father,' said she. 'One who doesn't bring home smelly strangers.'

"The miner was appalled and said, 'You don't mean what you say. Do you know that this stranger is an Elder and will grant us a wish? What do you really want?'

"His identity surprised the girl. She thought for but a moment before saying, 'I want lots of money.'

"The miner asked the Elder to grant her request, so Vogyn pulled from his jacket a coin pouch as large as his head and left it on the table. When he was gone, happiness entered the miner's heart. He told his daughter of the wonderful things they could now buy. A new door, a new roof, maybe even a shop in the city.

"'*I* made the wish,' said his daughter. 'It's *my* money. I'll use it for what *I* want.'

"A week later, the miner made baskets amid piles of the finest clothes. But all that the girl bought wore out in time, and she took the remaining wealth with her to the city. The miner assumed that she would come back someday, but though he waited," Hasyl lifted his head with an air of finality, "his daughter never returned."

The Skorgon stood unmoved like they hadn't heard a thing.

"That was a terrible story," Crell said.

Hasyl sighed. "It was, wasn't it?"

Crell felt bad for the poor old man stuck telling stories to his captor. Seeing the patient Skorgon on either side of Hasyl, wielding spiked instruments of torture, he also felt sick—no, no, he didn't. He was just going to oversee the Skorgon, anyway, while they did the dirty work. He'd get the information. Or else disappoint Nychta. He got up from the ground.

The Kyndelin's expression changed. "Agh, what is that—" He sniffed the air. "Busar-noa! This place smells like tortoise egg soup and rabbit sweat. Can't I be tortured elsewhere?"

Crell inhaled. "I don't smell anything."

Hasyl sniffed again, his wide nostrils flaring larger. "It's magic I'm smelling, that's why. And not only magic, but sorcery."

They could talk for a little longer, Crell supposed. He wasn't ready to hear screams yet. "Sorcery?"

"Someone around here got hold of Myrkhar's little sketchbook, eh? Wouldn't surprise me, what with all these Skorgon clicking their heels and reeking of death." He wrinkled his nose.

Crell's eyes flicked from one blank Skorgon to the other, and he held a hand over his heart in the old protective gesture. "They smell like death?"

"Where do you think they come from?" Hasyl shook his head. "You know the tales. Long time ago, an army of Skorgon sold themselves to Myrkhar. Then he found a way to make it so they wouldn't fully die. I wager they swarm back willingly enough from that wilderness place…from Rubetha."

Crell let his hand fall to his side. He didn't want to learn any more about sorcery. It would just make his work more difficult. "Why did you tell me that story?"

Hasyl opened his mouth in a silent 'ah'. "I meant to elaborate. Forgive my mind. It's had one century too many. Let's see…I wanted to stall this unpleasant business," he said dryly, "same as you. However, that is not all. I ask you, did the miner love his daughter?"

Crell frowned and thought back to the tale. "She didn't deserve it," he said, "but he loved her very much."

The skin around Hasyl's dark eyes crinkled with a melancholy smile. "No. He felt affection for her. Devotion. Not love."

"What's the difference?"

"Love is action and decision. Wanting what's best for someone and, if you can, helping them to achieve it. If you follow the *feelings* called love, you may end up doing hateful things to an alva."

Crell snorted with derision. "What are you talking about? You can't love without feelings."

"Feelings are important, cub," Hasyl said gently, "but they're as flighty as the wind. Reason first, and then feel."

Feelings had kept Crell alive and given him purpose. He knew them better than some old hermit did.

"Crell," came a measured voice. "You haven't started yet."

His heart jolted. "Nychta," he said. "I, um, I've been questioning the hermit." He turned and saw her in the doorway, small and calm, with an imposing edge to her bearing. He wanted to smile – but it wasn't appropriate at the moment. He wanted to bow – but it was too strange between old friends. He reminded himself that she was the same Nychta he had always known. The same with some exceptions, admittedly, marked by her new eyes. Her purple eyes used to be warm. Now they shone icily, drained of richness in contrast to her chestnut brown skin. At least they were never sad anymore.

She glanced at Hasyl. "The Book says we won't get anything out of him until his will is weakened. When you think he's had enough, tell a Skorgon to come get me."

Crell nodded firmly.

"Did you hear me, hermit?" Nychta said. "Give us the information right away and I won't need to set the Book loose in your head."

Hasyl stared at her, stony-faced. She scowled back.

"How…how is the summoning going?" said Crell.

Nychta blinked at him. "It's going. The weak Skorgon were much easier to summon than these ones, but in the end we'll have the most powerful army in Eventyr."

"Ah, okay," Crell said. "That's good."

"Act more like a general," she said in distaste. "What don't you get about the word 'army'?" With that, she left the room.

Crell imagined beating himself over the head with a rock. *Why* had he acted like a flightling? General Crell, General Crell. He was a general now. He looked at Hasyl, who wore a faint grimace, and said, "You talked a lot earlier. Why are you so quiet now?"

"I'm trying not to breathe in," Hasyl said. "The smell when she walked through the door—" He rolled out his tongue and made a gagging noise. "She's the Book-bearer, all right."

As a general should, Crell resolved himself to his task, but he wanted to finish the strange conversation. "I don't get it. A hermit trying to teach love?"

"Do you think that I was always a hermit? Once, I worked with the earth. With my claws and a pick. Alva surrounded me, and I was subject to my feelings more than I practiced love. Is it any wonder that a man who's learned his lesson would teach? Is it odd for him to wish that others would spare themselves his mistakes?"

There was a silence between them. Crell could think of nothing to say. This Kyndelin who sounded both sensible and passionate still couldn't dispel the dissatisfaction his words left with Crell.

"I told you the story," Hasyl said, "because it's important that love be understood."

Crell narrowed his eyes. That settled it. "No one can understand love," he said. He turned to the Skorgon. "Begin."

17

Chronicles and Crime

Fainfal's border with the Sangriga kingdom of Tyrlis lay two days south of Hasyl's home. Matil had plenty of time to read the hermit's journal while the three travelers picked their way through the vast, sun-speckled wilds. She kept the large book open on Dewdrop's shell, just in front of the saddle, and read interesting parts out loud to Khelya and Dask.

There were several entries detailing Hasyl's defenses against bandits, be they Eletsol, Obrigi, Sangriga, or other kinds of alva; many entries about pleasant meals shared with strange travelers; some that recorded the rebuilding of his house over the centuries or his meetings with the Korsens; beautiful illustrations that grew more common and more prominent as the journal went on; scribbles of Hasyl's ideas for contraptions; what seemed to be folk tales; absurd jokes; and 'chronicles' as the journal called them, interwoven throughout the book. At first Matil didn't understand why those last ones were included; they described very minor occurrences that unfolded over the course of a season or longer.

The first one was titled *Chronicle of a Year* and it was chiefly about the weather and the changes that came over this part of the forest during a year's three-season cycle. His writing for *Year* was terse and factual, but he indulged in naming the trees by his home. *Chronicle of a Flower* came next, dated twenty years after the first. It followed the growth of a flower – lushly rendered in the hermit's scratchy sketching and warm paints – from its first sprouting, through the storms it weathered, and finally to its death in a harshly cold Thrual. Softer words than Hasyl had used in *Year* conveyed his attachment to the flower. Another chronicle described the flashes that he witnessed of a particular squirrel's life. *'The dancer twirled out on an eastern limb of Braya Oak today, in fine spirits. I wonder what he calls that step.'*

One story, begun just a year after the squirrel's chronicle ended, went on for a few years in short but involved passages. *Chronicle of a Burrow*, it was called. Hasyl wrote down his observations of a rabbit family until an abrupt conclusion, after which there were no more chronicles for a long time. His other entries had gone back to being blunt, and there were no pictures for a hundred years. The next picture was of a robed, burly man with very small ears and – standing over him, dominating the page – a black badger with white stripes on its head.

'Hope fails sometimes when I cannot see the end,' were the words beside the man and beast. 'And I feel the forest tugging at my heart, begging me to waver. It is a sweet feeling. So sweet that I nearly lost myself. Tell me, Thosten. Why a Kyndelin? Why me? Is there an end at all?' And at the bottom of the page, in bolder ink, 'Wait a little longer.' Hasyl repeated that phrase in many of his following entries. The years turned with the pages, but even with his descriptions and pictures, Matil couldn't imagine what that time must have been like to live through.

At last there came the beginning of *Chronicle of a Thief*, dating back to five years ago. *'Today, I drew my wagon behind me. It brimmed with strawberries: large, glistening, and ruby-red, with a scent that would entice a perfumer. I was too taken with my haul even to look up for the loud buzzing I heard when I passed Rigan Beech. I discovered upon my return home that some cured meat, seed bread, and my favorite clockwork diorama were missing. It seems I should close the skylights when I leave.'*

Three days later: *'Things vanish every time I leave my house. Even locking the door has not helped. It's time to confront this thief of mine.'*

A day later: *'I caught him! You must be dying to learn of the horrible punishment I administered. Well, to catch him, I went out, hid myself, and watched the house. A slim Skorgon fellow landed in front of my entrance hut. The back of him, from head to waist, was covered by overlapping brown plates, and he wore trousers about five times wider than his waist,* cinched up with a piece of rope. He looked around constantly while picking the lock, so I had a good view of his gray-brown face. There was no mistaking the youth of his features. I wished to know then what sort of life this boy had led for him to steal from an old man in the middle of nowhere, and so far from Deep Valdingfal. Once he got inside, I followed him with all the quiet my creaking joints could muster. He didn't notice me as he raced down the tunnel and into the house.

'I called out to him then. I stood between him and the door and transformed, my bulk sealing the path out. He panicked and buzzed around the house. Here I kept a careful eye on him, but it seemed he didn't know how to operate the skylights. When he became tired, he went into a corner and curled into a protective ball, looking just like a woodlouse with that brown shell of his. So I transformed back, picked the creature up in my hands, shook him out, and set him on his feet. You never saw a more despondent face. I made him wash up and stay put at the table whilst I put together soup and porridge. Then we ate in silence until I asked, "Doesn't this taste better than stolen scraps?"

'"Yes, sir," he said in a voice as thin as his arms.

'"You could eat like this every day if you worked for it. But should you go on stealing, you'll be quite unwelcome in my house. Understand? Good. Soon as we're done, show me where you've put my things."

'He opened his mouth, but I stopped him: "And refrain from lying. You've not had time to sell them all."

'Without a word, he showed me to a tree where he's hung up some cloth among the roots, hoarding his stolen goods in a shoddy little shack. A few of the items were broken, like my diorama, and he'd eaten all the food.

'"You've done poorly by my property, cub," I said. "That puts you in debt."

'His black eyes filled with fear, bless his shell.

'I put on a very heavy air and nodded. "The Sangriga are too lenient when it comes to punishing criminals. I had best take you to the nearest Eletsol tribe. Make peace with your right hand, because you won't have it for much longer."

'I prepared myself in case he tried flying away. Instead, he fell to his knees. Tears poured down his face. "I'm sorry, I won't do it again. Don't take me to the Eletsol."

'"Would you rather repay your debt as my worker?"

'"Yes, sir! Let me work."

'Following the exchange, I put him in the visitor's room for tonight. I shall sleep just outside. If he tries anything, he'll have to contend with a very angry badger. The boy's name is Loop, he comes from Dwell in Nychtfal, and that's all he'll say.'

The next few entries showed that Loop was willing to work. He was so willing that Hasyl asked him why.

'"Because your cooking tastes better than stolen scraps," he said. He learns well.'

They fell into a routine where Loop helped Hasyl with chores and then sat down for an informal lesson in whatever came to mind. Writing was the first thing Hasyl taught, but Loop hated it. He took better to tinkering. Hasyl passed on as many skills as he could.

'I find the cub hopping here and there, all over the woods. His heart is restless. Quiet contentment means little to him.'

But Loop changed, like how Dask had changed.

'Tonight Loop shared his reason for being out here in west Fainfal. "Father died when I was baby," he said, his accent changing. He always spoke like a Ranycht, but I could hear Skorgon roots slipping in. "Mother brought me to Dwell and raised me there. We were part of gang that grew weaker and weaker until an enemy took over. It was fly or die. Mother escaped with me to the Fainfal border and—" He broke off to stick a fork in his boiled potato chunks, bring it to his mouth, and set it down again without eating. "They followed us. Before they attacked, Mother told me to go away. So I did. All the way here."

'At that tale, I leaned back in my chair. "Do you know if she—"

'"I heard her scream, and then stop." He shoved potato into his mouth.

'"I'm sorry, Loop," I said. I took a sip of dandelion wine. "Highwaymen killed my wife when she was coming home from the market."

'He nodded at me and we both made noises in our throats. Then we demolished our dinner like we'd never eaten before. We're friends now, I think.'

The second-to-last entry in the entire journal was titled *Chronicle of a Boy*. Hasyl had written it a year and a half after the first *Thief* entry. 'I had an errand to run at the Eletsol village and Loop refused to go. Still worried about losing his hand. This was precisely the sort of opening I'd been looking for, so I left him in charge of my house. When I returned, he was looking at a map of Eventyr. He'd tidied up the place, and *nothing was missing. It was my plan, then, to sit with him and tell him something of my purpose in this place. To tell him how long I have lived. To offer him part of my burden, should the worst occur.*

'*But he looked up before I could get past greetings, saying he finally felt ready to return to his birthplace, a city in Deep Valdingfal called Kharvev. He asked me to come with him. I don't know how I produced such a pathetic chuckle. "I must remain," I said. "You may leave."*

'*He was brought low for a bit. His mood bounced right back up, though, when we began packing for him. In addition to things he would need for travel, many of which he had gathered and fashioned with his own four hands, I gave him my best compass, a music box inlaid with gold – which will surely fetch a good price, and the clockwork diorama he once stole. He tried refusing that one, so shamed was he. Trustworthy fellow. We said farewell before sunup. He cried quietly, I shared my usual stern commands, and then I watched him fly past Braya Oak. I suppose that's it.*

'*Suddenly I cannot see the page so well. Can it be that I need eyeglasses after a thousand years? No. Just something that got in my eye. Thosten fly with you, Loop. Here concludes your chronicle.*'

Matil smiled even as she felt the beginnings of a sigh. Was Loop still out there, and how was he doing? Why couldn't she and her friends have arrived in time to save Hasyl? She turned the page. The final entry came from earlier this year.

'*My dreams have grown alarming, and I sense a change*

coming upon the forest. Mr. Korsen agrees. Thus, I will bind these pages into a book so that my story can be told. Not for my sake, but for the one who kept me alive and faithful through it all. Glory to the King Thosten.'

Matil flipped the last page and ran her finger across the inside of the cover. At the beginning of the journal, he'd said he would only write about things of importance. Why would he then write these inconsequential stories, however lovely and wistful they were? He mentioned his "purpose" and his "burden", but there was no talk of artifacts or the Elders...

A lump formed in Matil's throat and she looked up from the journal to take in the midday warmth that permeated even the forest's shade. The stories weren't inconsequential to Hasyl. They were a part of his life.

* * *

The forest thinned and allowed more sunlight as Matil, Khelya, and Dask continued south through Fainfal, and then they reached the border, marked by the Tynsen River. Once Khelya saw the rushing water, she refused to cross, but Dask pointed out how hard it would be to sneak over one of the well-guarded border bridges. She reluctantly lashed bark and twigs together in a serviceable raft and the three of them lined it with river-grasses as a disguise. They waited for the cover of night to pole the raft past a sleepy Sangriga outpost on the far bank.

In Tyrlis, they navigated toward the university town of Icto Lan, which wasn't far from the border. They reached their destination as late afternoon edged the trees with gold. The university was a forest of slender stone spires threaded together with breezeways and arched tunnels. Simple as the buildings looked, their great heights and aged stone walls made the campus impressive and elegant.

The trees were buildings in their own right, dotted with doors, windows, and protruding wooden annexes. Glowing alva bustled on and around the upper levels of the town, where butterflies capered alongside them. An abundance of meadow-grass, knobby tree roots, and fragrant herbs provided a screen through which the group could move, safe from the eyes of the busy Sangriga above.

Matil and Dask dismounted to lead the beetles. They passed into a blinding ray of sunlight and rushed to the other side, both of them squinting hard. When they saw that Khelya wasn't with them, they turned back. She had stopped in the ray and faced the sun, her eyes closed.

"Come on, Khel," Dask said.

"It feels *great*," Khelya said. "So warm…"

Voices approached from nearby. Matil and Dask grabbed Khelya's arms and dragged her under an array of ferns.

As she landed on her behind, her cloth headband fell over her eyes. She pushed it up and huffed at them. "Stop doin' that. I was almost—"

Matil held two fingers over her own lips and then put a hand on Dewdrop's head, between her antennae. The voices became louder. A large group of chit-chatting Sangriga in rumpled clothing floated past like shining dandelion fluff. Their skin was powdery-pale and their wings were shafts of light that gradually expanded and contracted. Even though they spoke the same language as Matil, she found herself understanding almost as little as if they spoke Eleti.

"Locomotion of solid luminescence is a notoriously complex process. I'm surprised you managed…"

"They say everyone died. Makes sense. Cross-plane intervention has quite the sanguineous record."

"Thought. That's what I'm talking about. Using thought to remotely control the passage of a physical object through space. Possible with Rhingan's trigonometric methods? Yes or no?"

"Your mum always sends the best dumplings. Have you got any left for supper?"

At least Matil could comprehend supper.

Two men followed behind the group. One of them wore a rather shabby shirt and breeches. He had his finger up and was using it to impale the air violently. The other looked ahead, the lines in his face dragged down by boredom. His green robe looked like it was made of fine material.

"That's a- a sign, isn't it?" the man in breeches said.

"Perhaps," the robed man said dully.

"But—you know there's- there's presently so much division among the alva," the man in breeches said, "and, when you remember how the Book was stolen, I really think—no, I'm *quite sure* that Eventyr will be, erm, *decimated.* In…probably in fifteen weeks. Probably. My calculations turn out with, er, three weeks as the margin of error.”

“The prophecy to which you refer states that the Elders will wake before then.”

“Exactly!” The man in breeches stabbed the air again. “The Elders will wake!”

The robed man covered his face with his hand. “I’m not feeling well today, scholar, so,” he began to ascend, “please excuse me.”

“Yes, of course,” the scholar said weakly. The robed man sped up, leaving him behind. “You are…excused…”

Matil, Khelya, and Dask looked at each other.

“Didja hear him?” Khelya whispered.

“I’ll follow him,” said Dask.

Matil nodded. “Don’t get caught.”

He rubbed his hands together. “I’d have to go outta my *way* to get caught.”

The scholar had already gone in another direction. Dask flew up into the air before gliding toward the Sangriga and using the tree trunks and foliage to conceal himself. Matil soon lost sight of him and settled down in her own hiding spot.

“Do you think he’ll be all right?” she said.

Khelya put her hands on her hips. “He’s gonna mess somethin’ up for certain.”

“He might not.” Matil trusted Dask. Ever since he had helped tell Brenna about her son Amacht’s death, she trusted him.

18

Library Bound

He'd looked pretty professional just then, hadn't he? Swooping, creeping, and tumbling with everything he had. If the fate of the stupid forest was in his hands right now, he could get the job done.

Dask kept the Sangriga scholar in view, but stayed extra-aware of the things around him. The sharp wind woke him right up. Wings of light drifted at the corners of his vision. Something had to obscure him at every turn, and he broke one cover to bolt for the next only when no one was looking. These sun-lovers would think he was an insect or a bird darting from tree to tree. Avoiding their sight was harder as he moved toward the town and the populace.

The Sangriga man's legs dangled like a mosquito's while he flew. He eventually slowed near an apartment house set in a tree and floated to a quiet eatery atop the building. As the sunlight faded, lamps flared up all around.

Dask sat in the crook of a branch to observe the Sangriga scholar eating out on the deck. With barely a thought, he let the darkness spread over him until he was near-invisible. The rich and spicy smells of the eatery wafted over to him. Dripping noodles disappeared into the Sangriga's mouth. Even though Dask didn't like Sangriga food, his hunger made any kind of grub look good at the moment.

The Sangriga finished his meal, descended to a particular balcony, and entered a flat. The windows went from dark to light.

Dask considered the apartment house. While some of the other flats were lit up as well, most were dark – which would be normal for Ranycht, but here it meant that the Sangriga were asleep or gone. Quiet neighborhoods like this one had upsides and downsides. Upside: Alva kept to themselves and probably wouldn't be watching for weirdos. Downside: *You* had to be quiet, or everyone around would hear.

Dask fluttered to the balcony, wingbeats as soft as a sigh, and then he crouched below a window. The shadows closed over him again. All he heard were soft footsteps from one alva. He moved his ears slightly. Furniture creaked and a moment later the Sangriga yawned. This guy must live alone. Perfect. Dask faded again so the Sangriga wouldn't see anyone when he opened the door.

Knock knock-knock.

"Oh!" came the man's muffled voice. "Er, let me, ah…I shall…open the door! Hello! Who's visi-" the door opened, "-ting?"

Seeing him standing in the doorway, Dask thought he looked like a chump. Puzzlement etched the guy's narrow face, and his gangly limbs were angled inward as if to minimize his own tall presence. His light brown hair appeared to have been so hastily smoothed down that a ratlick of hair stood up in the back. He had a short goatee, breeches, and a sleeveless tunic over a shirt, both wrinkled to the point that Dask guessed he slept in them.

The Sangriga would struggle, but Dask had to keep it quiet. Direct it into the flat, yeah, that was the key. And once they got in, the intimidation would begin. He smiled, satisfied.

With a hand outstretched to clap over the Sangriga's mouth, Dask launched himself at the guy. Darkness rolled off of him as he lunged. The man, seeing him, gave the tiniest squeak before Dask knocked him over. They thudded onto the wood floor, Dask muffling the Sangriga's mouth while twisting his arm behind his back. Dask braced himself for the fight about to go down…but it never did. He looked disbelievingly at the Sangriga, whose eyes had rolled back into his head. In his unconscious state, the man's wings had gone out like a candle.

Dragging the lanky man farther into the flat took the wind out of Dask, but it wasn't as hard as he thought it would be. It seemed he had gotten stronger since his days in the gang. He shut the door and moved the Sangriga through wadded-up sheets of paper littering the floor and into a corner, where he would be trapped. Dask went around the flat – finding tatty furniture and more crumpled paper all over – and blew out each of the magical Sangriga-lights he found. They reminded him of the first Sangriga-lights he'd really had a chance to look at, in his Corwyna jail cell. He shuddered. Not a nice memory.

Faint light entered through the windows, so he drew the curtains tight. This was a night that the man wouldn't be able to see through. To Dask's Ranycht eyes, it was a comfortable level of green-tinged dimness. He cut off the curtain cords with his Eletsol knife and used them to tie the Sangriga's hands and feet. Lastly, Dask pulled a soft armchair to face the corner and nestled into it, making sure his wings padded his back comfortably.

He hoped that Matil and Khelya hadn't been found. Khelya was an Obrigi in Sangriga territory, so he wasn't as worried about her. Matil…she would defend herself, but if they so much as scratched her…

Wing light shimmered beneath the Sangriga. His eyes fluttered open. "Eurghhh…where have I gone? Good Calo, it's dark—"

Dask slunk down to cover the man's mouth and pinned him to the floor with a knee on his chest. "I got a knife to your neck," Dask whispered, "and I need your help. So you aren't gonna make a single sound, got it?"

The Sangriga screamed in the back of his throat.

Dask thumped the guy's collarbone with the hilt of his blade. *"You wanna die, Sparkles?"*

Under Dask's hand, the man shook his head with widened eyes.

"Good choice," Dask said. "You'll be good and quiet?"

He nodded vigorously.

"Okay. I'll let you go. Light this place up first so you can see what to be afraid of."

The man's eyes glowed for just a moment, unnerving Dask, but all that happened was his wings brightening against the floor and a small globe of light fizzling into being above his bound hands. The knife blade glinted in the soft new light. The man observed his intimidator. His prominent alva's apple went up and down as he swallowed.

Dask let go of the man and sat back in the armchair with his feet hanging. Sangriga furniture was too tall. He scooted forward so that his feet touched the floor.

"Oh," the Sangriga said, crestfallen. "You've got feathers on my reading chair."

Itching under his arm at his right wing while prominently displaying the knife, Dask said, "Is it… problematic that I'm getting feathers on your reading chair?"

"No, it's…*perfectly fine*…that you're getting feathers on my reading chair."

"Well then, if that's settled," said Dask, "let's talk business. I need something here in Icto Lan. A frog pendant."

"Frog pendant…" The man sat up. "We don't have a—oh! You must mean the wooden toad! Why would you want that? We decided a long time ago that it's worthless."

"It's a frog pendant, isn't it?" Dask growled. "That's why I want it."

"Toad, actually, it's—"

"Where is it?"

"Right." He cleared his throat. "You wait here and- and I'll find it for you."

"Do you think I'm stupid?" Dask said.

"I'd hoped you were, but I suppose you're not. Let's be off." The man stood, lifting his tied hands to cradle the floating light globe, and moved to go.

Dask set his foot against the wall to bar the way. "Just tell me where it is."

He looked troubled. "Won't you have, er, difficulty finding it?"

"I'm a Ranycht. I can see in the dark."

"That's not what I—"

"Tell me!" Dask said. This exchange was taking too long. If Matil and Khelya were still all right, they'd be worrying about him, too. The thought suddenly made him feel… goopy, like honey on the inside. He twitched his ears to bring himself back to reality.

The Sangriga gazed at the light globe. "The last I remember of the pendant…it was in the treasury room in the back of the Library. The Library's northeast of here. You'll recognize it right off, it's quite an eye-catcher. White roofs and stained-glass windows."

"Northeast, Library, treasury room. I got it." When Dask got up from the chair, he was peeved to find out that his head only came up to his captive's chest. He stuck his wings out a little to look larger.

"Wait now, I'm not finished," the Sangriga said. "The treasury room's a bit confusing – honestly, we ought to reorganize – so you'll have to rummage about in the desks for a catalogue. And the desks are past the archived directories shelves, to the, erm, to the right? No, left. To the left as you walk in. Past those shelves are the desks. Once you find a catalogue, you might need to guess at the shorthand, but with some common sense it's simple enough. 'Up' is upper shelf, 'low' is lower shelf, 'five up two d' is fifth upper shelf, two rows deep, and so on. Finding the catalogue entry for the pendant could be harder…it's probably in the P section, but T's another option, if P doesn't have it. Also try F for frog and A for amulet. They might even've put it in J, for jewelry, or W for wood! Just a few weeks ago I was hunting for an ancient sang flute and had to go through each section till I found it. Someone had listed it under T for, get this, T for 'thingy'." He shook his head with a laugh. "Unbeliev-able." Something in Dask's expression caught his eye and he meekly shuffled backward into the corner. He cleared his throat before speaking again. "D-did you catch all that? Would you like me to repeat—"

"Lucky you," Dask said in resignation. "You get to show me where the frog necklace is." Picking up an extra length of curtain cord, he tied one end to his left wrist and the other end to the Sangriga's wrist-bindings.

"Lucky," the Sangriga repeated. He looked despondently at Dask's knife. "I am, aren't I?"

* * *

Silent buildings sprawled beside perfect stone paths and the rare guard floated among them on the cool night breeze. Below, Dask flitted from shadow to shadow while pulling his hostage behind him. The way most Sangriga moved through the air gave Dask toadbumps, but this Sangriga had his feet tied and was trying to match Dask's sneaking. As he wobbled along like an ungainly leaf, it spoiled the image of eerie Sangriga flight.

They entered the university grounds, creeping below its sky tunnels and towers. Soon, the Sangriga raised his bound hands to point.

"There," he whispered. "The Library."

Dask took a look upward and almost whistled. Out of all the spindly spires and flowing walls, the Icto Lan Library was the tallest and thickest structure, with its buildings ranging across the grounds and towering up into the great trunk of a knotty tree. Rays of moonlight fell through the tree's thin leaves high above and illuminated the Library's white-tiled roofs. Dask and the scholar passed beneath soaring bridges that connected the main building to towers surrounding it. Grand, colorful windows set beneath the coiling eaves showed pictures of alva, beasts, Elders, and complex symbols.

The Library was like something out of the old stories, Dask had to admit. Matil would love seeing it. Khelya, too. She'd stare for a while and then try making a model out of sticks. Though it was pretty, Dask much preferred the villages of Nychtfal, and fancy Sangriga architecture couldn't hold a daisy to his huge hometown of Ecker's Brug.

"That door, use *that* door," the scholar said, lifting his hands toward a skinny wooden double door on the main structure.

Dask narrowed his eyes. "Better not be a trap."

"Oh," the scholar said. "I suppose I should have been inventing a way to trap you. On the other hand, I would dearly like to learn what that pendant is useful for."

"I'm sure you would," Dask muttered. He slowly approached the door and opened one side of it to reveal a slim passageway. His sharp ears picked up no tricks.

The two of them entered. The Sangriga made a globe of light in his hands like before, casting a yellow glow on the stone walls. Ankles restricted by the curtain cords, he shambled a couple of steps and then turned to Dask.

"Would you untie me?" he said. "We could go more quickly then."

Dask left the wrist cords in place and still held the other end of the cord looped in his hand, but he bent down and sliced through the ankle cords.

The Sangriga cringed. "Ahh. I'd hoped you might untie what remains of my curtain pulls rather than…destroy them." He set the light globe down – it levitated slightly above the floor – scooped up the fraying cord remnants with his tied hands, and dropped them in a pocket on his tunic. With a steadying breath, he took the globe and started to creep down the passage.

They went past several doors before turning through an archway. It let them out under the lofty ceiling of the Library. It was vast, supported throughout the room by four-sided pillars that, Dask realized, were massive wooden bookshelves. The bookshelves started out wide at ground level, narrowing gradually until they connected with the ceiling's slabs of stone. It looked like there were at least a hundred bookshelf-pillars in the entire room. And between the bookshelves, wooden platforms hung from the ceiling by chains at each corner. The Sangriga's light globe cast deep shadows among the rows and rows and *rows* of dusty books, and his unsure gait lengthened until he strode with single-minded focus down the aisles. Dask hurried to keep up with the scholar's long legs.

Each bookshelf looked the same. It wasn't long before he was lost in this new kind of forest. They came at last to a spacious area filled with desks, chairs, and tables. The scholar made for the largest and oldest-looking desk and then put his light globe atop it in an elevated metal bowl obviously designed for that purpose.

"Help me look," he said, sliding open one of the drawers. "We need a big book with 'Treasury Catalogue' written on the front. There's no telling where they've put it this time." He rifled through the papers, books, and odd bric-a-brac filling the drawer, then quickly moved on to the next one.

Dask eyed the many drawers and reluctantly pulled one open. There was just enough time to notice that the thing on top said *'Catalogue'* before the Sangriga snatched it up.

"Well done!" he said. With a grunt he set the large book down on the desk and ran a finger down the lettered tabs on its side. The speed with which he flipped the pages and hunted through the tiny scribbles inside was supernatural.

"What time did you wake up?" Dask said.

The Sangriga didn't break rhythm as he answered, "Just after dawn."

"And you're not tired?"

"I'm absolutely done in, but isn't it quite energizing to have a mission? Ah-*ha!*" The scholar grabbed a piece of paper from the desktop and a stick of charcoal from the drawer, put them in his pocket, retrieved his light globe, and then floated away. Since Dask hadn't moved yet, he came to the end of the rope and tugged on it. "Follow me, please," the scholar said.

Shaking his head, Dask walked along behind the Sangriga. The rope barely kept the rabid firefly from spinning off into the shelves as he darted down the aisles. The two of them reached a wall with a line of doors from floor to ceiling. The Sangriga flew to the second one up and struggled with its handle until it popped open. Inside he went. Dask followed with a sweep of his wings and some maneuvering.

The room they entered was full of tall, spiral-carved columns. The two of them stood on a maze of walkways suspended over the first floor, each walkway leading from one column to another. Above them were several other levels of walkways. Stacks of dusty leather display cases filled much of the floor space. The cases had metal-reinforced corners and glass fronts.

As the Sangriga set off, he began to talk. "Welcome to the treasury room, visitor. I must tell you, I looked in the catalogue at all of the places I mentioned, starting with T for 'toad', of course. I didn't see our pendant anywhere. Then I got a feeling, went back to T, and, you won't believe it, there it was – under 'thingy'! Really, I've brought the state of our cataloguing to the attention of so many, but still it languishes. They just don't…listen to me." His pace slowed. "I think it's because I work a bit differently, you know. They trade favours, have connections and pensions, they're mostly from the nobility, and…" He looked nervously over his shoulder. "And you don't care, so I'll button up now."

A weird feeling descended over Dask as the Sangriga's words repeated themselves in his mind. A knowing feeling. He didn't like it. But the sad silence in which they walked was too familiar, and, before he could think better of it, he spoke. "It really stinks when alva tell you the world is so bad that you gotta go along with it. And you know they're wrong."

The Sangriga gave a glum nod. "It does stink, doesn't it? Like a rotted fish."

"Like a fungus shop," said Dask.

They both sighed.

As if struck by a bolt of lightning, the scholar visibly filled with vigor. "Found it!"

He floated ahead of Dask in an arc over the display cases to their right and landed before a tall, slim case, marked on the back with, *'Potentially Ancient,'* in white lettering. Once Dask had caught up, he saw through the glass that this case was full of pendants on strings. On each shelf, the necklaces were piled in disorder. The scholar took a small key from his pocket and opened the case's front. Dask grabbed a wad of the pendants to sort through.

"Gently!" the Sangriga said. "You're holding history."

"Old or new, it's junk," Dask said. He picked out a pendant, a lopsided metal lump. "See? What's this blob supposed to be?"

"That's…" His forehead wrinkled up perplexedly. "I don't know." He took it from Dask and laid it back in the case. "But I'm sure it meant something to someone."

For a few moments they slid the pendants around in their search.

"*There* we are," the scholar said, shaking the other necklaces off of a large, flattish pendant. He gave it to Dask.

The pendant was as big as Dask's hand, a fat toad of smooth-worn red wood with flared nostrils and slits for eyes. He turned it over a few times. It felt solid and reassuringly natural. No magical looloo business, no slimy spirits hanging around. He'd flown jobs for the gang transporting that kind of thing, and if they were uncanny, he could always feel them scratching at the edge of his senses.

Thankfully, that wasn't the case with this necklace. If it wasn't magic, though…it was useless.

Dask lowered the string over his head. As long as it got to Matil, he figured things would turn out – which reminded him of the need to hurry. The longer he was out here, the less safe they would all be.

"Now…" The Sangriga took the charcoal and paper from his pocket and began to scribble.

Dask glanced toward the exit and back at the Sangriga. "What are you doing?"

He held up the paper. "This is a permission slip. Not only does it provide you with the proper documentation to possess the item, it has the due date on the bottom so you know when to bring it back."

"Uh, thanks." Taking the paper and tucking it under his vest, Dask noticed a few very large display cases. Jars and weapons filled most of them, but at least one in the middle was empty. An entire Sangriga could fit in there…

"Won't you tell me why you need the toad?"

"I'm on a mission, like you said." He edged toward the big cases. "I guess I'm gonna see if the legends are true."

The Sangriga stood up straight and his wings brightened. "Legends? Which legends?"

"Hey," Dask pointed at the empty case. "I think something's in there. Open it up and let me take a look."

As the Sangriga walked to the case he took out his key again. "But which legends are connected to that toad? After all this inconvenience, you really ought to tell me."

He unlocked it with a click, opened the door, and stuck his head in. "I don't see anything."

"I was sure I saw..." Dask shoved the Sangriga in the back and pushed the flailing limbs into the case long enough to slam shut its glass front.

The Sangriga's struggling rocked the case, so Dask rapped on the glass. A terrified face peeped at him. Dask held up his dagger and then put two fingers across his mouth. He stood on some shorter cases to reach the top of the big one. With the dagger he punctured the case's leather top twice, making an X and folding its corners inward.

"You've been a real help, Sparkles," he said through the square hole.

The Sangriga shinnied himself so he could look up. "But—"

"Keep it down. You're in a library."

Dask took off the way they came in. Hopping from the edge of the treasury room's doorway, he glided along the wall, and the huge, pillar-like bookshelves whipped past his right wing. Soon he slowed and stopped to try some doors. The third one opened to the outside.

It was a swift and silent trip tracing his path back to the apartment building and, from there, to the place where he left Matil and Khelya. Plants reared up in the darkness around the base of the tree.

"I'm back," he said, short of breath.

Out of the plants and out of her fading stepped Matil. Khelya was right behind her, holding the reins of the two beetles. The sight of the beetles gave rise to a memory that he quickly put away.

"Guess what I have…" He pulled the toad out from under his shirt.

Matil's face lit up. "You found the pendant? You *found* it."

"Huh. Doesn't look too special." Khelya bent over and squinted at it.

Dask lowered his hand holding the pendant. "Oh, so should I put it back?"

"No!" Khelya said. "No, good work, you got it."

Dask grinned, going near to let them see better. A soft sound entered his range of hearing. He paused and moved his ears. He could hear gasping breath getting louder. He turned to see a spark hurtling through the tree branches in the distance, fast, but not as fast as a Ranycht would fly.

"Talrach." Dask hurried to the tree. "I don't know how the guards saw me. Hide."

Matil was already fading with a frightened glance at the ball of light, which resolved itself into a string-bean figure as it approached. She and Dask took Khelya's hands and ducked under the plant leaves beside the tree.

A thud on the ground close by made Dask's heart speed up. No, he had this, he could handle it. Whoever was out there swallowed up great lungfuls of air. Dask tried and failed to see through the foliage. He was starting to think—but it couldn't be that guy!

"I saw you down here," came the voice of the Sangriga Dask had abandoned. "I'm sure I did, I…"

With an unbelieving shake of his head, Dask slipped away slowly enough that his fading was barely disturbed. He crept to the side as the Sangriga went toward their hiding place. They switched places. Smoothly, Dask unsheathed his knife, held it by the Sangriga's torch-bright back, and grabbed the guy's arm.

The Sangriga whimpered.

"Rach, I'm about to go crazy," Dask said. "What are you, a trick-magician? How'd you get out of that box?"

"Well, er…" He twisted around to see Dask and smiled nervously. "You didn't lock it."

"Oh, thiffen," Khelya said. "I knew you'd mess somethin' up."

19

Quite Bright

Matil let go of her fade, seeing that it wasn't necessary anymore.

The Sangriga gawked up at Khelya. "An Obrigi? What sort of Obrigi is translucent?"

"An Obrigi who's got Ranycht friends," Khelya said glumly.

"Friends?" He looked at Matil and excitedly shook his hands, which were tied together. "I've *heard* of you three! You're the trespassers who escaped the Corwyna Prisons!"

"Great," said Dask, letting go of his arm. "We're famous."

The Sangriga focused on Dask. "What in Eventyr are you planning to do with that artifact?"

He pointed at the Sangriga with his knife. "Hey, you said it wasn't worth anything. What if we just want it to look at it? What's it to you?"

"Well, I helped you find it *and* gave you the permission slip to borrow it."

Khelya bowed slightly. "We think it belongs to the Eletsol," she said, "so we're takin' it to Fainfal. It's supposed to help us wake the Elders."

The Sangriga jolted. "Wake? Elders?"

"*Khel*," Dask whined.

"Please don't try to stop us," Matil said. "We're looking for the Heilar as fast as we can."

"To wake them?" the Sangriga said. "From the Hibernation? The Great ruddy Hibernation?"

Dask folded his arms. "Stupid, huh?"

The Sangriga breathed in deeply before speaking. "What makes you think you can do it? What proof, how much research have you done? Why do you think the toad thingy belongs to the Eletsol? If it does, then how did it get *here?* What does it have to do with the Elders? How will you find them? Have you got a map or something? Was it all hidden in some kind of code? Because I have theories." He laughed. "Oh, I have theories. But why are *you* searching? This is all so—"

"We got what we wanted, so we'll be going now," Dask said. "Hand me the rope, Khel. He won't get free this time."

Matil looked apologetically at the Sangriga. Even with those piercingly bright wings, he didn't seem bad. Like the councilwoman and her agent who helped them escape the first time they were in Tyrlis. "Sorry," she said. "Thanks for helping Dask."

The Sangriga took a step forward. "But—"

"Rope," Dask said.

Khelya reluctantly pulled rope out of her pack. "Here we go, wrongin' Sangriga again."

"Wronging Sangriga? Did you forget they lined me up for execution in Corwyna? When you punched out that guard, it was the best thing for everyone." He took the rope, crouched down, and began wrapping the Sangriga's legs.

"No, wait!" The Sangriga tripped backward over the rope and fell on the ground. "It makes so much sense. The writings the Elders left behind were all in pieces. No one understood them. But based on what you've told me, I can already see how they go together! This is the breakthrough that we in the University have been waiting for. I'm Scholar Simmad, a specialist in Elder studies, and you *must* let me work with you!"

Matil blinked and opened her mouth but couldn't think of a response.

"He's out of his mind," Dask observed.

"I dunno," Khelya said. "Maybe we *could* let him come with us."

"Oh. Okay." Dask stood. "Matil," he whispered loudly, "let's make a run for it."

"But," Matil said, "what's so bad about bringing him along?"

"I'm the only sane one left, aren't I?" he said.

"I'm serious, Dask," Matil said. "Tell us what you think."

He squared his jaw. "We're not taking this murderer with us."

Matil felt ill hearing the word. Her thoughts jumped to Nychta.

"*Murderer?*" Scholar Simmad said, getting to his feet. "I am no murderer, sir!"

"You and the rest of your night-forsaken kind might as well be," Dask said.

He shrank back. "I know Sangriga and Ranycht haven't been *friendly* in the past – Dark Districts, Westfalinn, and all that – but I- I think alva should be judged on their own faults and merits. For example, I've never done anything to warrant the title of murderer. Unless one counts the time I wrote an epic poem and killed off all the characters. Eh-heh." He cleared his throat. "Please…may I accompany you three?"

Matil looked between Simmad's longing face and Dask's unwavering glare. "Just a moment," she said to Simmad and Khelya. After taking Dask's arm, she pulled him away from the others.

He tossed Khelya the rope. "Tie him up," he said.

They walked behind a thick root, where Matil faced Dask. She spoke carefully. "I think we should let him come."

"Why?" said Dask.

"He seems to know a lot about the Elders. We might need someone like him."

"*Someone like him* is the last thing we need." He glanced in the direction of Khelya and Simmad. "What if he's dangerous? He might be waiting for the right chance to rat us out. Maybe there's reward money if he turns us in."

"Might and maybe," Matil said. "I'll watch him. If he's dangerous, we can handle it. Okay?"

"You don't understand," Dask said.

"I do," she said. "You're being stubborn because he's a Sangriga. I know how much you dislike them, but this one…"

Dask rolled his eyes. "Don't say he's nice. You don't even know him. What if he *is* a killer? A really bad one who sneaks in alva's—"

"I was going to say he seems harmless. But you're right, I don't know." Matil remembered the genuine passion in Simmad's eyes when Khelya mentioned the Elders. "I still think it would be all right for him to come along. He found the pendant for you and then followed you back here. It sounds like he can carry his own weight."

"Doubt it," Dask said. "I kidnapped him, I should know. He's weak, he talks too much, and he doesn't have *anything* useful to say."

One of Matil's ears twitched. He kidnapped the Sangriga?

"Believe me," Dask went on, "he's a chump. You're telling me we should take a chump with us."

She leveled a serious gaze at him. "Why not? You and Khelya stayed with me."

"Matil…you don't understand."

"You said that already."

"Listen." Dask stepped closer. "You barely know what they did to the Ranycht. You haven't lost *everything* because of them. Even after all that's happened, you have me and Khelya, and we take care of each other. You've never been alone." He shook his head. "I just can't handle one of them coming along like he's one of us. I can't look at their faces without…seeing the fires again."

A shiver ran down the back of Matil's neck and she found she couldn't meet his eyes. He was right. It would be cruel to hurt him by bringing Simmad. "Let's go, then. I'll tell him he can't come."

Dask's ears lifted. "You'll do that?"

"I will," she said.

"I…thanks. You. Thank you."

Matil didn't want to let the Sangriga down, but it would be better this way. She smiled reassuringly at Dask as they went back to the others. Khelya was tying off Simmad's leg bindings. She murmured apologies.

The Sangriga wore a determined look. "I'll- I'll follow you to Fainfal!" he said.

"You won't be able to find us, and then you'll get stuck in the wilderness without even a bowl of noodles." Dask gave him a disgusted look. "You might as well stay safe at home."

"But…" Simmad hung his head. "Home. I suppose you're right."

A new voice from above made them all freeze. "Ho there! What are you doing out so—"

They looked up at a stunned Sangriga guard in bronze armor. He shook himself out of it and grabbed a horn from his belt.

"Let's split!" Dask jumped into Olnar's saddle.

Matil put her hand on Dewdrop, and then searing light engulfed her. She cried out in pain and covered her eyes. A shrill note resounded between the confused shouts of her friends.

"Intruders! Intruders! Collaborator!" The guard winded his horn again, but the horn's blaring broke off abruptly.

Large hands threw Matil over Dewdrop and the beetle pitched into motion.

"Good, no, that way!" Simmad said. "Yes, straight on! Now turn left!"

Matil gripped the far side of the saddle, sliding across the seat on her stomach as Dewdrop turned sharply. Her eyes burned with the light. She kept them crunched shut.

More horns sounded behind them but soon receded. Wind whipped over Matil. She had never before gotten Dewdrop to top speed. Her heart raced with the beetle and she wished that she could see what was going on. A jumble of emotions flooded her without relenting. Out of them rose one so sour and cold that she gritted her teeth. She hated this light-blindness. It made her weak. It threatened to overwhelm her with even more blinding fear. For the moment, that frozen anger kept her head on her shoulders.

"Let's stop here and let your friend get in the saddle," Simmad said.

They slowed. The air changed around them from open and smelling of grass to feeling contained and earthy. Matil let one eye squint open. She flinched. It was all wrong. Bands of light imprinted her vision and the burrow they had entered was *dark*. Not in the usual way, where she could tell that there was very little light even though everything remained sharp and rich. No, this was the real meaning of dark. Shadows shifted the more Matil tried to look, and the faces of her companions wavered like poor reflections.

Khelya crouched and scuffled farther into the burrow with Simmad tucked awkwardly under her arm. She set him down, which let his wings light the burrow. Matil and Dask slid from their beetles.

Dask rubbed his eyelids. "Was that what I thought it was?"

"A Sangriga magician," Simmad said. He wobbled, his legs still wrapped in the ropes. "Only a feeble blast, though. We're fortunate that watchman wasn't more powerful."

"Fortunate?" Dask laughed. "Yeah, we're sure fortunate a guard showed up! What are *you* doing here, anyway? I bet you led the guard right to us."

Simmad pointed to the burrow entrance with his tied hands, eyes very round. "He called me a collaborator! I *am* a collaborator! If I went back, I'd be severely punished and perhaps even lose my spot at the University! I can't go back now, not without bringing something, some proof that I'm a true scholar."

"Mr. Simmad helped us get away," Khelya said. She sat down with a sleepy yawn. "When it was hard to see, he gave me directions so I could pull the beetles. Can't we take him with us? Please? It would make up for me grabbin' that guard and throwing 'im."

"You threw the guard?" Matil said, blinking up at her. She was still trying to get rid of the light remnants.

Dask snorted. "Nice."

"But I didn't want to," Khelya moaned.

"Hey, why are you so concerned about Sangriga?" Dask said. "You didn't have any problem holding an Obrigi bandit at knifepoint or taking down Skorgon."

"Sangriga are different. They're good guys. They make the rules. They gave the Obrigi everything we have."

"Good guys," Dask said incredulously.

"I wouldn't say that." Simmad scratched his goateed chin with the rope binding his hands. "It's more of a symbiotic alliance, isn't it? We give to the Obrigi, the Obrigi give to us."

Khelya took on a very small look for one so large. "Really?" she said with a tinge of hope. "We help you?"

"Of course! Though…" He lowered his hands. "I don't know why, but some of my colleagues are dead set on keeping the Obrigi out of our universities."

Dask tapped his head. "Think about it. It's 'cause the Sangriga are tall dungbasks with wings. Now let's fly outta here before they find us." He pulled his knife on Simmad.

"Ah!" Simmad stumbled backward. "N-no need to get stabby! I'll leave if you want me to, I promise!"

"I'm cutting you loose," Dask said curtly. "You can do what you want afterward. Hold still." He cut through Simmad's bindings, sheathed the knife, and went back to the beetles and Matil. Now that her eyesight had fully returned, she looked at him in disbelief.

"You mean I can stay with you three?" Simmad said, brushing the ropes away.

"Can he?" Khelya said.

"Yeah, he can," Dask said unenthusiastically. "Three cheers for stick-ears."

"Oh, thank you," Simmad said. "I won't give you cause for regret!"

Matil smiled at Dask in gratitude. He gave her a small, crooked grin in return. Their expressions softened as they stood still. Matil realized that Dask's eyes weren't just green; they were the leaves on a tree, bright and shaded, close and far away. A vague memory washed over her. She no longer saw Dask but someone else's worn-out orange eyes. Her heart was stung, and sad pain welled up in it.

She averted her gaze. That strange state of mind fell away, and she was left feeling like an empty box. Simmad spouted words at Khelya in excitement while the Obrigi nodded happily. She turned toward Dask again, not quite looking at his face. "You're- you're okay with letting him come?"

Dask's wings were hunched up. "It's nothing," he said, sounding how she felt. Something wasn't right, but just as she hesitantly went to steal a glance at him, Khelya waved her friends toward the beetles.

"We should get goin' before they find us here," she said.

"Yes!" Simmad said. "Abso-*lutely!* Let us away thither!"

"Take your thither," Dask grumbled under his breath, "and stick it up your nose."

The four of them traveled north through the meadows of Tyrlis for much of the night. Clouds skimmed over the half moon, but, even when it was concealed, a sourceless illumination softly outlined the grass, bushes, and trees. Taking cues from the clouds, owls and bats hunted overhead like ghosts and shadows.

Despite Dask's distaste, he had let Simmad sit on Olnar with him, back-to-back. Simmad's wings radiated light and as time went on Matil could tell that Dask was uncomfortable. She tried to give Simmad one of their Eletsol leaf cloaks to cover his wings with.

Simmad waved it away. "No, thank you, that won't work. Our wings aren't affected by anything up to a certain thickness."

"You guys have complicated wings, don't you?" said Dask.

"I suppose in some ways...oh, do you mind terribly if I examined *your* wings? You see – as one can imagine – I don't often get the opportunity to observe a Ranycht. Or a Ranycht without wings. *Or* an Obrigi in a half-faded state! Perhaps this would be the research paper to begin my career!"

Dask looked taken aback. "I—yeah, I *mind!* I don't want any Sangriga *ever* poking at my wings. And whaddaya mean 'begin your career'? You don't have a job at your age?"

Simmad blinked rapidly and made no sound. Matil hadn't seen him this quiet yet. It wasn't just that he didn't speak; his bright, intense expression had switched off.

Since Dask was at the front of the beetle, facing forward, he couldn't see Simmad. "Hello?" he said. "You fallin' asleep back there?"

"It's..." Simmad rubbed his face with his sleeve. "I *do* have a job..."

"What do you do at Icto Lan?" Matil said.

He timidly looked down at her. "I read, mostly. The Elders and related legends are my specialty. I have several theories, as I've mentioned, but…no notable discoveries."

"You must know a load of things about the Elders that regular alva don't," Khelya said with some awe.

"Well, I- I do, don't I?" His face brightened again, along with his wings.

"Ack!" Dask shielded the sides of his eyes with his hands. "Turn those things down, I can't see."

"Sorry, sorry!"

"We should stop chatting, anyway," Dask said, hunching over Olnar. "I think a village is coming up."

They did come by a quiet, luminous village, so they stayed far away from the outskirts to avoid the gazes of the watchmen. Simple but graceful buildings arched across tree branches. Windmills lined the upper boughs. Matil wondered what it must be like to live in those ethereal homes. With the village safely behind them, the journey took on a dreamlike flow. Matil's eyelids fell and rose, fell and rose as the beetles and Khelya marched. They finally shot open when Simmad let out a pathetic cry. She halted Dewdrop and turned around to see him sitting up on the ground behind Olnar.

"Mr. Simmad!" said Khelya as she rushed to his side. "You okay?" She pulled him to his feet and lightly dusted him off.

"He's fine. He just went to sleep and took a little tumble." Dask patted Olnar's head. He saw Matil looking at him and smiled cheekily.

She tried to suppress her own small grin and then found Dask still watching her. His green eyes searched hers. Sorrow pricked at her heart again as the memory returned. A man with orange eyes. She looked up through the trees to break eye contact with Dask. Finding the moon low in the sky, she said, "I think we've gone far enough away. Let's stop here."

They set out four blankets – the Eletsol had packed extras for them – and each traveler bundled up. Simmad was out as soon as his head touched the ground, and Khelya offered to take first watch. Matil longed for rest, but her mind was restless.

From somewhere behind her, she heard Dask's blankets rustling.

"Matil," he said in a voice too low for the others to hear.

Her first urge was to answer him, but the pain came back, small and lonely. Hatred returned, holding fear at bay. The eyes appeared first, and then the entire face of that alva from her old life fastened itself in her thoughts. She kept her breathing steady and lay still. Eventually, she heard the sound of Dask settling back down.

* * *

"We can't stay here," Matil said.

Crell glanced up from his plate of pickled cabbage, his large orange eyes looking troubled. All around them dishes clanked and the sounds of muddled voices in before-dawn conversations were somber. The common room was dark, lit only by the roaring fireplace. It kept everyone warm, but the sight of the licking flames made Matil feel cold.

She stabbed at her own cabbage. "It hurts too much to stay." Her eyes stung as she tried to hold the tears back. "I think we need to do something."

"We *are* doing something. We have work now." He gave her a small smile. "We'll make it, Nychta." She wouldn't meet his gaze, and his smile turned to concern. "What's wrong?"

Matil shook her head, slid off the chair, and ran through the inn's door. Time. She needed time to think. She jumped up and flapped her wings, hiding on the inn's roof just as Crell burst out.

"Nychta!" He unfurled brown wings with black markings and took off flying from the balcony.

Matil flew in the opposite direction, hurtling through the leaves for a long stretch, until the sun had risen and her wings could barely flap. She lit down on a branch, curled up under her wings, and covered her eyes. Images from *that day* became real in the darkness behind her hands. Beings made of pure light danced like demons and breathed fire. Their shouts and awful words scorched Matil's ears, while smoke filled her nose and mouth. She needed to escape.

But she realized now that this evil should never have happened. This time, as the world crumbled all around, her numb fingers became hard fists. This time she saw herself flying *at* them instead of away. She pulled the night sky with her and drowned the burning sun in a sea of ink and stars. The capering creatures died with wails of remorse.

Now Matil was at the inn's balcony. It was late afternoon and Crell sat slumped against the wall. He looked up at the sound of her footsteps and his eyes widened.

"Nychta," he said, jumping up. "Don't leave like that! I didn't know if I'd ever see you again."

"I'm sorry I flew off," Matil said. She had to tell him. Would he understand?

"Just be careful. Let's stick together from now on."

"Yes. Stick together." His words encouraged her. "I figured something out, Crell."

"Yeah?"

"I know what we need to do." Cold and hot built up inside of her at the same time.

Crell looked at her blankly.

"If only they'd been executed, I wouldn't feel so—" She reached toward her heart. "The magistrates failed. The magistrates let them go home, even though *we* can't go home because of them."

"And there's nothing we can do about it." Crell sat down with his legs hanging from the balcony. "I wish I were stronger. I could've protected us all."

"We can *get* stronger!" Matil started pacing back and forth, her wings itching to fly again. "We *can* do something. My father said that Ecker's Brug is full of powerful and dangerous alva. We should go there and find them. Someday they can help us punish the Sangriga."

He puckered his face in thought. "Punish?"

"By giving them what they gave us," she said.

"Giving them…" Crell said. "But…the Chivishi…"

"The Chivishi would say that it's right." She stopped pacing. "Doesn't it always talk about justice?"

"I guess. But what they did to us…how could we—"

"If we sit here quietly and work for the rest of our lives, nothing will change," she said. "They'll just come back again and again until we're all gone. They need to know they can't get away with it!"

"Please calm down," he said, standing. "Sleep. We stayed up too late." He put a hand on her forehead. "The sun's made you feverish. C'mon, you'll feel better in the evening."

Matil batted away his hand. "I'm not feverish! I thought a lot about it, and I *know* it's the right thing to do."

"No. All we have left is ourselves and each other. That's what we need to focus on."

She gave him a disgusted look. "You're just like the magistrates, aren't you?"

"What?" said Crell.

"You're going to let them go!"

"Stop it, Nychta."

"Good job, Magistrate Crell. Good job watching us all die."

"I said, stop it!" His voice rose.

"You're not even a magistrate," she said bitterly. "You're a *Sangriga*."

"Nychta!" He seemed ready to hit her. Instead, he kicked the banister and began walking toward the inn. "Go to bed," he tossed over his shoulder.

When the inn door slammed, Matil felt loneliness open like a terrible chasm in her stomach. The same thing in the past had come close to swallowing her whole. As she slipped toward it and as her throat tightened with small gasps, a cold, hard hand seemed to grab her. It wrenched her back from the gaping hole. It took her in its steely arms and whispered in her ear. Justice.

She stood, knees shaking, on the branch of a tree. Her bag was packed and slung over her shoulder. Outlined against the red and purple western sky was the inn, where Crell was content to stay.

"You said…" Matil wiped her eyes. "You said we should stick together."

She looked past the inn to the golden half-sun visible above the tree canopy. For one last moment, she let herself cry. Then the cold hand grabbed her again and turned her around. Deepening blue spread across the sky. She cinched her bag's strap, pushed off from the branch, and flew into the welcoming arms of night.

20

Seekers Found

The breeze threatened to blow Lyria off-course, but it was a small inconvenience. She found that it woke her up to fly straight to the teardrop-shaped Ambermeet rather than through one of the administrative buildings in the trees flanking it. Morning light came through the trees and a few clear rays hit the warmly-glowing walls of amber. The Ambermeet hung suspended from a branch, fastened in place at its tip with bronze fittings. A broad bridge of wood and metal ran through the massive, jewel-like Council hall, holding it secure at the bottom and leading on either side to doors in the neighbouring trees. Windows speckled the tree-buildings, some windows shut tight, others kept open while Sangriga floated in and out of them. The Obrigi of ages past were great craftsmen, and this place reflected their ambition and attention to detail.

While Lyria flew, a few other Council members arrived at the bridge in palanquins borne through the air by their servants. She recognized Duke Bevan by his frizzy and grey-streaked yellow hair. Poor Bevan had to disembark from a cramped palanquin beside Lord Cad Gan as the latter stepped down from his large, curtain-draped litter, assisted by fastidious maids. Bevan's face showed its usual envious pucker. If she didn't constantly remind herself of the nobles' pettiness, she might herself grow resentful wishing to be one.

She rose over the bridge and floated back down to land on its smooth wooden beams. Her triangle-topped staff met the bridge with a *thunk*. Spirited shouts ascended from the ground nearly a greatlength below, where a grubby group of commoners had gathered. They'd started protesting every morning since the tax increase was proclaimed, and their number had grown since then. Soon there would be enough of them that the guards would interfere. As Lyria paused to watch the upset commoners, regret hit her like a wave on Lake Vangara.

"I'm sorry," she said quietly. "I tried."

A careful and familiar voice drew her attention. "Lyria."

Nearby was a woman in a purple Council robe with her hair done up in braids that circled her head. It was the same hairstyle this woman usually wore, just as Lyria didn't often deviate from her simple bun.

"Branneth," Lyria said as she fell in behind the other Councilwoman.

The two walked across the bridge near each other, but never side by side. When they reached the archway into the Ambermeet, Branneth moved to the side and turned to face Lyria. A councilman floated past them with a greeting.

"Did you hear about the intruders at Icto Lan?" Branneth said, the light of news glimmering in her cobalt-blue eyes.

Curiosity caused Lyria to forget her awkwardness. "Not yet, no."

"It's mind-numbing how little happens out there most of the time, but," Branneth lowered her voice, "having ears in the university has finally paid off. The incident happened two nights ago. Three outlaws got in. Two Ranycht and an Obrigi. Sound familiar?"

She didn't have to pretend to be appropriately shocked. "You don't mean the ones who escaped earlier this year?" Blazing sun, what were *they* doing in Icto Lan?

"Of course I mean them, mudhead. Er…Lyria." Branneth looked up at the light streaming through the leaves.

Lyria paused before going on. "What did they do?"

"The reports say they met a traitor and then ran off with him to the north. They likely came from the north in the first place, by way of Fainfal."

Traitor? Fainfal? Now she was itching to know if they had a plan or had simply gone mad. If only she'd known earlier that they were so close.

Branneth continued. "Can you believe a respectable San-griga scholar would up and fly away?"

"*Scholar?* From Icto Lan?"

"Naturally. Not a very important scholar, granted, but that's what spies do, isn't it? Slink about in the background so no one notices?"

"I…suppose you must be right," Lyria said. She tapped her staff with her finger. "You called him respectable? That's hardly the word for a fellow like him. Reckless, perhaps. Coarse and disloyal, certainly. A mercenary scoundrel."

Branneth laughed. "You haven't lost your delightful way of cutting alva down, Lyria, well done. We should be getting to our seats, but…I thought I might share."

Lyria thanked her quietly, and then the two parted as they entered the Council chamber. The news still ran through Lyria's mind. Assuming it was true…

The scholars in Icto Lan were famed for their studies on the Elders and related artifacts, such as the Book of Myrkhar. What could have compelled the man to join the outlaws? She knew only the vaguest details of their travels, but all signs pointed toward a mission of significance and urgency. It would require this scholar to be a brave sort, unafraid and capable. Perhaps he even knew the dangers of the Book and was willing to do what he could to stop it.

Lyria almost tasted the freedom and simplicity of such a life compared to the cloying perfumes and maze-like politics of the Ambermeet's golden hall. If the Icto Lan situation was as she deduced, then this runaway scholar was quite remarkable.

* * *

Wide-awake Dask made a snoring noise to underscore the steady torrent of words flowing from the Sangriga behind him.

"You know," Simmad said, "it's fascinating how much influence different Elders have had on different kinds of alva! Icto Lan is named after Icto the Great Scholar, of course, because he founded it, and in Nychtfal," he gestured at Matil and over his shoulder at Dask, "Shora established Ecker's Brug and its system of judges. Falgar founded Corwyna with the Obrigi, though it was then known as Ared Thunn."

"Ared Thunn," Khelya breathed. She was following Dask and Simmad's beetle in order to hear the Sangriga talk.

The day after Simmad joined them, they had told him about Mr. Korsen and Hasyl the hermit – he nearly keeled over with joy when he held the journal – and explained Matil's connection to Nychta. Then the four of them continued into Fainfal, generally moving eastward toward Ansi's clan. They expected to meet Eletsol on their way there. Simmad said that he knew enough of the Eleti language to communicate, and Dask planned to pass them off as a very small traveling circus.

"That great city Ared Thunn," said Simmad, "was wonderfully industrious until the Hibernation, when Falgar's blessing left the Obrigi. The Time of Loss hit your alva the hardest." He nodded sympathetically at Khelya.

Her face grew troubled and she looked down at him with sudden urgency. "You know a lot about the Elders, so you'd know…you'd *know* if the Elders are still here, right? If they're really sleeping and ain't just…well…dead or something?"

Simmad's blue eyes looked back at her keenly. "Interesting you should mention death. It's one of the less popular theories regarding the fate of the Elders, but it is in line with the scant archaeological clues known to us. So I can't honestly say I *know*. Why do you ask?"

Matil's heart sank. Dask turned to watch Khelya.

The Obrigi sighed, shifted the bags hanging from her shoulders, and said, "Just…curious. I think I could use a bite. Anyone else hungry?"

They lunched beneath a spray of ferns, eating the last of the mouse jerky that Ansi and Teres had given them. It was around noon, so Simmad's wings had been faint in the light, but under the shade they illuminated everything. Despite giving the wings a few uneasy glances, Matil didn't say anything.

"Remember the Sangriga who helped us get outta Tyrlis a while ago?" Dask said. "The one who could make his wings go away? Sparkles here needs to do that. Those back-torches are too obvious."

Simmad appeared hurt. "Well, maybe. I-I'd prefer it if you called me—"

"Can you do it?" said Dask

Matil began to braid her hair. "It's a good idea, since we usually don't want to draw attention to ourselves." She eyed Dask. "Would you please stop calling him Sparkles?"

Dask sat back and rubbed his fingernails on his tunic. "I'll stop calling him Sparkles when he stops sparkling."

"My aunt taught me how to dim my wings once," Simmad said. "Hopefully it'll work."

"Hopefully?" Dask said. "We need more than hope."

Simmad lifted his chest and nodded. "I'm absolutely positive that I can remember. After that…well, I couldn't actually manage it last time."

Dask looked wearily at Matil and Khelya. "This guy."

The Sangriga stood up with a self-conscious stoop. He closed his eyes and scrunched up his face. "Sun is shining… sun sets…sun *sets*…" He opened his eyes, twisted his head to get a look at his glowing back, and shut his eyes again. "Bother." He straightened himself up. "Sun…*sets*. Sets! Good night, sun! Lovely to see you, but I'm afraid it's time… for…you…to…" With each word, his wings grew weaker. "Go!" They became so dim that Matil could barely notice the faint light they cast. Simmad's eyes popped open, and he surveyed his work. "Brilliant! Or, I suppose, it's the opposite of brilliant! You get it, of course, because my wings were brilliant before – brilliant as in bright – but now they're… do you get it? Er, never mind." He spun around, trying to see his wings. "I did it!"

Khelya watched him proudly. "See, Dask? He's an expert."

"Hardly!" Simmad slowed down and stopped. "But you're kind to say so."

"Can you keep it up?" Dask said.

"Hmm, not for long," he said. "It's too difficult."

Dask shook his head scornfully. "Fine, here's what you'll do. You'll keep those eyesores turned off for as long as you possibly can…"

Simmad began nodding.

"…and when you can't do it anymore," Dask added, "we'll tie you to a rock and leave you there."

He paused mid-nod. "Oh."

Matil looked askance at Dask. He lifted his hands as if to say, *Just trust me.*

Khelya had missed their exchange and was blushing heartily. "We ain't gonna tie you to a—Mr. Simmad, Dask's jokin'. Whatever you can or can't do is okay."

"It's your first time dimming your wings all the way, right?" said Matil.

"Yes," said Simmad, glancing between Khelya and Dask in confusion.

Matil smiled. "You'll get better."

"W-well, in time, certainly," he said.

She made herself look serious. "We don't have much time."

"You're right." Simmad squared his bony shoulders. "I'll get to work on it right away." He squinched one eye shut with the effort. His wings, which had been growing in light as he spoke, suddenly vanished.

"Now that Sparkles isn't so sparkly," Dask said, "let's get moving."

They got the beetles together and led them out from underneath the fern.

Simmad looked at the quiet forest surrounding them. "In the last couple of days I've felt…odd. Can't quite put my finger on it. It's as though the woods are breathing down my neck…" He shivered.

"I feel it, too," Khelya said.

"It's always like this," Dask said. "That's Fainfal for ya." He started climbing into Olnar's saddle.

"Wait," Matil said before she mounted up. "I've wondered if we should have the necklace out for when we meet any Eletsol. The last few times, they were so quick that we couldn't do much besides get caught."

Dask rubbed at his stubble. "I don't know…see, we wanna keep it safe. In my experience, keeping something out in the open makes it less safe."

"That's true." Matil pulled out the red wooden pendant from a pack on Dewdrop and let it dangle as she observed it. Her ear flicked around. She'd heard a leaf brush against something.

Dask, Khelya, and Simmad yelped in unison. Matil looked up and held back her own squeak.

Slowly, silently, about a dozen alva advanced out of the grass and tangle from all directions. They were Eletsol painted with green and black patterns, half-crouching and holding their curved blades before themselves. At a certain distance, they came no closer.

"Hm, well," Dask said out of the side of his mouth, "it only now occurred to me that what we're doing is very dangerous."

"Sun preserve us," Simmad whispered. He cleared his throat and spoke up weakly. "Elamys…"

One of the Eletsol lowered his sword and pointed at the pendant. He was a man wearing a colorful beaded headdress.

"Dyndal," he said.

Matil looked around at her friends and then said, "Kal."

Eletsol jumped into the air, hollering like madmen. They clanged their swords together and one by one flew down to get a better look at the pendant, only to whiz back up in new heights of exultation. After the warriors had calmed down somewhat, the man in the headdress positioned them around the four outsiders and the beetles. He ordered everyone away from the bushy ferns. Matil looked around at the warriors as they marched, her heart pounding.

The commander brought the formation into a clearing overshadowed by a large, craggy ridge of rock and soil. Roots curled in and out of the ridge face, belonging to two trees at the top. Brown huts built from tree bark strips covered the ridge, from the ground at its foot to the stony crevices all along and up to the knotholes and branches of the trees above. The commander gave another order to his warriors, and half of them swarmed the ridge, joyfully shouting to those within the huts. Alva peeked curiously out of the huts. Matil and her friends were soon surrounded by Eletsol men, women, and children – the whole village.

Before the babbling crowd could get too close to the outsiders, the villagers parted respectfully for a little old man to approach. His bald head rested snugly among the cloths and furs that draped from his shoulders to the ground, and his eyes were concealed by eyebrows like huge cotton puffs. The wings on his back were red petals and a bit shriveled.

When he reached the outsiders, he said slowly, "I am Uro, tain-man of this clan. Is it true you have Dyndal's sign?"

Matil lifted her hand, which was sweaty from clutching the toad.

Uro's furry eyebrows lifted until his eyes could be seen. "We must leave at once," he said, eyebrows falling. He faced the villagers and spoke Eleti. A murmur spread through the crowd, and they squinted at the toad. A few of them beamed. When the meaning of Uro's announcement sank in, the villagers became as ecstatic as the warriors had been, whooping and shouting to the sky.

"Wow," Dask said over their noise. "Great plan. Let's leave."

Simmad looked at him. "But where are we going?"

"*That's what I wanna know*," Dask said.

"Remember when Ansi told us about Dyndal's tomb?" Khelya said, reaching up to tighten her headband.

Simmad's mouth formed an 'o' in surprise. "Tomb?" he said.

With a glance at Khelya, Dask said, "The Eletsol are pretty sure the Elders died off."

"Mm, yes," he said, "I've heard a little about the Eletsol's folklore, their idea of the Elders' fates. I wonder why they believe that when all of the stories—"

"Anyway," said Khelya, "I'd guess we're goin' there. To the tomb."

Uro turned to her and nodded. She didn't look happy to be correct.

* * *

The villagers buzzed to and fro with piles of goods in their arms, while some on the ground hoisted bundles and blanket rolls onto Dewdrop, Olnar, and their own pack-mice. Uro had ordered a few of them to take care of the outsiders. They bowed and adorned the outsiders with beaded necklaces before leading the group to sit down in the shade. They returned a little later to serve the outsiders cool blueberry juice in bowls fashioned from acorn caps.

Matil sipped the tangy liquid, pausing to grin at her friends and the activity around them. Dask seemed disgruntled when he saw that the only others not working were young children drinking from their own bowls. He got up to help the adults, but they sent him back where he dourly gulped down his drink instead. Khelya drank the blueberry juice slowly, one of her eyes squinting as if she didn't know what to think of its strong flavor. Simmad left his juice untouched for a long time while he observed the industry of the villagers, but after taking a swig, his back straightened up.

"I believe I taste hints of rose and pine," he said, delighted.

Some of the Eletsol, like Uro, wore long layers of cloth, leaves, and grass. Matil wondered why, because the weather was too warm for so many clothes, but when these alva rested, they caused nearby foliage to grow over and shade them. They were magicians, as was Uro. A villager helped the old tain-man onto one of the mice, where he perched with ease. The party – making up maybe half the village – was finally ready to leave.

"Noosh-noosh," said a mouse-driver to get his mice moving.

"Noosh," said another.

A straggling magician flew out of the village after the departing group, flittering haphazardly in a tangle of his wings and flapping garments.

Daytime faded into evening. The party traveled well into the night and then Uro directed them to make camp. Matil fell asleep in no time, and it seemed like she was woken in no time. She kept the last watch, looking out for her friends while one of the Eletsol watched over Uro's alva. The morning was still dark when the Eletsol began to stir. Light crept in through the undergrowth while the party ate a quick breakfast. The Eletsol became jubilant after Uro urged Matil to hold up the pendant again, and once done eating, they moved with eager swiftness.

As Matil walked behind her friends in the early light, she rubbed the back of her right arm and then stopped, her hand touching above her elbow. She felt a patch of rough skin. Straining her neck and shoulder, she tried to see the back of her arm. There it was, a long blotch just darker than the warm brown of her skin. It began near the elbow and extended upward almost a hand's length. Could it be a birthmark? She looked at it, wondering why she hadn't noticed it before. A point in the back of her head itched feebly. No, it…tugged at her. Pulled her in another direction.

Her ears lowered in alarm and she stumbled. The thick, sunny forest seemed like a terrifying blaze of colors pressing in. It took a moment for her to calm down enough that she again heard the birdsong and beast chatter tucked away in the leaves and branches. A regal red butterfly flimmered across the journeyers' path.

It was the pull to Nychta that Matil felt scratching at her mind.

Nychta had tried to take away part of herself in a powerful ritual she couldn't complete, causing Matil to appear; Matil, the part of Nychta she didn't want. Through the ritual, the two of them were still connected, still drawn together.

Seeing signs of animal life and feeling how weak the pull was, Matil was certain that Nychta and the Book of Myrkhar weren't nearby. But they were near enough. She took a last puzzled glance at the mottled skin on her arm and sped up to walk between Dask and Khelya.

Dask looked over at Matil and, upon seeing her expression, his own ears went back. "What's wrong?" he said.

"I- I feel Nychta's presence," Matil said.

Shock crossed his face.

"Thiffen," Khelya said.

"What is it?" Simmad said from Khelya's other side. Khelya turned to explain it to him.

"Can you tell which direction she's in?" Dask said.

Matil had been rubbing at the back of her head as though she were brushing off a clinging gnat, but now she gave up trying to get rid of the pull. She focused on it with a cringe and then pointed to their right.

He squinted toward the sun and then where she was pointing. "Southish, southwest. And we've been heading northeast for the most part."

"That's incredible!" Simmad said. He leaned around Khelya to gawk at Matil.

"I don't think she's close," Matil said. "I don't think she's been looking for us. She has the hermit." She hung her head. "Nychta's probably already killed him, though."

"Hold on." Dask put a comforting hand on her shoulder. "I doubt he's gone yet. If the journal is right, that hermit's old enough to know loads of information that Nychta wants. Anyway," he gestured at Khelya, who carried the journal in a bag on her back, "we haven't…you know, we haven't gotten to thank him yet."

Khelya put her hand on Matil's other shoulder. "We'll keep you safe," she said.

Matil began to feel reassured, but it curdled into guilt. She didn't want them to worry so much about her.

Even as the Eletsol marched and flew and sang around them, the four outsiders took on an anxious silence. After midday, the pull disappeared.

21

Bridging Gaps

Even before Matil and her friends first entered Fainfal, she had stopped counting the length of their journey. The changing weather, slowly heating up day by day, kept track of the time well enough.

Since leaving Uro's village a few days ago, every time they happened upon Eletsol who wore paint in different colors and patterns, Uro would call out in a strong voice. Whether friendly, hostile, or only curious, the Eletsol heeded his words and let them pass. They would examine the four outsiders intently, and many joined their train with bells, horns, drums, and pipes. Simmad facilitated the barest of conversations between the two tongues, but it was enough for the outsiders to join the festive mood. No longer a mere outsider in Fainfal – more like an honored guest – Matil took the time to admire the Eletsol, especially their flower-like wings and curved ears.

The women congregated around Matil and Khelya, getting used to the ghostly Obrigi. They invited the pair to sit in their crowded, two-wheeled wagons and made noises of awe over them. Three of the women could speak Alvishu, one of them very well, and they talked about life in the various clans. Despite Matil wearing Dyndal's sign, they seemed shy to speak on the topic of Dyndal with alva who were not Eletsol. Two women gave Khelya and Matil Elestol-style braids that went up the back of the head, while Matil braided a little girl's glossy, crow-black locks. The woman braiding Khelya's hair threw away her old cloth headband, sending the Obrigi scrambling out of the wagon to pick it back up.

During those few days, Dask raced many other alva and lost only to the fastest flyers. He attributed the successes to his ritual of shaking hands with Matil, Khelya, and even Simmad, and then as many Eletsol as he could. Simmad sought out Uro and other Eletsol who could speak Alvishu, and learned words in Eleti from the young ones who were mesmerized by his wings.

Matil asked Uro if there were any Vima or Taina with them; she hadn't seen the telltale orange or white body paint. He called to another Eletsol, who went to find someone else before returning with the news.

"Those clans are still in war," Uro translated. "Even for the sign of Dyndal, they cannot come."

Matil nodded, her ears drooping.

He watched her from underneath his eyebrows. "How do you know of them?"

"We have friends in the Vima," she said. "And we were there when they, uh, overthrew their chief."

At night the party, lit by torches and buzzing nets of fireflies, came to a wide, deep brook running northwest across their path. While everyone waited, the magicians split into two groups, one of which flew to the other side of the brook. They took positions near the water and extended their arms toward the underbrush. With the magicians' sinuous movements, plants and reeds leaned and wound their ways across the brook. Each magician – their number had multiplied since leaving three days before – wore a hard look of concentration. Everyone else watched the formation of a bridge in quiet excitement, and Matil's eyes shone with how beautifully the plants laced together.

There was a sudden splash as one magician pushed another from a different clan into the river. Construction of the bridge halted while many other magicians swarmed into a brawl. A few more Eletsol were knocked into the river and burst out, faces red, but harsh rebukes from their leaders got their attention. They gave up the fight as abruptly as it started and soon the bridge was complete. The magicians stayed in their places, slowly waving their arms to hold the plants steady. The pack bugs and animals crossed with a little prodding, and small groups of Eletsol had already flown over to set up camp.

Matil and Khelya passed over the bridge beside a rat whose harness Khelya clutched in one hand while stiffly walking along with her eyes shut and face turned to the sky. Her other hand was locked on Matil's shoulder, and Matil patted Khelya's clammy fingers while eyeing the quivery plants that served as a railing for the bridge. It was nerve-wracking to traverse a bridge that hadn't existed until moments ago but Matil tried to enjoy the experience. Moonlight fell through clouds and trees to hit the black water like shards of white pottery. The Eletsol urged their beasts forward with gentle "nooshes" and "ep-ep-eps". Sweet herbal scents drifted on the warm wind.

"It's nice, isn't it?" Matil said.

"H-h-how is it *nice?*" Khelya tripped slightly, causing her hand to yank out of Matil's. "Ah!" She pulled herself closer to the rat, who squeaked and quickened its pace until a girl flew in to stroke its twitchy muzzle.

Matil hurried to catch up. She looked over Khelya to make sure the Obrigi was fine. "Sorry, I meant that…it's nice to have a friend who's not afraid of the same things I am. That way we can look out for each other."

Khelya pursed her mouth in thought. "Yeah," she said shakily. "I guess it is nice." Eyes still closed, she smiled. "Thanks."

"Thank *you*," Matil said.

"See?" said Dask, landing behind them and folding his wings. "I leave you alone and all I hear are pleases and thank yous. If I weren't around, you'd die of boredom."

Khelya laughed. She opened her eyes and shook a fist over her shoulder at Dask. "I'll show you bor—" She suddenly realized what she was doing and her arms flew out to grab at Matil and the rat.

Matil ducked instinctively. The rat gave a panicked skreak and scampered ahead. Khelya missed them, freezing in place with both arms out. She shut her eyes again.

"Are you all right?" Matil said.

Khelya's eyes scrunched tighter. "I give up."

"And not a moment too soon," Dask said. "Welcome to the other side, my lady. Hope you enjoyed your crossing."

Slowly, she looked down at her feet. She stood at the end of the bridge. Nearby, a magician was so focused on holding the bridge that he didn't even wipe the sweat rolling down his face.

Khelya stumbled, jelly-legged, onto solid ground and sank to her knees. "I don't ever wanna get on another bridge unless I made it *myself*."

Simmad met the three of them when they entered the ramshackle camp-in-progress. His knee pants were splotchy with dirt, grass, and juice stains. He still wore his blue tunic, but he'd tied the undershirt around his waist. His thin, pale arms were covered in symbols of different colors, sizes, and designs.

"Look!" he said, waving his arms about like an Eletsol magician. "The tain-men taught me about heraldic devices of the clans and even drew them for me!"

"Drew them *on* you," Dask corrected. "Huh. They even put 'em all over your back."

"I know!" Simmad turned, showing off the symbols across the back of his tunic. His wings beamed as much as his grin and, when he noticed their brightness, he concentrated to make them disappear.

Matil went up to look at his arms. Each symbol was like a flower blooming on him. "They're very pretty."

Khelya leaned down toward Simmad so she could peer closely at the symbols in the torchlight. Dask followed the others and glanced at the symbols with at least a little interest.

Simmad smiled timidly at the three crowding him. "Yes, they're…they're aesthetically pleasing *and* quite meaningful." He pointed at a red, seven-pointed star. "This clan's name is Taivalaan. Its literal meaning is 'by the sky lights'. The whole clan lives in one of the tallest trees in Fainfal and their wise men chart the stars throughout the year. The seven rays represent the chief and the six patriarchs that rule them. Not a large clan, but they're highly influential."

He continued to explain symbols while they walked toward the Eletsol unpacking food and twisting plants into bowers and tents. Men unhitched animals, leaning their two-wheeled wagons on the ground. Others in the campground pulled out pipes, drums, and stringed instruments to play spirited accompaniment for voices already lifted in song. The singers strung hammocks through the trees. Some Eletsol formed instruments on the spot, magically twining together grass and twigs.

New sounds floated from the brook, chimeful and jangling music in a timing and key that clashed with the Eletsol melody. Both songs ceased as the musicians became aware of each other. Matil looked and saw a flat-bottomed barge floating down the current, long poles sticking up and paper lanterns strung from corner to corner. Lounging on the deck and surrounded by crates were a few dusky Ranycht and several dark-haired Nervoda, their pallid faces standing out like bones in the night. Harps, tambourines, and other delicate instruments sat in their laps.

"A-hey-o!" a Ranycht with a black head kerchief shouted. "We goin' by safe and peaceable, awright? We don't mean no harm!"

"Aw-haw, aw-haw," said a few of the other barge-alva. A Nervoda poked his head out of the cabin.

One of the tain-men flew to the edge of the brook and bowed. "Outsiders may pass!"

Matil watched with great interest. "Who are they?" she said.

"Traders from Vangara." Dask gave the barge a side-eye. "Those boxes are full of 'luxury products' like eel and jewelry that go for almost nothing around the lake. Nobles in Tyrlis buy it up like they buy favors from the sun Elder. The traders usually cut through Nychtfal, though. I wonder what they're…oh yeah, remember the wall we set up with the Obrigi? Going around it is probably faster than trying to go through."

The Eletsol musicians tentatively started up again. The barge-alva imitated them and then played their own music for a few beats. The back-and-forth went on until a new song emerged, a sprawling blend of tunes that came from uncoordinated musicians improvising with each other. The Eletsol sang even more loudly. Many flew and spun in the smoke from the campfires, their flower petal and leaf wings fluttering. Some Nervoda rose from their pillows, scintillant mist gathering around them as they floated and wove through the air to the music's strong beat. All of the Ranycht whooped and danced on the deck.

Matil realized she was smiling and couldn't stop if she wanted to. Dask laughed at the wild antics of everyone involved and Simmad was humming and swaying along. Matil turned to Khelya to cajole her into dancing together – copying the funny kicks and graceful hand motions – but stopped short of speaking. Khelya's head was tilted to the side. She wore a slight cringe.

Matil tapped her arm. "What is it?"

Khelya startled out of her reverie. "Oh," she said, "you know how it is between us Obrigi and this kinda artistical thing."

Right. Obrigi saw no point in music or other arts. Apparently it had been that way since the Hibernation, when they lost the blessing of inspiration given to them by the Elder Falgar.

Khelya sighed. "The music wouldn't bother me if I weren't trying to listen."

"You're trying to listen?" Dask said.

"Yeah, I am," she said defensively. "I just wanna…understand it, is all."

He nodded, but still looked confused.

"It won't work, anyway." Khelya put a hand on her stomach. "Wonder when the food'll be ready."

Once the barge neared the dense forest beyond the campgrounds, the barge-alva waved and hollered goodbye. They passed behind a tree and now all that remained was their music, until that, too, was swallowed by the night.

Matil and the others were about to turn away when a voice rang through the campground. The Eletsol musicians stopped playing.

"Hey!" the voice said again. A Nervoda man swooped along the surface of the water. A curtain of mist swirled around him, droplets catching the light of fireflies and torches. He wore a leaf cap and well-worn jerkin and trousers. It was one of the barge-alva. He stopped and hovered at the shore, announcing to the Eletsol, "Thought we'd letcha know to keep yer eyes open! There's word from upriver that Skorgon are about. Real mean ones."

"Thank you for this warning," Uro replied.

The Nervoda bowed in mid-air with a lazy grin and dove into the brook to catch up with the barge.

Matil turned to her friends, her insides tight with worry. "Skorgon?"

"Not all Skorgon are Nychta's Skorgon," Dask said. "This far east, they're probably a gang of highwaymen."

"I do hope there won't be any fighting," Simmad said.

Khelya shuddered. "Me too. To be honest, I never wanna see another Skorgon in my life."

Matil stared at the ground, frowning. Dask came over and touched her arm.

"It'll be okay," he said. "You don't sense Nychta, right?"

"No," she admitted.

"So don't worry." Dask looked around. "You know, I'm with Khel. When's the food—"

"Dels!" the group of Eletsol cooks yelled. "Dels! Dels!"

Teres had taught Matil and the others that 'dels' meant food.

Everyone piled their bowls with greens, berries, and a small slab of meat. Uro sat with the bearers of the sign for dinner. He spread his hand out toward the gathering. "All this you see…this peace is not ordinary," he said. "Rather than eat together, these clans would war. The sign of Dyndal has united us more truly than when we have celebrated Velana Festivals at his tomb over the generations."

"What is the pendant meant for?" Simmad said. "Why does it have such an effect on the Eletsol?"

"Dyndal promised." Uro nodded, eyes barely showing under his brows. "Though dead, he would return to guide us."

Khelya frowned. "Why didn't he tell anyone else?"

"Because," he said, using a knife to slice a chunk off his sizzling meat, "Eletsol are the best at keeping secrets." He picked up the chunk and dropped it back on his plate. "Ah." He blew on his burnt fingers. "Helkuum, helkuum."

After dinner, which ended a long time after everyone had actually finished their food, alva dropped off to sleep here and there. A slow drumbeat began. It poured through the camp as everyone settled themselves either sitting or lying down. A few watchmen stood straight in the trees and among the alva on the ground. Khelya offered to take first watch for Matil, Dask, and Simmad.

A woman remained standing on a low branch in the center of the camp. Her yellow hair hung to her knees in two braids. She took a deep breath and, swaying with the drum's pound, let loose a clear note. The song she sang had just the traces of a tune and didn't sound like it was in any language. It was strange and lovely, reminding Matil of hooting owls and trees forever stretching higher in a midnight sky. The woman's voice was the loneliness of being awake while everyone else slept. Matil lay underneath her blankets, staring up at branches heavy with darkness and patches of stars returning her gaze.

* * *

Matil and her rangy teacher, Etsel, strolled through a narrow street so deep in the city that there was no sky above them, only crisscrossing bridges and alva flying from level to level. They were surrounded by the wood, stone, and glass of run-down but warm storefronts. Low-burning braziers at street corners offset the dying year's chill. The street was a bustle of Nuen Festival shoppers bundled in their wings and heavy coats.

"You do what you can," Etsel said, pointing at the various busy shops. "Take work from the alva who'll pay ya, but don't get too enterprising or the gangs'll feel your downdraft. They like keepin' jobs to themselves." He waved at a shopkeeper who had stepped out to empty a bucket of dirty water into the gutter. "Mr. Criffer! How's life?"

Mr. Criffer wiped his hands on his apron. "Sorry, Ets, I don't need nothin' done today."

"Hey, okay, I'll see ya tomorrow."

He squinted at Matil. "Who's the kid? She yours?"

"*Nooo*, sir. This is Manners. Y'see, I finally picked up etiquette."

Matil smiled shyly. "It's nice to meet you."

The older man wheezed out a laugh. "'Bout time our Ets got some manners, huh? Listen, I think she could help around the store. Shora knows my apprentice needs a good example."

Matil blinked and looked up at Etsel. Had Mr. Criffer offered her a job?

"How's the pay?" Etsel said.

"Aw, don't ya trust me?"

"'Course I do, Mr. Criffer, but my little friend has a healthy sense of skepticism."

Did she? Matil resolved to think more skeptically.

"Smart kid," Mr. Criffer said. "Howsabout…five relds for a day's work and seven if she's good? S'all I can afford right now."

Etsel nodded slowly. "She's a hard worker and doesn't eat much. You can feed her, right?"

"Yeah, sure. C'mon in, kid." Mr. Criffer carried his bucket into the store.

"Don't molt this one up," Etsel whispered. "Do good and

ya got yourself an income. I'll be back here for you by the time he closes up shop, all right?"

A lump formed in Matil's throat so she could barely talk. "Th-thanks, Etsel. Thank you so—"

"Ah, cut it out." His wings twitched. "Just, y'know, uh… do good."

"I will."

* * *

"The Eletsol are still moving," Crell said, "and more of them are joining every day." He walked beside Nychta down the gloomy tunnels of their temporary base. "My scouts learned that they already went to the tomb of Dyndal this year, so why are they going again? Do they know about us?"

"My leftover self went to Icto Lan, and I bet she's with the Eletsol right now," Nychta said. "Somehow she found out the hermit's secret. They have to know about us."

Crell remembered the girl, the one so much like Nychta used to be. Those purple eyes. He shook his head. "Then that's why they're gathering. They want to keep us out. Are we too late?"

"No," Nychta said in an airy tone, "we're just not early. The Book and I made plans. I'll leave today to find Kanay's prison and unchain her before anything else happens. Next, I'll go to Igsun and Stal. Our enemies are so busy looking for the Heilar that they've forgotten about the Saikyr."

255

"Kanay, Igsun, Stal," Crell murmured. "Do you believe… the Elders really exist?"

"I don't care," Nychta said. "It doesn't matter if Kanay, Myrkhar – any of them – are Elders or earthworms. The Book is powerful and it says that they're powerful. We need them." Her pale eyes seemed to shimmer in the dimness. "Crell, it's working. Everything is starting to pay off. That fake thinks she's fighting me, but all she's doing is helping me. Helping *us*."

Every step Nychta took and every one of her gestures was controlled and purposeful. Crell had always seen it in her, but it was different now. It was as if purpose had taken over her whole being.

He closed a hand around the hilt of his sheathed sword, trying to feel the same resolve. "I'll gather the Skorgon."

"Set the best ones aside for now," she said. "The Book says you'll need at least four hundred for this strike. Afterward, the rest of them will go on to Nychtfal. We have enough now to make the High Court listen to me." She smiled. "Can you believe it? The *magistrates*…the magistrates will finally give us justice."

The back of Crell's neck prickled. Her plan would come true. Good. It was good because once they completed the plan, they could go back and start over. They could live a new life.

"Before we go," she said as she stopped, "we need to get rid of the hermit. The Book's done with him." They stood right outside of the cave where they kept Hasyl.

"Yes, Nychta," Crell said. Stepping in, he motioned to one of the Skorgon guards standing over the tattered lump on the floor. "Kill him."

One of the Skorgon raised a hooked blade.

"Stop," Nychta said. "Crell, you do it. Meet me in the map room when you're done."

Crell nodded before he could think too hard. As Nychta walked on past the hermit's cave, he moved farther in, drawing his sword and stepping over the rocks littering the dirt floor. Hasyl's slitted eyes flicked up at him. The once-heavy Kyndelin had diminished. His bony frame lay drawn in and breathing shallowly.

The physical torture had done much, but it couldn't break him. After Crell oversaw Hasyl's pain, he'd hoped that the Book of Myrkhar could get the information without further violence. Instead, the hermit's screams had been worse. Nychta had held the Book in front of Hasyl, who twisted in agony. Crell had flinched and kept his eyes averted. Nychta and the Skorgon watched.

At least the hermit wouldn't have to live with his wounds any longer. Crell raised the sword. Probably…he should probably cut off the head. Hasyl would die immediately.

Crell tried to steady his heartbeat. A thought crossed his mind before he could squash it: He should be holding a forging hammer instead of a sword.

"Don't kill—" Hasyl inhaled raggedly, "—your own soul."

He gritted his teeth. "Be quiet."

Soft footsteps made him turn and lower the sword. Nychta entered the cave. Had she come to give him a different assignment?

"He's still alive," she said matter-of-factly.

Crell couldn't respond. Nychta was right – she *must* be right. She must be right. She was Nychta. They had known nothing would come easily.

She nodded at the two Skorgon. "Stand him up."

The guards grabbed Hasyl by his arms and pulled him almost to his feet.

"Look at him," said Nychta. "He's not even useful to his own side."

She reached out and curled her right hand around Crell's on the hilt of the sword. Her soft touch clouded his mind, and he wondered why she would choose to hold hands at a time like this.

In a swift move, she grabbed his arm with her other hand and shoved the sword through the hermit's chest. Hasyl groaned and slumped over the blade. After a moment of staring, Crell jerked his hand from the sword-hilt. Nychta was left holding it alone.

She gave him a hard look, something he had seen from her only once before, and pulled the sword from Hasyl's body. The two Skorgon dropped the limp corpse with a thud. As she roughly handed his sword back to him, the blood coating its blade dripped onto the floor. Crell fumbled with it, accidentally cutting himself in his attempt to keep from dropping the sword.

Nychta's cold eyes searched his own. "You said you wanted to stick together."

The words steadied him. "I do." He gripped the hilt firmly.

"Then follow my lead. You've protected me, Crell, but now I need to protect you. Let someone live, and they won't stop until they've taken you down. I learned that lesson the hard way. *You* get to learn it the easy way." She looked beyond him at the Skorgon. "Take care of the body." Without a second glance she left the cave.

A loud *ting-ting-ting* startled Crell. He looked down to see that his hand was limp and empty. The sword lay on the ground, its blade vibrating from impact with the rocks.

22

The Young Spirit

Two days passed since the travelers crossed the brook, and alva continued to join their number. There was tension and hostility with some of the clans, particularly the reddish-skinned Eletsol who had come from the east. The western Eletsol almost turned them away because the easterners didn't believe that the Elders were dead. Their beliefs and presence made Khelya hopeful, but Dask reminded her what Uro had told them: That the easterners had never before been allowed to see Dyndal's tomb.

On the morning of the third day, Matil, Dask, and Khelya – the bearers of Dyndal's sign – rode in an open wagon driven by a dozing Eletsol man and pulled by a mouse. Dewdrop and Olnar were tethered to either side of the wagon and bore weapons, food, and blankets on their ample shells. The sign-bearers' wagon was near the front of the procession, after about four rows of three wagons each. Behind their wagon, the line of alva and animals curved away into the undergrowth. Magicians sat interspersed among the wagons, moving plants out of their way and sometimes using stems or foliage to lift the wagons over rough terrain.

The morning sun made it through in some places, warming the path. The sign-bearers' wagon bumped over grass roots and dirt while Matil and Khelya chatted idly. Dask lay stretched out on the bench beside Matil, shading his eyes with one hand.

Simmad flew up and alighted in the wagon. A thin old man with wrinkly yellow petal wings followed him in. Matil, Dask, and Khelya looked up at them.

"I found a storyteller!" Simmad said. "He speaks fluent Alvishu, and he would be honored—"

"I would be honored," said the old man, "to share a tale of Lord Dyndal."

"That'd be great, sit down, uh…" Khelya pulled a blanket off of the bench beside her.

The old man sat. "I am Likku of clan Heiga."

"Pleased to meet you," Matil said cheerfully. "I'm Matil."

"I'm Khelya."

"And I'm Dask," he said, sitting up.

"Excellent!" Simmad took the space next to Dask. "Are you ready?"

Dask slid away from Simmad. "Does it have to be about Dyndal? Why not a wizard fighting monsters?"

"I thought it would make an excellent introduction for all of you considering where we're headed," Simmad said.

Dask folded his arms in curt acceptance.

"This is a story of Lord Dyndal the Young Spirit," Likku said in a sonorous tone. "When Dyndal became a man, he wished to find a wife. Among daughters of the Elders, there were great beauties, great minds, and great hearts, but he met none who could laugh and sing and dance as though no one else in the world mattered."

"I've read many variations of this story," Simmad whispered. "Each one is the same up till about this point. I haven't yet heard an Eletsol version, so even I don't know what will happen next!"

Likku blinked slowly at Simmad and then said, "One day when Dyndal was going deep into Valdingfal, the only place he had not yet looked, he found himself flying with the sky below him. He turned right-side up and was suddenly flipped over again. A woman's voice burst out in a waterfall of laughter."

"Waterfall?" Simmad said. "Do you perhaps mean 'cascade'?"

"Waterfall," Likku said. "Dyndal tried twisting and turning to see this woman, but he kept on being twisted and turned the other way round. At last he stopped flying and dropped. He landed on a tree branch. But this tree branch began to move, and then another branch on the same tree moved. The branches cradled Dyndal like a child in its mother's arms. 'Teeli reeli roo,' the woman's voice sang. 'How tired are you?'

"Dyndal said nothing. He lay there with his eyes closed. The woman said again, 'How tired are you?' Two bright yellow eyes looked down through the leaves at Dyndal. '*Very tired*,' she said. 'My lullaby worked!' She appeared from out of the leaves, a beautiful woman with dark hair and a joyous smile. She had sharp teeth like a snake's and wings like a carrion-bird's. When she flew down to Dyndal, she reached out to touch his face. His eyes flashed open and he took hold of her wrist."

"'Will you dance with me?'" Simmad said.

Likku blinked at him again.

Simmad turned red. "Sorry."

"*Dyndal said*," Likku went on, "'Dance with me, strange creature.' The woman laughed and agreed. They had no music, but they danced through the trees of Valdingfal for three days, each trying to be more ridiculous than the other. The light that they created with their magic settled in Deep Valdingfal to become the cold fire that lives in the mushrooms there. Finally they sat down on the tree branch where Dyndal had fallen three days before, and Dyndal said, 'Become my wife, strange creature.'

"The woman laughed and refused. 'I go where I please, not belonging to anyone.'

"Dyndal asked the woman, 'Who are you?'

"'Kanay,' she said. Kanay was the daughter of Esren, Elder of Rivers, and Kiha, Elder of Storms."

"Esren," Simmad explained, "died fighting the Saikyr when Kanay was a child. Her mother, Kiha, remained neutral in—"

"*So Dyndal told her he would return.*" Likku glared at Simmad. "He went to Kiha and begged for Kanay's hand.

Kiha said, 'I can do nothing. She is wilder than I.' Dyndal went to Falgar, Elder of Handcraft, and asked for a beautiful song or piece of jewelry that could win Kanay to his side. Falgar said, 'Lead her and see if she will follow. If she does not, leave her be.' Dyndal was disappointed, so he asked his sister Hanem, Elder of Flight, what to do. 'Always chase her,' Hanem said, 'but do not catch her until she lets herself be caught.' To him, that made sense. It was a game. For a year, Dyndal danced with and talked with and chased Kanay. Though she ran from him, she never left him.

"The next year, Dyndal had more responsibilities with the Heilar, protecting the alva of Eventyr. He didn't come to chase Kanay as often, and she grew lonely and angry. While she sulked, a stag walked by and saw her sitting on the branch where Dyndal had fallen. He raised his mighty head to look up at her. 'What is wrong?' he asked.

"Kanay said, 'One who claimed he loves me is not here to be with me. He must have grown bored – or perhaps he has someone else!'

"The stag considered her words and said, 'Should he come back, tell him to fetch you the crown of Calo. If he does, he truly loves you. If not, he does not love you enough.'"

"The *intrigue*," Simmad said.

Likku ignored him. "The next time Dyndal appeared, Kanay was nowhere to be seen. He called out for her. Her voice sang from the trees in reply, 'Teeli reeli roo, I will marry you.' Dyndal's heart leaped and he told her to show herself so they could marry as soon as possible. But she said, 'I will marry you *if* you give me something I dearly need.'

"'Anything,' Dyndal promised.

"'The crown of Calo.' And with her words, Dyndal was brought low, for he would not and could not do as she demanded. He tried to explain, and Kanay grew so upset that she simply fell silent. She watched as he pleaded and begged with her, and then as he sang of his love for her, and then as he finally left with sorrow on his shoulders. Not long after, Dyndal and the Heilar fought a battle against the Saikyr. The trees all around them came to life, taking the Heilar by surprise. Dyndal knew that it was Kanay.

"His heart broke, but during the battle he asked that Calo and Falgar create a false crown. Falgar took off his iron circlet and together he and Calo changed it to appear as the crown of the great Elder. Dyndal took it and held it high. When Kanay saw the crown, she went to Dyndal, pleased that he truly loved her. At the same time, the Heilar struck from both sides and the Saikyr were forced to flee. The false crown, quickly made by magic, turned back to the iron circlet in Kanay's hand. In her anger, she attacked, and Dyndal made no effort to move. The Elders Falgar, Chalena, and Shora shielded Dyndal from Kanay's wrath and cast her away. Thus they won the battle, Kanay joined Myrkhar, and Dyndal ceased looking for a wife."

"He never found anyone else?" Matil said. The story made her heart ache a little.

"No." Simmad looked upward. "A bitter sort of tale, but

we need those to teach us what alva are really like. That some become possessive of loyalty they don't return, and that even the fellows fighting for good can be ruthless."

"You sound like you've thought a lot about this," Dask said. "It's just a story."

"I, er, wrote my junior scholar thesis on the longevity and necessity of folklore," Simmad said. "This tale was one of the examples I used."

"Hm." Dask stretched his arms over his head. "I think we did you a favor getting you away from all those books."

Simmad brightened. "And now I'm out in the field!"

"Thank you for telling us the story," Matil said to Likku. He nodded in reply.

Khelya shifted beside Matil. Her nose was wrinkled in thought.

"What is it?" Matil said.

"My telvogir used to tell that one," Khelya said, "and I always cheered for Dyndal, but I just realized how sad it ends for him. *And* for Kanay."

"I don't think Kanay really cared about Dyndal," Matil said. "She wasn't being fair to him."

"He could've given up anytime," she said. "It ain't unfair if he goes along with it. They both messed it up for themselves."

"Just a story," Dask repeated loudly. "Doesn't mean anything."

"Now, I must take issue with that assertion," Simmad began.

The sound of shouting came from somewhere in the forest ahead of them. Three Eletsol scouts shot out of the undergrowth to the right of their wagon. The scouts headed straight for the lead wagons, continuing to raise an alarm. Within moments, whatever the scouts had shouted was spreading through the procession. The man driving the sign-bearers' wagon reined in the mouse and brought the wagon to a halt.

Likku heard the news being passed along and simply translated, "Skorgon."

Matil put a hand on her knife.

Khelya gasped and stood, causing the wagon to wobble. "Matil, they're gonna try takin' you!"

"Sit down." Dask climbed onto the side of the wagon and opened his wings. "I'll find out what's going on. You keep Matil covered up."

Likku said farewell and left to rejoin his own clan while the three in the wagon passed around blankets and put them on like cloaks. Simmad dimmed his wings. Khelya's blanket slowly became as transparent as she was.

Matil kept her eyes roving, looking for signs of an immediate attack on the procession, but none came. Eletsol men picked up their weapons — spears, bows, axes, and poleaxes — and gathered in groups. Hundreds of them hovered over the procession, their various garb and painted designs distinguishing the clans from each other. They were like a gigantic patchwork cloth floating above. A small band of warriors split off to stay with the procession. The rest of the force went forward through a curtain of ivy, into the forest.

Dask landed in the wagon. "The Eletsol are going to meet the Skorgon and see what they want."

"We already know what they want," Khelya said.

"Khel," Dask said, "what if they talk and it turns out we don't need to fight?"

Khelya didn't look convinced.

He folded his wings. "We only gotta worry if we hear—"

There was a deep blast from a horn.

"Okay, they started fighting," Dask said.

Matil tried to control her panicked breathing. "It's my fault they're here," she said, reaching again for her knife. "I should fight, too."

Dask put his hand over hers on her knife's handle. "You have the toad thingy. We can't risk it getting captured, can we?"

She frowned. "I guess not."

He stepped back and opened his wings again. "And *I* can't risk *you* getting captured."

"Wait," Matil said, fear rising in her throat. "Where are you going?"

"They have a mission for me," Dask said. "I'm one of the fastest flyers here, so I'll take messages back and forth to the fighting. I can keep an eye on the Skorgon and warn you guys if we need to split." He looked at each of them. "Um… stay together. Don't go towards the battle. If you have to go *away* from it, find Uro first."

"Should I—I mean—I can go with you," Simmad said. He stood up, squinting nervously.

Dask shoved him back down. "Stay here. Protect the ladies." He winked and took off.

Simmad nodded. "Protect…" He looked up at Khelya. She shrugged.

23

First Blood

The air grew hot as the day wore on. Matil was sweating, but she didn't want to take off the blanket she was hiding under. Seasoned and scarred Eletsol warriors kept the sign-bearers' wagon fenced in, and everyone in the procession was unusually quiet.

A few times, to Matil's relief, Dask sped out from the bushes and landed by the lead wagons where the chiefs, tain-men, and commanders strategized. He would give them a missive written on a leaf, wait for them to hand him a response, and then bolt away. Whenever he left, she clutched her knife's handle. At some point, Khelya put her big arm around Matil's shoulders, and from her contact, Matil began to turn transparent without even trying.

Clouds moved through the sky, changing the light to gray. Matil strained to hear anything from the forest. There came a long stretch without any sign of Dask, but Eletsol began to carry back their brothers, who were either limp or struggling in pain. A group of women immediately went to care for the wounded fighters. Matil wished she could join them. If Dyndal was really dead…then what was so important about his pendant? Shouldn't the Eletsol worry more about the living? Would it be better to just hand Khelya or Simmad the pendant and give herself up to the Skorgon?

And then what? Who would stop Nychta? Who *could* stop her? Matil's stomach turned as all her questions led her right back to sitting still and waiting. Something else stirred in her as well. A twinge of envy.

Nychta could do as she pleased. She had earned the command of armies and magic. Matil was something lower, more childish – relying on everyone around her and subject to *their* wills. No wings with which to fly and hardly any past to build on. She was even depending on legends and bedtales to save the forest. Fear and doubt and disgust with herself loomed like one of the dark clouds above.

Nychta had gotten rid of her for a reason.

The whirring of wings met Matil's ears, and she clutched the blanket tighter. Out of the ivy burst many warriors.

Matil went weak with relief. Her hands trembled while she watched scores of Eletsol fly back to the procession. They appeared triumphant but tired, and they kept careful eyes on the way they had come. Matil thought she saw feathered wings and dark skin among the warriors, and then several men descended. Behind them flew Dask, all in one piece.

Matil took off the blanket and jumped out of the wagon. Khelya and Simmad did the same. The warriors protecting them said something in a hard tone and gestured with their weapons to keep the three from going farther.

Dask flew in the center of a group of warriors covered in orange and white designs, and beside him was a man with jagged leaf-like wings and golden-brown hair.

Matil and Khelya looked at each other, their faces brightening with joy.

"Ansi!" Matil said.

Simmad squinted. "Who?"

"Remember the Eletsol chief with the crazy sisters we told you about?" Khelya said. "The one who helped us find Mr. Korsen?"

"That's him?" Simmad said excitedly.

The orange-and-white group flew lower to join other Eletsol, who exclaimed and bombarded them with questions in Eleti. Dask and Ansi landed in front of Matil and Khelya and folded their wings. Sweat beaded their faces. Their chests heaved as they gasped for air. Ansi's forehead was lined with dirt and green Skorgon blood.

"I didn't think you were coming!" said Matil.

Khelya nudged Ansi's shoulder with her fist. "It's good to see you. So what happened? Why're you *here?*"

"I return from battle and, of course, Ansi gets all the attention," Dask said.

Ansi cleared his throat.

Dask held up his hands. "Kidding. He's the hero, saved the day, all that good stuff."

"Thank you," Ansi said primly.

Matil edged around to stand next to Dask. "I'm really glad you made it back," she said in a low voice.

He smiled down at her. "Haven't you noticed that I always come back?" he said. "It's an inescapable law of nature."

Ansi gave the three of them a relieved grin. "My entire body is sore, but your faces are a salve to me."

"He and his men flew all night and all day," Dask said.

"Yes," Ansi said. "And I see that a light-wing has made it into Fainfal. A rare sight."

Simmad bowed. "Hail, great chief, I am Scholar Simmad of Icto Lan."

"I am Ansi the Smart of the clan Takkamakaini. I see you show proper respect." He smirked at Matil, Dask, and Khelya. "You could teach these three something."

"Pfft." Dask punched Ansi's arm.

Simmad coughed uncomfortably, but stood a little straighter.

"Did you come to bring the sign to Dyndal?" Matil asked.

"Ah…" Ansi looked ill at ease. "Is there a place to sit and take refreshment?"

They led Dask and Ansi to the wagon and gave them skins of dandelion-apple juice. After they had time to catch their breath, Ansi spoke.

"Let me go to the beginning," he said. "A few days ago, there were Skorgon at the border in greater numbers than usual, bringing fear to the Eletsol. We have a bad history with Skorgon raiders, and these were thought to be more of the same. At that time I was gathering support from vassals of the old Takkamakaini clan in exchange for promises of protection. One of these clans called on us to protect them against the Skorgon. When I arrived with my men, the Skorgon were no longer a threat to this clan. They had only passed through, led by a Ranycht."

Matil's heart beat faster. Crell.

The forest was marked with signs of their going," Ansi said, "so it was easy to see that they traveled toward the tomb of Dyndal, where I had heard the clans were gathering. Very suspect. I took my men and followed them."

"All night and day," Dask said.

"I will sleep well when I get the chance." Ansi rubbed his eyes. "But we followed their trail and at long last we heard the sounds of combat. A force of armed Skorgon attacking Eletsol of many different clans. My men and I were of one heart — fly onward and fight. We found the Eletsol and Skorgon matched almost evenly, and the battle might have gone badly. My men and I struck where we saw weakness. The Skorgon fought fearlessly to the death. The battle did take time, but we Eletsol decimated their force, and the Ranycht commander finally retreated with what few Skorgon remained."

Dask nodded. "It was unbelievable."

"And then I saw Dask," Ansi said, gesturing at him. "It has been a storm of events." He leaned forward and clasped each of them by the hand in turn. "May…may I see the sign?"

Matil nodded and pulled the pendant out from under her tunic.

"Dyndalittu," Ansi said wonderingly. "Bearers of the sign. The tatuvar have come to life." He gave them a deep bow.

"When we take this pendant to Dyndal," Simmad said, "will there be a ceremony, a sort of rite? Or will something happen instantly? And what will that something be, if anything? Uro and the other Eletsol have been loathe to tell me about the tomb."

"Too many questions at once," Ansi said. "I…stand with the others that I dare not speak of the sacred things. As to what may happen, it is said that the spirit of Dyndal will bless us. Dyndal was one of the great good beings. But when was the last time great good came without great evil? I am both desperately happy and quite afraid." He chuckled. "Somehow it is right that you are the bearers of Dyndal's sign. You are friends to the Eletsol."

The orange-and-white-painted warriors approached their wagon.

"Ah," Ansi said. "These are my men. They have been eager to see the ones who spoke with the Watcher."

Some of the warriors had staves wrapped around their chests.

"Magicians!" Matil said.

Ansi hit the lip of the wagon enthusiastically. "Yes. A few of the Taina have joined us already."

One warrior asked a question. Ansi replied in Eleti and each man held a fist to his heart.

Dask pointed with both hands. "Ansi, buddy. You're getting some respect."

"Respect," Ansi said. "It's a difficult thing to earn and keep, I find. Every day I must strive anew to lead well."

"Looks like you're doing a good job," Dask said. "I know I wouldn't be able to."

Ansi rolled his eyes. "Yet you thought *I* would."

"Hey, was I wrong?" he said.

"No," said the Eletsol, looking very pleased. "Do you have more of that drink for my men?"

They pulled out a barrel of juice and let Ansi's warriors help themselves to it.

"It's exciting," Matil said. "The Vima and the Taina working together. Is Teres all right, too?"

"Yeah," said Dask, "how's the lovely lady doing?"

"She's pressed with responsibilities, as are we all." Ansi lifted a shoulder of his sleeveless robe to wipe the sweat from his temple. "But she tells me she is content and hopeful."

Dask glanced at him. "Any progress?"

"We have yet to find Dag," Ansi said, "though her men are weakening and the war bends in our favor."

"No, I mean—that's great. Is *anything else* progressing?"

"Dask, you always speak so strangely. I will say…one of my captains – brother of Teres – has put in a good word for me with their father."

Dask laughed and slapped Ansi's back. "You're the traditional type. I like it."

At twilight, they went and presented Ansi and his men to Uro. Soon the warriors were drinking hearty soup and dropping off to sleep on borrowed blankets. The last of the Eletsol who had gone to fight returned, and parties went out and back, transporting the dead and wounded. They had a few scares when alva reported seeing Skorgon, but by nightfall the Eletsol were satisfied that there were no fighters in the area. The Ranycht commander had also disappeared.

Matil slept until Khelya woke her to keep watch. It was warm out, but Matil rubbed her arms as she sat in the wagon, hoping she wouldn't see any Skorgon. Among the hundreds of Eletsol sleeping in and around their wagons and animals, her friends lay on the ground in their blankets, Khelya on the near side of their wagon and Dask and Simmad on the far side. Matil leaned over to get a better look at Dask's dark face and long nose. His black hair had fallen across his eyes. She again felt a surge of relief that he'd made it back safely.

Crell entered her mind and a knot of pain entered her heart. She remembered Amacht, the spy's son, and the knot grew larger. Nychta was the cause of this pain. Nychta… and Matil.

She couldn't let anything happen to Dask.

24

Deep Routes

"It will be another long journey," Ansi said. He stifled a yawn. "We must leave soon."

He barked something in Eleti at his men, who were shoveling mashed radish and roast rabbit meat into their mouths. They each responded, "Kal, ferra!"

"If you're still tired, you can sleep in the wagons as we go," Matil said as she stepped down from their wagon to stand with Dask, Khelya, Simmad, and Ansi.

"I...don't think he's coming with us," Dask said. He looked at Ansi. "Are you?"

Gloom fell over Ansi. "You're right. I am not. My men and I are needed with our alva."

"But- but what about Dyndal's sign?" Khelya said. "Don't you want to come and see?"

"I *would* come with you." Ansi shook his head. "With everything in me, I want be there to witness it. But I must go back."

Simmad listened to the exchange, fidgeting worriedly with his hands.

Khelya also looked troubled. "Maybe Dyndal can help your clan," she said. "When we bring the sign, I'm sure he'll be able to do something."

"Khel, Ansi's gotta be there for his alva," said Dask, "because the Elders *aren't*. Even if they showed up in a blaze of glory to right all the wrongs in Eventyr, they still wouldn't replace Ansi. His alva are fighting for their lives right now."

Ansi put his hand on Dask's shoulder. "Kal. It is regrettable to miss the giving of the sign, but I know it's the right decision."

"See," Dask said, "this is why I couldn't be a leader. Too many hard decisions that affect other alva."

"We are all leaders of our own lives. Even that simple duty requires making sacrifices to do the right thing." Ansi surveyed his warriors, who stood talking to each other a few paces away. "It is time to go. Please, if you will…show them the sign."

Matil again held up the red wooden toad that hung around her neck. Ansi motioned for his men to come closer. They moved forward with heads lowered and palms raised reverently. They whispered to one another in Eleti, smiles spreading across their faces.

"Thank you," Ansi said to Matil.

She let go of the pendant. "Thank you for helping to protect us."

"Yeah," Khelya said. "Thanks for…for goin' out of your way, Ansi. I hope your alva are safe and sound when you get back."

Ansi inclined his head. "I hope you remain safe as well. Though you have the sign, don't let your guard down. I wish us to meet again in the future."

Matil smiled brightly. "We'll come see you when we can. Tell Teres we said *heisia*."

"Of course."

"See you around," Dask said, one side of his mouth lifting in a smile.

"See you around, buddy," Ansi replied.

Simmad bowed at the waist. "A pleasure to meet you, Chief Ansi. May the sun shine warm upon you."

"And on you as well, good scholar." Ansi flicked open his green, veined wings.

His men opened theirs, a line of flower petals blooming on their backs. Ansi gave Matil and her friends one last nod and flew away. The Takkamakaini warriors took off after him in a swarm.

"Colthal," Dask said quietly.

Simmad blew out a breath. "I can't believe you spoke so casually to an Eletsol clan chief."

Matil, Dask, and Khelya looked at each other.

"He's our friend," Khelya said.

"And I keep forgetting how important he is as a chief," Matil confessed.

"No one's really a chief when you've done time with 'em." Dask started walking back toward their wagon. "But it doesn't matter, chief or not. He's important either way."

The procession moved faster that day, and scouts and warriors were more conspicuous in case the Skorgon returned. Matil wondered just how far away Dyndal's tomb was. Uro wouldn't give an exact answer.

Early the following morning, the leaders stopped the procession again. A boulder towered over the travelers in the unsure light, a gigantic sentinel standing watch for an impenetrable copse looming behind it. The forest had grown dense, and the alva were moving in a narrower line, two wagons side-by-side. But now everyone was confronted with this impasse. Eletsol flew from their places in the procession to crowd the boulder, almost concealing it from view with their flittering wings.

Matil and a snoozing Khelya were the only ones in their wagon. Matil looked around for Dask and Simmad, and, not seeing them nearby, got out of the wagon to find out what was going on. She edged through the sleepy-eyed and quiet crowd. When the Eletsol noticed she was trying to get through, they moved out of the way to let her pass. A few steps away from the boulder, the crowd stayed back so that there was a clearing for the leaders of the clans, who stood facing the mossy rock face.

A plump woman with ragged pink wings like carnation petals stepped out from among the leaders. She walked sedately to the boulder and ran her hand down a line carved in the rock. Wind swirled up around her, stirring her hair, wings, and skirt, and then gusted toward the copse to rile the leaves on the right side of the boulder. The unearthly wind brushed past Matil. She shivered.

The gust of wind seemed to signal which way to go. The procession could have easily gone around the copse, but instead, magicians gathered beside the boulder and made pulling and twisting motions with their hands and arms. Leaves died and fell away, branches corkscrewed and bent backwards, and a path through the copse began to open. The party siphoned into the thin, dark tunnel. Their heads ducked beneath leaves, spiky plants, and branches where caterpillars scrunched along. It reminded Matil of a dream she'd had where her father made her a playhouse inside of a rosebush. The thorns had been sawed away and the small space had given her comfort, like she couldn't be harmed inside of it. A similar feeling came over her as she looked up through the snarl. Something fleeted on quick feet high above them, and the whole copse shook.

Matil went back through the alva and the wagons, where Dask and Simmad were waking Khelya. They decided to walk together on one side of the tunnel, marveling at the magic of the Eletsol. The four of them spoke loudly to each other until they noticed that quiet had fallen over the rest of the party. They didn't ask why, and no one explained. At times the leaders would again stop at a rock inscribed with a simple line or shape and then trace it to call forth the wind that guided them in another direction through the thick foliage.

"We know the Eletsol go to this tomb for their festival every year, right?" Dask said. "Why do they need magic rocks? They could write down the directions or put up some signs."

"By Woveg," exclaimed Simmad. "I believe I know!" Matil could hardly see his wings. He was much better at dimming them. "There have always been stories of places one can't find in the mundane way, by simply flying about. Perhaps when these stones are activated, they open up a path to the next stone, and so on until we've reached the destination!" He clasped his hands and looked ahead, starry-eyed. "I wonder how many other legends are true; such as—oh, the diamond-winged birds of gold...or the sorcerer's sidewise waterfall!"

Though it must have been at least noon, the darkness of the copse closed in around them. The Eletsol lit torches and Matil blinked at the flames, wondering how many they really needed. A tickle began just below her collarbone, where the toad pendant hung from her neck between her shirt and tunic. She had doubled up the long cord to make it shorter. The pendant seemed to be the source of this strange feeling, so she took it off and examined its red wood. It tickled her hand.

"What's wrong?" Dask said.

She focused on the tickling. "It feels almost like when I sense Nychta."

"Again? *Talrach*."

"But it's not. That's a pull and this is more of a...hope. I think it hopes I'll go somewhere."

"I reckon that magic finds its way to you," Simmad said, scratching his goatee in contemplation. "It would make sense, since you're a magical construct."

Matil's ears lowered and she looked down.

"No, she's not." Dask's wings flared out a little. "She's an *alva*, same as anyone else."

An alva…

Simmad pulled his hands together, looking ashamed. "I'm terribly sorry. I- I didn't mean—I promise I won't make that mistake again, Miss Matil."

"I knew we shouldn't have told him," Dask said.

"It's okay," Matil said. She smiled at the ground. She was an alva. "Thanks, Dask."

Dask touched the pendant for a moment. "Hey, I feel it, too. Weird. It didn't seem magical before."

Simmad reached over to feel the pendant as well. "You're right! I wonder what's set it off."

Up above, back bent to avoid the foliage, Khelya was clearly lost in thought. She hadn't seemed to hear their conversation. Now she spoke. "What do you think Dyndal's place'll be like?"

"Well, what's his most common title?" Simmad said.

"Dyndal of the Green, right?" Khelya said.

"Right! He is known as such for his connection to nature and the spirit of youth. But I've always hypothesized that his favorite color was green, so don't be surprised if the color green features prominently in his place of rest!"

Dask chuckled. "His favorite color? Is that seriously the kind of thing you studied?"

"It's—I didn't—you know—just..." Simmad took a breath. "It's one of the things that came up in my- my side studies. After weeks of helping senior scholars research micro-nations and unusual systems of governance during the Middle Hibernation Age, a junior scholar might like to...have fun thinking his own thoughts."

"He might, huh?" Dask said quietly.

The pendant's tickling had steadily increased, and holding it by its cord didn't help much. The Eletsol around Matil suddenly raised their voices. She found herself looking around, searching for something up ahead.

The copse thinned out and the magicians could clear the way faster. Finally, there were no more plants, only pebbly dirt that came to an end at a sheer crag, massively tall and dripping with ivy. Beyond the heads of those in front of her, Matil saw an opening in the cliff. It was the huge entrance of a cavern, a triangle-shaped mouth, like someone had levered the rock apart. The split narrowed as it went upward until it was a mere crack. Thin sunlight streamed down on the face of the crag, making the cavern entrance look dark and cold.

Some Eletsol flew overhead into the entrance while the rest waited to enter on foot or in wagons. The entrance at the ground was so wide that more wagons could fit side by side than in the tunnel through the thicket. Matil shuffled on impatiently through the thickness of the crowd, driven by curiosity and the pendant's insistence. The closer they came to the cave mouth, the farther right she swerved.

Eventually the pendant led her to a skinny rock standing about the height of her shoulders. She reached out and put her hand on the cool stone. At that moment, letters carved noiselessly into the rock and spelled out a word that Matil didn't know: *'Velana'*. The tickling melted away.

"Matil?" Khelya said.

"Where'd she—Matil, you…found a rock." Dask scratched his head. "Okay."

Simmad gasped. "It looks *ancient!*" He crouched down to look at the standing stone closely, his wings brightening up.

"What does 'velana' mean?" Matil said.

"'Awaken'," Simmad said. "It's an old word. Fell out of use in Alvishu after the Age of Goec."

Awaken. Did that word mean the Elders could really… come back? Matil put a hand on the cord around her neck. "This is where the pendant wanted to go. This is the right way." She let her hand fall and continued slipping through the crowd.

"Hey," Dask said, "wait up!"

Matil entered the cavern, her friends hurrying to keep pace. Everything was lit by dim orange torchlight. The space inside could have fit a small city and the voices of the Eletsol echoed off its vaulting walls, but the cavern was sparsely scattered with huts across the walls and uneven ground. Ledges, niches, and tunnels led off in every direction. The procession – all the alva, animals, and wagons – pressed into the cave. The ledges filled with Eletsol. The leaders of the clans gathered on a plateau in the center of the cavern, appearing to wait for something.

Leaf banners hung from the jagged ceiling, each blazoned with a triangular, fan-shaped symbol in bright yellow paint.

Three dots in the symbol and a curl on either side made it look almost like a face with eyes and ears. A few unfamiliar alva emerged from deeper in the cave to meet the leaders of the party. They were decorated with yellow paint and dressed in green kilts and capes.

Dask looked around the cavern. "Well," he said to Simmad. "You were right about the green."

Uro called out from his place hovering by the green-clad alva. "Bearers of the sign, follow me." He shouted something else in Eleti.

The Eletsol in front of them stepped aside to allow Matil, Dask, Khelya, and Simmad to pass. The sign-bearers walked slowly at first, intimidated by the entire party acknowledging them, but they hastened when they saw Uro and a group of tain-men and leaders from other clans waiting up ahead at a tunnel opening.

He nodded to Matil and the others. The entire group followed a yellow-painted Eletsol. They entered the tunnel, leaving behind the caravan of clans, who started to make camp in the great cavern.

Matil had never been in a cave system so vast. Her eyes swept along the rough dirt-and-rock walls that stood more than twice Khelya's height. She realized that what looked like natural erosion on the walls was actually relief sculpture. Forms of alva much larger than life stood out from the stone in fluid poses. They were towered over by noble figures that stretched from floor to ceiling. Rising and falling between the pictures, letters were carved so deeply that they appeared black, and they spelled out words Matil couldn't understand.

Some of the giant figures had magnificent wings, others were wingless. Some bore the visages of animals, and others had beautiful, alva-like faces. They danced across the walls and, with fierce weapons, fought beasts baring claws and teeth.

The silent drama filled Matil's vision as they walked, until the mural came to an end. The tunnel had widened into a damp-smelling cavern that felt like an underground meadow. Pale mushrooms in all sizes were dotted around the floor and walls, and vines splashed with bright flowers of purple, red, and yellow somehow flourished without sunlight over the walls and ceiling. A burbling sound to Matil's right drew her eye toward a small hole partway up the wall where water rushed out. It fell into a stream that flowed along the right side of the cavern and disappeared into the wall at the far end.

On the left side of the cavern, ledges and ramps had been carved from the dirt. Stacked on every ledge were woven-grass shelves full of scrolls. Eletsol in their green kilts and yellow paint came and went, sitting on floor cushions to read scrolls or talk with one another.

Uro and his fellows led the sign-bearers across the cavern to a torch beside the stream, where a black-haired Eletsol sat on the bank with his legs stretched out into the water. He wore a long, delicately-crafted tunic made from whorls and slivers of flower petals. The tunic was fastened with small animal teeth above and below his blue wildflower wings.

Uro leaned toward the sign-bearers, thick eyebrows firmly in place over his eyes. "It is the tomb-keeper. He stays here and meditates over the teachings of Emperor Ivu for much of the day."

Matil, Dask, Khelya, and Simmad all tried to get a better look at him as they walked closer. The yellow-painted Eletsol leading the group spoke to announce their presence, and the tomb-keeper turned to look. He was a boy with clear gray eyes. When he stood, he rose to the height of Dask's shoulders.

Dask gave Uro an incredulous half-smile. "The tomb-keeper, huh? Does he get nap time off?"

Simmad cleared his throat with a pointed look at Dask. He turned to Uro. "He's young."

"All tomb-keepers are young. The chiefs of this clan train a keeper in rites and duties from childhood, and then they choose a new child when the present one is too old. It is the tradition."

The leaders spoke to the tomb-keeper. The boy examined his odd assortment of guests with eyes narrowed. At a pause in the conversation, Uro told Matil to take off the pendant and show it to the tomb-keeper. Matil took the pendant from around her neck and bundled up the cord in her hand. As the toad dangled, bathed in firelight from the torch, the boy's eyes and mouth opened in surprise and wonder. He calmed his expression with a deep breath and knelt. Looking at the pendant, he said something in a confident voice. Matil only recognized the words 'Dyndal' and 'velana'.

The tomb-keeper got to his feet and called one of the green-kilted Eletsol to him. The Eletsol's eyes opened wider as the tomb-keeper spoke, and then he was gone, flying through one of the tunnels. The tomb-keeper took Matil by the elbow of her free arm. He lightly pulled her away from her friends.

"Whoa," Dask said, moving toward Matil. "Where's the kid taking her?"

Uro indicated a tunnel opening at the far end of the cavern. "We will gather the drummers and proceed to Dyndal's chamber."

Simmad's eyes bulged out like he was about to explode.

"You mean he's right in there?" Khelya whispered.

With a nod, Uro said, "Our greatest treasure. Dyndal's remains."

A disturbed expression slowly congealed on the Obrigi's face.

With the tomb-keeper and Matil ahead of them, the Eletsol leaders and the sign-bearers walked quickly to the tunnel. The sound of running water receded. This tunnel was not as tall as the other one, but it seemed much broader. Plant life continued to grow in here despite the lack of natural light, and Matil saw more carvings underneath the vines, these ones static and sober. First a giant Eletsol man was portrayed holding out a hand over which some object floated – Matil recognized the object's slit eyes and squat form at once. It was the toad pendant. The rest of the carvings featured alva prominently, all different kinds of alva bent in mourning over large figures lying on their backs.

After a rightward curve in the tunnel, it ended at a mass of thick roots and vines interspersed with pale pink blossoms. The tomb-keeper let go of Matil and stepped forward, raising his hands.

Uro brought Dask, Khelya, and Simmad up to Matil. "The three chiefs of the clan covered the tomb with a lock — a great knot which none besides them and the tomb-keeper know how to undo."

The boy moved his right hand one way and his left another. For a long moment he went on making hypnotizing motions, but nothing seemed to happen. Then a root on the wall of plants slithered off to the side. A thin vine uncoiled. In the dim green atmosphere, the plants appeared to steadily untangle themselves. Bigger roots and stems started to curl away from the center, showing an empty chamber on the other side. The plant life slithered aside, its strands laying back against the tunnel walls obediently, as if trained. The tomb-keeper let his arms fall, breathing hard with the exertion of magic. The way was clear.

He took Matil into the next chamber. From the tunnel the ground sloped down, an immense, bare space. Flowers, berries, and leaves were thick on the walls. The near side of the chamber was wide compared to the narrow far end. On a ledge at the distant end stood a raised bier made of blooming plants woven tight together, raising up a supine occupant covered in leaves. Sunlight spilled down from a large crack in the roof, and particles floated in the rays over what appeared to be a man of Obrigi height lying on the bier. Each Eletsol, especially the young tomb-keeper, looked on the bier with solemnity. Dask crossed his arms. Simmad craned his neck forward to look while Khelya trembled. Matil took her by the hand.

They all walked down the slope without a word, the padding of their feet the only sound in the huge place. When they were halfway down, grinding noises echoed out from behind them. Matil and her companions looked back. Eletsol carried or wheeled in drums big and small, the wheels bouncing over the bumpy floor. The drummers passed the chief's group quickly and made it to the ledge at the end of the room. The ledge had two ramps, one on either side, for them to roll the drums up. They placed the drums in a semicircle behind the bier.

Everything was set up by the time the group stood before the waist-height ledge. Someone coughed in the chamber, echoing loudly. Matil gripped Khelya's hand harder in surprise. Behind them, the room had filled with Eletsol of all clans, and the front of the crowd was only a few steps from her back. She had watched the drummers too closely to notice the muted alva assembling on the slope.

It seemed that the entire crowd stared at the man on the bier. At no point had Matil been able to see what he really looked like, obscured by leaves as he was. She *could* see, from his bare torso and one arm lying over his stomach, that his complexion was light tan, almost golden, and his body's outline was visible enough to tell that he was bigger than Khelya. Could this really be Dyndal? He didn't seem like an ancient corpse. Matil glanced up at Khelya, whose expression had lifted in hope.

The tomb-keeper spoke with Uro and some other Eletsol, and Uro turned to Matil. "They will take you to give him the sign."

She didn't have time to ask what he meant before two men in green kilts and yellow paint lifted Matil into the air, one on either side. Her stomach swooped and she gasped as the floor receded beneath her. The two Eletsol flew up to the ledge and brought her lower to hover over a space near Dyndal's left hand. The body's appearance struck her with its stillness and height and shining golden skin.

Matil realized why they had brought her up here. She leaned forward to lay the wooden pendant on the bier at Dyndal's side. The men flew her back down to the others, a gentle rush of wind stirring her hair.

"You okay?" Dask said.

Matil gave a breathless and smiling nod.

The tomb-keeper's blue wings fluttered as he jumped up and glided to land on the ledge. He turned to the crowd. "Velana," he sang in a high, clear voice.

The drummers hit their drums once…twice…

Pause.

Once…twice…

Pause.

Now they pounded out one-two…one-two…one-two… until it was a regular heartbeat rhythm. The tomb-keeper burst out singing a verse. All the Eletsol repeated it with a roar, the tune and unfamiliar words amplifying around the chamber.

The song began as a slow call-and-response that picked up as the drummers pounded more and more often. Soon they were singing without pause. The voices swelled and the drums sounded on every beat. It might have been Matil's imagination, but it really seemed that the reds, pinks, greens, and yellows of the plants began to glow vividly.

Over the body on the bier, in the fragile light, the air shimmered. Joining the chorus of Eletsol was another voice, faint at first and then growing strong, a voice that sang recklessly. It slid in and out of the song, almost a drumbeat itself. It stirred in Matil the ache to sing as well, though she didn't know the words; to laugh, though she wasn't sure why; and to fly, though…of course…

The new voice came from the shimmering air, which resolved into the cloudy specter of a man spreading muscular arms and expansive wings. His wings splayed out from his back, each a half-circle made up of many layers of smooth leaves riffling in a gentle breeze. The dark orange hair on his head stood up, so unruly it seemed to defy gravity, and his eyes were closed with the passion of his singing. His ears curved back like those of an Eletsol. The only clothes he had on were baggy pants rolled up at his shins and a wide sash wrapped around his waist.

This was Dyndal.

The song fell in volume, turning from a gale of sound into a zephyr, soft and warm. Dyndal's voice disappeared below the quieting Eletsol voices until the Eletsol brought their melody to a close. He hummed the tune one last time, making the once-rousing chant sound almost sad. When he, too, finished the song, his mouth spread in a smile. He opened his eyes, and Matil was taken aback.

His eyes didn't have pupils. Instead they were like pools of water lapping at the shore, green as grass in a meadow and flowing with fathomless, whispering life.

25

Velana

Dust motes swirled within the nebulous, golden form of Dyndal. His eyes were the most substantial part of him. His body was like a ray of sunlight itself, as transparent as Khelya but gently illuminating the area around the bier. He considered the Eletsol looking up at him in wonder. He smiled wider, showing his teeth, and then his extraordinary eyes found the four sign-bearers. He burst into full-bellied laughter.

"Kiitras," he said between guffaws. "Ah, to wake up and laugh. Thank you."

All of the Eletsol fell to their knees with shouts and cheers. "Ferra palikun!" they cried. "Ferra Dyndal!" They bowed their heads to the ground and went quiet. Khelya and Simmad quickly clambered down with them, though Matil hesitated.

Dask had his eyes narrowed at Dyndal. He noticed Matil glancing at him. "It's a decent illusion," he said in an under-tone, "but just watch. He won't step out of the light."

Dyndal once again looked across the crowded chamber, appearing quite pleased. He glanced at the bier over which he floated. His body lay still beneath him. "Ah myska," he said, startled. "Is that my flesh?" He spotted the pendant on the bier and moved down through the air until he stood beside it. With a quick movement he grabbed the pendant – but the pendant didn't move. He looked down at his tenuous arms and spoke something in another tongue. Again he tried to touch the pendant, succeeding in picking it up. Distress turned down his mouth. He set it down. "Not yet," he said. The wavering green color of his eyes was disturbed by an influx of blue. "I am not myself."

What did he mean? Why was he…standing beside his own body?

Simmad reached up and tapped on Matil's arm. "You really ought to bow," he whispered.

Dask shrugged. "Hey, we've got bad knees."

Matil shifted her weight. She had been standing so long that kneeling now might look funny. Either way, it didn't seem that Dyndal cared. He was focused on the pendant.

The tomb-keeper lifted his head and spoke to the specter in a halting, awed voice. Dyndal looked blankly down at him. The boy repeated himself.

"Ah!" Dyndal said. He replied in slurred Eleti.

Now the tomb-keeper looked blank.

"What language would you like, great Lord Dyndal?" Uro said, rising into the air.

Dyndal laughed in relief. "Common Alvishu, yes. It seems the Eletsol languages are much changed."

"True, my lord. Eleti became the Eletsol tongue only a few hundred years ago."

Dyndal leaned forward. "'A few hundred'? How many years has it been in whole?"

"A thousand at the least," Uro said.

"Much time has passed." He gazed around the chamber. "It is also kind of you, but you need not bow any longer."

Uro relayed the word to the rest of the Eletsol. They looked at one another and then stood up to give another cheer.

When the shouts ended, Uro gestured at the young tomb-keeper and three very old men in green robes on the other side of the bier. "The Dyndalsada greet you with the host of the ancestors," Uro said. "They wish to show you every honor and beg that you lead us to a new age of prosperity."

"I would very much like to," Dyndal said. "After I find my sister."

Uro's eyebrows drifted upward. "Sh…Shora?"

Dyndal nodded. "We must wake the others."

"*Others?*" Uro said.

Dyndal stepped off the ledge and landed without impact in front of Matil and the sign-bearers, standing a head taller than Khelya. The group of leaders who stood closer to the ledge turned around to face him with heads still bowed. Dask blinked. Matil inspected Dyndal. The specter no longer stood in the light, but he was holding together perfectly. He didn't seem like an illusion.

Dyndal turned to Uro while pointing at them. "Would these carnival alva be the ones who brought my frog?"

"Yes, your greatness!" Simmad said. "But, er, I believe it's a…toad…" Forehead turning bright red, he moved halfway behind a stunned Khelya.

"Toad, frog, doesn't matter," Dask said. "He called us carnies!"

"Oh, are you not?" Dyndal scrunched up his mouth. "That is unfortunate. Carnival alva are my favorite sort of alva. Who are you, then?"

Dask cast him a dismissive glance, but held his hand out to each of the four as he said their name. "Dask, Matil, Khelya, Simmad."

"Some time you will have to tell me your story," Dyndal said. "The four of you look like the lead-in to a very funny joke."

"A-a-are you a ghost?" Khelya said.

Dyndal turned his green gaze on her transparent face. "Are *you* a ghost?"

"No, no, no-no, I…" She winced. "They said you were dead, sir."

"Who did? I will show them I am not dead!" He flexed his arms.

Uro's voice shook. "You did, Lord Dyndal."

"*I* did? Hah! No. I would never make sport of life and death."

"Our history tells of the day so long ago, when you took us to this place and asked us to guard your body. 'The Elders and I now die,' you said. 'Valdri ja vi tega kaalu.'"

Dyndal looked impatient. "That is not what I said."

Dask's ears shifted toward the spectral Elder in surprise.

"But…so it is written," Uro said, slowly descending to the ground.

"Valdri lae ifen kaana tag," said Dyndal.

Uro balked. "I am sorry, I do not understand."

"*That* is what I said, in the Eleti I knew a thousand years ago." Dyndal glanced through the room at all the quiet Eletsol. "This 'ja vi' that you speak…I remember it not. Valdri lae ifen kaana tag: 'The Elders and I sleep for now.'"

Simmad looked up sharply. "'Drivaldri ir mu nu julan.'"

"The same thing in ancient Alvishu, yes," Dyndal said.

Khelya's expression lifted with a puzzled smile.

"That's what's written in our oldest manuscripts of the Chivishi," Simmad said. "Did any writings survive from before, to compare the old form of the Eleti languages to the new?"

A stunned look stole over Uro's face. He called to the tomb-keeper and the three old men on the ledge. They flew down, keeping a respectful distance from Dyndal, and exchanged words with Uro.

When they were done speaking, Uro said, "When Emperor Ivu united the clans and chose one language for us, he directed translations of the old language, but we have no writings from before."

Simmad jabbed a finger at him. "I'd bet that the lost writings match up with the ancient Alvishu manuscripts. If I could research it more deeply…"

Dask snorted. "So the Eletsol think the Elders are dead because someone switched the words around?"

Matil squeezed Khelya's hand and grinned up at her, but Khelya couldn't tear her eyes away from Dyndal.

"I am alive," the radiant specter said. "The Eletsol faithfully kept me safe, and it is a thing to be grateful for indeed." Dyndal lifted his arms and faced the crowd. "I am not dead!"

Some of the Eletsol understood and began whispering to those beside them, but they were still baffled.

"Great Lord Dyndal," Uro said respectfully, "whatever you told us in the past, you are now a ghost. There is your body. Does this not make you dead?"

Dyndal examined his own crystalline arm. "Mm, I see where there is confusion. No, this body sleeps while my mind wakes. My magic allows part of me to appear in the world separate from myself. The Hibernation has yet to end, but…I am not dead."

Dismay began to steal over Matil. They hadn't woken him after all?

A dubious-looking Uro translated to the Eletsol crowd. Some stared, others gasped, and several yelled joyfully.

"Before I leave," Dyndal added, "we shall celebrate! I declare a seven-day feast!"

"Seven days?" Matil said. "We can't…" She looked up at him while her hopes fell. He couldn't save them. Not like she had hoped. "Um, Lord Dyndal, I don't think we have seven days."

"I am finally, *finally* in this world again and you say I cannot live?"

"No, but—"

"Then let us begin festivities!"

"Hey, Your Royal Green-ness," Dask said. "You heard of the Book of Myrkhar?"

Uro lifted one eyebrow to stare at Dask.

"Of course I have." Dyndal frowned. "Featherlord."

"*Featherlord?*" Dask said.

Simmad raised his shoulders. "You did start it, Dask."

"There's an alva named Nychta Olsta who has the Book," Matil said urgently. "She's trying to take over Nychtfal with the Skorgon."

"They always do that sort of thing," Dyndal said. "We put in place someone to contend with Book-bearers. He has never been defeated."

Simmad tugged his goatee. "D'you- do you mean Bahantros?"

"Yes."

"Two hundred years ago the hero Bahantros fell, Lord Dyndal. He died from his wounds after killing a Book-bearer."

"Bahan is dead?" Dyndal stared at Simmad. Sharp silver streaks ran through his eyes. "Then...the Book-bearer can no longer be killed."

"That's why we need to hurry," Matil said. "Nychta and the Book are close. If they find you or me, we'll be in trouble."

"Why are they looking for you?" Dyndal said.

She twisted her fingers together and took a breath. "Because I'm part of Nychta. When she cast the Book's spell, she split in half."

He nodded with dawning realization. "You are the outcast portion? The spell failed? That is even more cause for celebration!" He began to sing. "*The Book-bearer can be slain!*"

"She…can?" If they had only known sooner, they could have saved Amacht.

"It is not easy," Dyndal said, "but I trust it can be done. Because of you, she is not yet full of the Book's power."

Matil's heart lifted. Dask gave her an encouraging smile. She faced Dyndal. "Then there's another reason to find the other Elders as soon as we can."

"Oh, very well. It does not have to be a seven-day feast. We can stay for five days."

"That's still too long," Dask said.

Dyndal shot him a look. "After being apart from others, it is natural to want to talk and dance and sing with them. But because I am understanding of your point, I propose a simple one-day feast."

Matil tugged on the edge of her tunic. "I guess we could stay the night."

Covering his mouth, Simmad said, "I can't *believe* you two are haggling with an Elder."

Dyndal shook his head with exaggerated seriousness. "It is not right, is it?"

Uro was translating the proceedings to the Eletsol leaders. The tomb-keeper watched and listened closely and even let out a disappointed noise after Uro translated Dyndal's cut of the feast from seven days to one.

"Now you must tell me of yourself," Dyndal said to Khelya. "Alva sometimes fade slowly from history, but I have never before witnessed it with my own eyes."

Khelya scuffed her transparent boot against the ground.

"We were helping her to fade," Matil said guiltily, "and we did it so often that now she stays faded."

"Why do you not end the enchantment?" Dyndal said.

Khelya gave a short laugh. "I can't."

"You can."

She stared at him. "But…sir, I've tried."

"Obrigi don't have magic," Dask said. "Maybe you could tell Matil and me how to fix it."

Dyndal knelt so he could talk directly to Dask. "The Obrigi *do* have magic."

Khelya stood completely still.

"Well, not anymore." Dask shook his head with impatience. "It's been a long time since you were around. Things have changed. You've changed."

"Of course things have changed," Dyndal said. "However…if your magic alone were shrouding her, you would be able to take it away as easily as you put it in place."

Dask lowered his eyes thoughtfully.

"Er, Lord Dyndal," Simmad said, "Dask is correct. Obrigi are- are different from all other alva in this regard.

In the place of magical skills, they have remarkable physical abilities."

Dyndal hopped to his feet and faced Khelya. "Let not your friends speak for you. If I say that you have magic, do you believe me?"

She looked away, twisting her hands. "I- I believe you, sir."

"Aha! No, you do not. There is the problem."

"How could I not know I had magic?" she cried. "Why does everyone say we don't, if we actually do? We lost the blessing, sir. Our magic's gone."

"In the Chivishi," said Dyndal, "it is written that each kind of alva has power in their own realms. Each kind. Believe what *it* says, if you do not believe me." He suddenly gasped and covered his eyes. "Do not tell me that the Chivishi is also lost!"

"No," Khelya said quickly. "We still read the Chivishi. Does that…really mean the Obrigi have power, too?"

Dyndal nodded. "Verily so."

Simmad began to stroke his goatee with intensity. Uro had become so absorbed in their conversation that he'd ceased translating. The tomb-keeper tapped on his shoulder.

"The power that keeps you half-concealed is yours," Dyndal said. "It is yours to disperse."

'Mine,' Khelya mouthed. Out loud, she said, "So, I can…"

Color and substance slowly began to infuse Khelya, like a mist-veiled dawn entering into full day. Her skin, hair, and clothes became rich and warm. Her outline filled in. She was solid again, and she seemed to stand taller. It was strange to see her blonde hair and kind face so clearly after so long.

"Khelya!" was all Matil could say.

"You've done it," Simmad said. "Miss Khelya, you've done magic!"

Dask smiled at Khelya. "I, um…I was wrong. Good work, Khel."

Looking down at herself, happiness grew on Khelya's face. She burst out with a cheer.

Dyndal raised his fists into the air, seeming to relish in Khelya's success and the Eletsol crowd's whispers of awe. Once he lowered his arms, he said, "I suppose the power of the Obrigi is not as noticeable as shadow, light, or water. But that does make it interesting."

Khelya gripped her own forearm as if testing out the skin and bones. "I don't feel magical."

"What *is* her power, exactly?" Simmad said.

"Obrigi can cause things to happen that otherwise would not," Dyndal said.

Dask put a hand to his temple and looked up at Dyndal. "Do you know what the word 'exactly' means?"

As they spoke, a strange dizziness snuck up on Matil. The light over the bier changed to a sickly green, and she wondered if it was all just her. But the others seemed disoriented, too, pausing and looking around slowly. The crowd began to whisper.

"Do any of you feel a tingling down your back?" Dyndal said.

Behind the bier, the vague shape of a woman wavered into being among the flowers on the wall. She blended in so well that it was hard to tell what she looked like, but her large, angled eyes of topaz-yellow stood out. They had no pupils, like Dyndal's eyes, and their shimmering depths were shot with red.

Dyndal noticed her with a yelp. The Eletsol drummers and the crowd saw her and, yelling a strangely familiar word, they flew back through the tunnel at the end of the chamber, parents dragging their children along. Some of the leaders went with the crowd, while four others, including the tomb-keeper and Uro, stayed by Dyndal.

From the woman's mouth erupted a trilling, songbird laugh that ended in a crow-like cackle. She stepped from the wall onto the bier. Her body looked as transparent as Dyndal's, but it gave off no light. Instead it was like a cloud of smoke, concealing light. Matil had a hard time comprehending what she saw, so she focused on one part of the woman at a time. A full-sleeved, mottled-brown dress cascaded around the woman's tall, thin figure, the edges strangely hard to pick out. Its rippling folds moved like no fabric could. One moment it covered her feet, but the next it retreated up to her knees.

The woman raised her head to meet the sunlight and stretched with a yawn, up, up, up, much farther than she should have been able to. Snakelike markings covered her pale, greenish skin, and dark, matted hair fell to her waist. Her hands and feet were scaly talons the same color as her skin. Her face was wide, the nose and mouth flowing together like a snout. Fangs made her big smile dangerous.

"Do not run, my sweetlings," the woman breathed, her voice carrying through the chamber. "Kanay…is…*here*."

26

Kings of the Forest

Kanay was…she was the one Dyndal had loved in the story. Matil's ears went back. She felt queasy. The way the woman spoke was all wrong.

"Kanay the Imponderable?" Simmad whispered. He sounded utterly fascinated.

"Oh, *thiffen*," Khelya said.

Dyndal cleared his throat and moved out in front of Matil. "Go away. You are not welcome in this place." He couldn't meet Kanay's eyes. His bravado was gone.

"Mmm." Kanay pursed her mouth with disappointment. "I expected something in the way of: 'Good morning, dearest. I hope you are sleeping well in that *foul demon-pit* you can never escape.' To which I would reply: 'Love, my love, my cherry blueberry treat…you are hilariously mistaken. Hah! Haha. For the first time, Lord Myrkhar cannot be prevented from shaping Eventyr.

Your safeguards have all failed. And unless you are an idiot – with you it is hard to tell – you are aware that when Calo wakes the Heilar, he also wakes the Saikyr.'" A hungry smile spread across her face. "'As soon as our eyes open, yes, not a moment later…we will break free from the waning power of our foul demon-pits!' Anyway, that is what I *would* have said. Instead I will ask a question. Why am I not welcome, dearest Dyndal?"

The Eletsol leaders standing between Dyndal and the bier made noises of alarm as Uro translated Kanay's words to them in hushed tones. They trembled watching the two apparitions. The tomb-keeper looked hopefully to Dyndal, whose eyes were beginning to burn with orange around the edges. Dyndal finally matched Kanay's gaze. His hands formed fists at his sides.

"Such a relief," he said, "my shining star. If our conversation had gone on so, I would be concerned. Not worried, only concerned. But to answer your question, you are not welcome because it is no doubt you are a bad influence. Our young friends here should avoid keeping company with murderous traitors." He held up a hand. "Murderous traitor? Is that right? Or should I say traitorous murderer?"

Kanay giggled and then jumped down from the bier to the floor. The four remaining Eletsol backed toward Dyndal while the tall, cloudy Elders stared at each other over the alvas' heads.

"I hate it when you make me laugh," Kanay cooed.

"At the present my form does not have any blood, but somehow it still *boils*." Her sleeves changed into huge, mangy vulture wings, her taloned arms and legs bent, becoming more animal, and her dress tightened into a green serpent's body frilled with brown feathers. While she transformed, she floated, wings moving slowly as though treading sap. "Use the first one." The corners of her mouth stretched along her cheeks. "The second one has too many sssyllablesss."

Suddenly she shot forward in the air, extending her claws and passing right through two of the Eletsol – one of the leaders and, standing behind him, the tomb-keeper. They howled in agony as her talons sliced them from chest to stomach. Horrified shouts went up from some of the others in the chamber and Matil, in her shock, couldn't tell who had cried out. Simmad hit the floor in a dead faint. Uro and the other Eletsol leader, a tain-woman, fumblingly dragged the fallen ones away from the Elders.

Matil unsheathed her dagger and lowered into a ready stance. Her mind was sharp, at work finding advantages and escapes, but overshadowing all those thoughts was the fear that her knife offered no protection. Letting the darkness of the cavern cover her, she watched her skin fade away. She reached up and held on to Khelya's hand. Khelya looked down and nodded once, her face white with panic. Matil's invisibility spread along Khelya's arm. Dask faded as well. He set his heel against Simmad's limp shoulder, and the unconscious Sangriga began to disappear.

Kanay wheeled toward Dyndal. Her eyes were giddy spirals of yellow and red – his were fiery storms of orange and green, and in his hand a long blade of grass appeared. He slashed at her, using it like a sword. Kanay slithered out of the way and sailed through the cavern, showing off with baffling twists and loops. Dyndal, his face hard, moved between Kanay and all of the alva in a protective position.

"Face me, Kanay," he said resoundingly. "One of us will banish the other from this place, and I intend to make you the banished."

She tittered. "By all the stars and teacups, why would I let you banish me? There is such fun to be had," her voice became a growl, "*here*." She dashed down to the faded alva.

Though the three alva couldn't be seen, Kanay hurtled straight toward Khelya. They scrambled in different directions and lost their fading as Kanay swished between them with a mocking laugh. She turned back to them, preparing another attack, but she paused when her feverish eyes landed on Matil.

Dyndal sliced toward Kanay. She snapped back at him. They danced through the chamber, intent on each other's movements. Kanay's tail whipped behind to slap Dyndal, which made him falter long enough for her to hook her tail back and sweep his legs out from under him. His stunned landing made no sound.

Kanay slithered through the air toward Matil, who stumbled back. The Elder stopped just short of crashing into Matil's face. Kanay sneered. "So *this* is the creature –

lost by the Book-bearer. Mmm, we'll have her caught and readied for the dagger in no time at all. Hello, ugly. My name is Kanay. Kanay-Kanee-Kanoo."

Matil edged away. She tried to fade, tried to find shadows that would hide her. Each time her terrified mind took hold of them, they slipped away.

"Rude little thing," Kanay said. "Say hello back to me!"

Her throat went dry as Kanay slunk through the air, tongue darting out. The serpent's open mouth glistened in the low light. Her eyes turned pure black. "I must not touch you, speck. But I can loop around your mind and *crush* it in my coils. Yes, I can. You will never think again. Is it not small, then, what I ask of you? Simply…s-s-s-*sssay hello.*"

"Hello," Matil said, wincing.

Kanay gave a screeching laugh. Dyndal pushed himself up with a shake of his head and rushed over to grab her by the tail. He thrust the blade of grass through her body, right between her wings, and she wriggled madly. Holding on, he began to glow like fire. Matil tripped backward onto the ground in an effort to slip away.

"You mean," Kanay gasped painfully, "to send me off? But we were all – getting – along – so – *well!*" The glow enveloped her. She turned and bared her teeth in a savage grin, her body blurring. "Enjoy your last days as kings of the forest, lovey-doves."

She washed away, but her voice pulsed around the chamber. "The Saikyr will soon sssucceed you." And then it, too, whispered into nothingness.

"She is banished," Dyndal said. "For now."

Simmad sat up, looking dazed. Matil wobbled over to him and Dask and Khelya.

Dask took Matil by the arm. "Are you all right?"

She nodded and tried to keep her limbs from trembling.

The four sign-bearers stared at the nearly empty chamber that Kanay had left behind, as well as the injured Eletsol and the tense, gleaming form of Dyndal.

One of the Eletsol lay still with a bloodied chest and glassy eyes. Seeing that he was already gone, the others hurriedly knelt to examine the tomb-keeper. Dyndal got on his knees as well.

A slash across the boy's chest and stomach oozed blood. He grunted in pain with his eyes pressed shut. His skin, beaded with sweat, looked completely white against the stark redness. Uro spoke rapidly to the woman on the other side of the boy, and the two of them pushed their hands toward each other, palms facing the wound. The skin moved together and crusted over. The two of them sat back, drained, but the boy still whimpered.

Forehead wrinkled with worry, Dyndal placed his hands on both ends of the wound. It shimmered and the tomb-keeper breathed in relief. The scab flaked off. While the wound healed, leaving a knotty line down the boy's front, Dyndal grew more vaporous in appearance. He finally pulled his hands away like they were heavy weights and sat with his eyes closed.

"Lord Dyndal," Uro said when a moment had passed. "You should not have worn yourself out so."

"His splintered bones would have killed him," Dyndal said in a low voice.

"But—"

"I will regain my strength, and he will live."

Uro lowered his head in acknowledgment. "Thank you, my lord."

Dyndal opened his eyes, which had darkened like roiling storm clouds, and turned slowly to Matil. "We leave…now."

"Lord Dyndal!" Uro said.

"Take me…take my velanach to Ecker's Brug," Dyndal said. "Shora is there."

Transfixed, Matil nodded once.

"You will see me again soon, alva. Colthal." Dyndal closed his eyes again and his body dispersed into a golden mist that drifted to the smooth rock floor. Up on the bier, the pendant flared with light and then fell dark.

* * *

Khelya carried the boy tomb-keeper down the tunnel. The injury had taken a toll on his strength, and he slept. Uro and the tain-woman hobbled beside her while Dask, Simmad, and Matil trailed behind, Simmad slowly regaining color in his face. Matil carried Dyndal's pendant with two hands, watching it warily.

"Dyndal will remain a secret with us," Uro said. "But the enemy will look for you. I can show you the most fast way out, and then…please hurry to Shora." His eyebrows uncovered his eyes as he looked up. "Praise the ancestors. Will we truly witness a second Age of Elders?"

They came to the entrance cavern, where the Eletsol clans were gathered. Guarding the way was a huge formation of fighting men. Some stood while many hovered in the tunnel mouth, peering into the darkness. Uro shouted to them, and the men in the center came forward to help with the wounded boy. Several flew down the tunnel to retrieve the dead from Dyndal's chamber.

Matil and the others passed through the army, hundreds of warriors stepping aside to let them in. Most of the Eletsol had seen Dyndal and Kanay, and it seemed they were preparing to fend off the Saikyr. Fearful alva speaking Eleti came up to surround the weary bunch. The tain-woman addressed the crowd. Uro gave orders to a few nearby alva.

An Eletsol led up Dewdrop and Olnar, and began to tie supplies to their harnesses. Matil rubbed Olnar's antennae, who took the affection stoically, and hugged Dewdrop's hard head. Dewdrop ran her antennae along Matil's back and arms. Strange, wonderful, and horrible things had happened today, and for a moment Matil clung to Dewdrop like the beetle was a stick that would save her from drowning.

Dask came over to pat Olnar's shell. "We're waking up the Elders, boy." He sighed. "I'm still trying to wake *myself* up."

Matil looked at him curiously. "I guess…now we know the Elders are real."

"Well, we've seen a couple of magical spirits. That doesn't mean a whole flock of wish-granting Elders is out there." He scratched the back of his neck. "But it's great if we can find a way to stop Nychta. And I believe *you* now. I'm sorry for… you know, when you saw Mr. Korsen the first time. I'm sorry for saying you didn't see him."

She smiled up at him and let go of Dewdrop. It was time to leave.

Khelya stood by with a determined expression. Simmad's hands shook. Matil looked down at her own hands, one of which held Dyndal's pendant. She went over to Simmad and passed him the pendant. His hands abruptly stopped shaking as he noticed her and then gazed at the pendant.

"Can you hold this while we get ready?" she said.

"I…yes, Miss Matil," he said, slightly bewildered. Like she had earlier, he gripped it in both hands. "Thank you."

Uro addressed them quietly. "None of our alva know where Dyndal is now. I've explained that he will return when the time is right."

"And—" Khelya self-consciously cut herself off.

Uro looked up at her. "Speak."

"You'll, uh, make sure everyone in Fainfal knows the truth, right?" A faint smile lit her face. "That the Elders ain't dead?"

He shared her smile. "The tidings have already taken wing."

The story will continue in

Wings of Eventyr

Ellias Quinn is an American storyteller. In her childhood amidst the rain and the woods, she stumbled into Eventyr's border – bruising her head in the process – and through the years has had the great fortune to learn from the bantam residents about its history and cultures. Now, she is humbled by the privilege of relating certain great events from Eventyr's past for the benefit of humankind.

Ellias's favorite time of year are the days just out of Vana, when the sun shines warmly through the cold air, as Thrual creeps in and paints the leaves. On those days she enjoys sitting down with her family to a meal of thick squirrel steaks broiled in the Obrigi tradition.

www.ingramcontent.com/pod-product-compliance
Lightning Source LLC
Chambersburg PA
CBHW051637180726
48284CB00006B/1763